V IS FOR VILLAIN

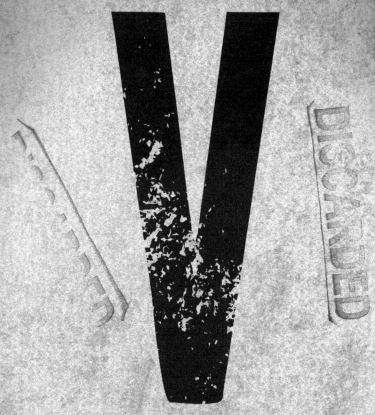

IS FOR VILLAIN

PETER MOORE

HYPERION | *Los Angeles* | *New York*

Again, for

Ellen

& Hedy

& Jake

with all my love, always.

First Edition
10 9 8 7 6 5 4 3 2 1
G475-5664-5-14074
Printed in the United States of America

Library of Congress Cataloging-in-Publication Data
Moore, Peter, 1963–
V is for villain Peter Moore.—First edition.
pages cm
Summary: "Brad Baron and his friends discover dangerous secrets about
the superheroes running their society"—Provided by publisher.
ISBN 978-1-4231-5749-6—ISBN 1-4231-5749-4
[1. Superheroes—Fiction. 2. Ability—Fiction. 3. Brothers—Fiction.
4. Good and evil—Fiction.] I. Title.
PZ7.M787515Vaah 2014
[Fic]—dc23   2013026304

Reinforced binding

Designed by Abby Kuperstock

Visit www.hyperionteens.com

Here are a couple of quotes for you,
just to get us started off right:

There is nothing either good or bad,
but thinking makes it so."

WILLIAM "BIG BILL THE BARD" SHAKESPEARE,
Hamlet, Sap of Denmark
Act III (methinks);
no recollection of which scene

And this cheerful little tidbit:

If only I had known the magnitude of the forces and
powers our work would unleash, I would have shut down
the project and destroyed every scrap of research.
We have tampered with the very essence of what limits
mankind. Our species cannot survive without those
limits, and if the human race extinguishes itself,
I fear it is I who must bear the blame."

DR. J. LASLO KOLVASZ-ZIMMERMANN
Chief Biophysicist and Director,
The Kraden Project
Final letters, August 1964

So, what I'm going to write is the truth. Every word. Honest.

Do you believe me?

Seriously?

Huh. Okay, then . . .

PART
1

N CHAPTER 1 N

Flashbang

I swear: the game was made to kill kids like me.

Gym class at the Academy—"Physical Training," or "PT" for short—is kind of like a microcosm of the real world. If you have enhanced strength, you get an A. If you don't have it, you get broken bones and bruises. Since I'm in the second category, I didn't exactly look forward to the forty-four-minute periods dedicated to Survival of the Physically Fittest.

The Fliers were using the gym, practicing for the Flight Maneuvers certification tests that a bunch of the seniors would be taking within the next few months. So the rest of us who had PT—juniors, like me, mixed with seniors—were out on the flashbang field. Not that the kids outside were second-rate, in terms of powers. Almost every one of us was a solid Hitter.[1] Some were playing hard because that was just how they were: born-hero types. Others were playing hard so they could score points for their PT cumulative grade. As far as I knew, I was the only unpowered kid on the field, and that meant I would have to play hard, too, just to get off the

---

[1] Hero-in-Training: Teen

field intact. Or I could try to stay out of the way of the action and survive the period.

"Hey, Baron!" Mr. M bellowed at me. The former Mister Mastodon (of the Liberty Sentinels) had voice-amp powers that could rattle glass when he shouted, which made him pretty perfectly suited for a PT teacher. "What's the deal? You stuck?"

"Huh?" I called, without a whole lot of effort or volume. I knew what he meant. I was hanging around in the left back-field, not wanting to get too close to the middle of the field, where the four offensive players from the opposing team were trying to break through our forward line.

Mr. M shouted to me: "You think Blake Baron would've been caught dead standing still for one *second* during a game of flashbang?"

"I'm not Blake," I said.

He laughed, way louder than necessary. "No, *Brad*, you're not Blake. Blake would be charging down the field, mixing it up, getting physical," he boomed. "You should be ashamed of yourself. If your brother saw you just standing there like that, he'd puke."

"I don't think he'd really care," I said. Which was a lie. He'd either be embarrassed or disgusted, or both. Blake had been a star when he went to the Academy. Even back then, he was twice the size I am now and busted out with new powers practically every day: enhanced strength, invulnerability, speed, and dexterity. Me? I had brains, but that wasn't going to do me much good in a game of flashbang. Cunning wasn't valuable in a situation that called for brute force.

"Wrong, chief," Mr. M said. "Blake took pride in being here—he worked hard. *That's* what it takes to be a hero. Now get your butt in the game or I'll make you goalkeeper. How's that sound?"

It sounded to me like a guarantee that I would get killed. "I read you, sir, loud and clear. I'm getting in the game right now," I called. "I am *pumped*! Ready and rowdy, sir." I even saluted. Not really as suicidal as it might sound: Mr. M probably couldn't spell *irony*, much less recognize it. Still, I trotted forward from where I was but kept my distance from the action, figuring at least a little movement would get me off Mr. M's radar.

Unfortunately for me, a completed pass to Donna Dersh sent her running toward my new position, followed by a stampede of kids right behind her. Her teammates were blocking mine from reaching her and stealing the flashbang. She threw a lateral to a guy on her team. He caught it with one hand and did a quick pivot away from a player on my side. He faked left, then right, and came running in my direction, and I saw his face.

It was Rick Randall: a likely contender to get recruited to the Dawn Patrol or another coveted hero-league position straight out of high school. I could see the rugby ball–shaped flashbang, gripped tight to his ribs with one hand. It was glowing green, which meant it wasn't set to go off within the next few seconds. Randall would have to pass it or make a straight run for the goal right away. He had more than enough time to cut across to my side of the field. Clearly, he figured he had a much better chance of getting past me than any of our other defenders. He was right.

Rick Randall was big. The guy was powered: six foot four and probably two hundred and forty pounds of solid enhanced muscle.

Coming straight at me.

You are so *not Blake Baron.* Perfect. I had been hearing voices once in a while lately. I was getting very nervous about it, wondering if I was going nuts, and this was not the ideal time for hallucinations.

Because I didn't have a single physical enhancement power, there wasn't a whole lot I could do to stop Randall. I ran through my options in my head: (a) try to slow him down enough for the other defense guys on my team to get to this side of the field and take him on, (b) square off with him and hope not to die, or (c) just get the hell out of his way.

Maybe the crap Mr. M had said got under my skin, but instead of getting as far as possible from this hurtling locomotive, I ran toward him from a flanking position, hoping that he would change direction. Not because I believed he was afraid of me, but, at the least, I might be an irritant that he'd rather avoid.

I saw him glance down at the flashbang, notice me, and start to slow.

The flashbang in his hand had just switched from glowing green to glowing red. And that meant it could go off at any second. Randall was still a good thirty yards away from our side's goal. He must've decided that he didn't want to risk going for the goal with a live flashbang in his hand.

I didn't realize what he was doing until it was too late.

If his two-hand "tag" hadn't knocked the wind out of me, then hitting the ground would have. Before I knew what was happening, he'd drilled his knee on my chest and pinned my right arm to the ground. A perfect force reception, and I could only watch as he pressed the flashbang's contact plate against the lock plate on my wristband. The high-pitched squeal signaled that the flashbang was locked on.

"Nice one, Rick!" Mr. M called. "That's the way to do it."

Rick Randall rolled to the side, got to his feet, and ran like hell to get clear of me. The ball was flashing red. Forty-five seconds left before it would go off. Anyone who was within ten yards when it detonated would have ringing ears for days. Anybody with enhanced physical powers who was dumb enough to look at the ball when the flash went off would see floating white spots for the rest of the day. But the real fun part was the bang: anyone within ten yards would be hit with a concussive force blast that would cause full-body aches for at least a couple of days.

The others on the field would just shake it off after a day or so. But for someone without physical powers, like myself, the effects of the flashbang would be much more than an annoying penalty for slowness, hesitation, or bad tactics. For me, it would be temporary blindness, loss of hearing, and profound pain—right down to the bone marrow. So I wasn't just going to stand around and wait for the damn thing to go off. But when the flashbang was locked and activated, the only way to disable it was to run it through the opposing team's goal. Not kick it, not throw it, which I couldn't do anyway, since it was locked onto my wrist. *Run* it through. And that meant I had to get past everyone on the other team.

Not too likely. But still, there *was* a chance, however small. And this was an opportunity for me to impress the other kids, to show them that even if I didn't have physical powers, I could still make a run and maybe even score.

But Hitters don't like to lose. They especially don't like to lose face. And they *most* especially don't like to lose face to kids with no real powers. They ran at me—eight of them? Ten?—and started bodychecking me, one by one. They dashed away, no one staying long enough to risk being caught in flashbang range. Bumper cars. I was getting knocked all over the place, not making much progress toward the goal. My teammates kept their distance, keeping out of the whole thing to avoid the blast of the flashbang, which would be going off at any moment.

Suddenly, the blue lights on the posts lining the field started to flash. At the same time, my feet felt the vibration from the electromagnetic lattice under the ground as it powered up. The power field engaged and pulled down on our vests, wristbands, and ankle bands, making us feel heavy, like we were fighting against increased gravity. I looked at Mr. M, who, being a typical sadistic gym instructor, was grinning. The purpose of Gravitygain was strength training, but I always believed the PT teachers used it to amuse themselves.

Kids with enhanced strength obviously had an advantage and were able to power through it. All I knew was that I was stuck to a beeping, blinking flashbang about to go off and I had to get rid of it *fast*, and the last thing I needed was to be slowed down. If one of the guys knocked me to the ground, I'd never be able to get back up.

"Let's go, Hitters!" Mr. M shouted. "You gonna let a little extra gravity slow you down? Get moving. Look alive." He clapped his hands, making a sound like staccato gunshots.

If I could make a straight run, lurch past the three guys who were between me and the goal only twenty yards away, I figured maybe I would have a chance. If I really dug in, I had a shot at diving through the goal and deactivating the flashbang before it detonated. There was a chance I could actually make it.

I can't wait to see this! It was a voice that seemed to come from my right. I heard it, but it hadn't been spoken aloud. Still, out of reflex, I snapped my head toward where it had come from.

And that was when my chance to score evaporated. There were rapidly approaching footsteps from my left, but before I could even look that way, Rick Randall slammed into me with a perfect form tackle.

I hit the ground. And I mean *hard*.

A loud crunch reverberated in my head. It was the sound of three vertebrae in my neck being shattered when they smashed against the ground. A chill like ice water shot down my spine.

I heard Mr. M's baseball mitt–sized hands clapping. "Nice tackle, Randall. Nice! But I'd get away from there if I were you. Look alive, kid. Run."

I could hear a bunch of Hitters laughing and high-fiving, and Randall's thudding footsteps retreating as he made his run for safety. That was when it occurred to me: the worst was still to come.

The flashbang suddenly vibrated and let off a high-pitched squeal. Then there was an astonishingly loud sound like a prolonged gunshot in my ears. My eyes were clenched shut, but it didn't matter. The bright light easily penetrated my closed eyelids; it was like looking directly into the sun. The concussive force of the detonation rattled every atom in my body, and just before I blacked out, I had one last thought:

I really, really, really hate this game.

CHAPTER 2

Repairs

I was out of school for almost two weeks. There wasn't really any way for me to go to class in my condition.

The flashbang was directly next to my face when it detonated. That left me blind for almost forty-eight hours, almost completely deaf for the same period of time. And to top it off, I bit my tongue most of the way through, so it was all swollen and stitched up, and I couldn't talk.

Deaf, dumb, and blind. Emphasis on the middle one.

Thanks to Mom, who has a certain amount of pull in the medical field, the hospital got me fixed up pretty quickly. Osteomend helped my broken ribs heal faster. In about two days, otoneuro-growth stimulators repaired my hearing, and steroidal retinal enhancers cleared up my vision a day or two later.

And that was when Mom explained to me why I couldn't move my head and why my arms and legs felt numb.

The doctors had to install complicated artificial vertebrae apparatuses: titanium rings, hydraulics, and some kind of smart nanotechnology. Pretty fancy.

Injections of Myoplexin sped up the healing of the muscles they'd cut through in my neck when they put in the hardware. All damage considered, it was pretty remarkable that I was discharged after only five days.

Still. Five days in the hospital. Big-time fun. I was supposed to rest up for two or three weeks once I got home, but I didn't really want to. It was humiliating enough being squashed into a big splat on the field. The sooner I could get myself back to school, the better shot I had of looking, well, maybe not tough, but at least resilient.

The question was, though, was I trying to prove it to the other kids or to myself?

I still felt kind of sluggish, so I didn't argue with Mom when she said I should take at least the rest of the week off.

Blake called a few times to check up on me. He couldn't come home to visit, but that was totally understandable. The Justice Force was in the last planning stages of a top secret siege it had been developing for a while, and he just couldn't get away.

It was good to know that he was thinking of me when he had such major things to deal with himself. But every time he called, I was left thinking, This never would have happened to him. I mean, obviously. It couldn't happen to him. With his strength and speed? If there were any way for him to get hurt like this, he never would have been taken into the Justice Force to replace Dad as Artillery.

Even though I wasn't supposed to, I kept touching the big scar on the back of my neck. It wasn't too sore, but it was new and I couldn't keep myself from feeling it, kind of like how it was hard to keep your tongue from going after that loose tooth when you were a little kid.

The doctor had told me that if the damage had been just a tiny bit more, if my neck had been forced another millimeter or two, I would have ended up a quadriplegic. So even though I was left with a whole lot of titanium just under my skin, I had to consider myself lucky.

Uncoded

My third night home, I woke up with my T-shirt soaked. Even though the sheets were cold from my sweat, the room was hot.

Ever since I woke up in the hospital, I had been thinking about what happened on the field, and more important, why. It was weird: I had heard that voice in my head, but it'd felt as if it had come from someone on my right side. *I can't wait to see this*, it had said. This had been happening more and more, sometimes a couple of times a day. It was making me nervous.

It wasn't all the time, and the truth was that I couldn't correlate the incidences with any conditions or situations. The only factor that was common to all the times it happened was that the voices were usually emotional: either highly angry, deeply sad, or even ecstatic. In other words, high emotion. I didn't recognize any of the voices and it happened mostly outside the house, a lot in the hallways at school.

At first, my thought was that I was developing aural powers, but I realized it couldn't be that. The voices weren't external noises that were just low volume or far away. But it didn't feel exactly like I was hearing the sound. It was more like I was feeling the *idea* of the sound. That wasn't how things worked for Audiates. But it *was* how things worked for people who were—to use the clinical terms—wacko crackers, around-the-bend loony tunes. And I was already enough of a smudge on my family's reputation. The last thing they needed was for me to be insane, too.

I dug out the book, buried under a pile of old PT class T-shirts, from the bottom of my closet. It was an actual book, with paper pages. I didn't want to risk leaving any trace on the Internet, either by computer searches or e-book downloads. The book was *Psychopathology in the Undiagnosed Person* by Dr. Miklos Kohane. According to Doc Kohane, auditory hallucinations were usually a symptom of a few heavy-duty psychological conditions, none of them good. I'd been having them for a couple of months by that point, and that worried me. I read the book some more. I was relieved to find that my not having "command hallucinations" (*"Go kill the president!"*) was a good sign that I wasn't a serious danger to myself or others. Yet.

I read until I couldn't take it anymore. If I wasn't, in fact, crazy at that point, it was probably just a matter of time before I went off the deep end. There was no way to avoid it if it was in my genes.

If it was in my genes. That was something I could at least find out.

I took off my sweaty T-shirt and put on a fresh one. Then I went downstairs.

The bottom step creaked loudly. Mom called out from down the hall. "Brad? Is that you?"

Good. She was home. I called back, "Yep, it's me. Where are you?"

"In the study." I went to her office and took a seat in the chair in front of the desk.

Mom was sitting on the short couch, her legs tucked up under her.[2] She had a reading lamp on and a copy of *American Journal of Metahuman Genome Studies* open, four or five more volumes on the floor next to the couch. There were dozens of Post-it notes sticking out of the journals.

Although she was a geneticist, not a psychiatrist, I needed some answers about the voices and I figured Mom might be able to help. I did what I could to sound casual. "Hey, remember that time I went to the lab with you and we looked at Blake's DNA image?"

"When you were writing that paper for school."

"Yeah. So, I was just wondering, did you ever run *my* DNA?"

"Well, yes. Soon after you were born."

"Can you bring it up on your computer here?"

"Now? I could, but I would have to log in to the GenLab database, do a search to pull it up, and then tomorrow, I'd

---

[2] Mom is really little, but that doesn't mean she isn't tough. Intellectually, anyway. The thing is, her mother was powered, but her father wasn't, so as much as she wanted to go the hero route, her physical powers just weren't strong enough. Instead of becoming a traditional hero, she took a different path.

have to explain why I was accessing the server to read gene maps that aren't among the ones we're studying. Why?"

"I was just thinking that I'd like to see it."

She closed the journal she was holding. I noticed, though, that she kept a finger tucked in, to mark her place.

"Honey, looking at your DNA won't change anything. All it's going to do is make you feel worse. It won't give you powers you don't have."

Huh. Okay, so she thought this was about my being upset that I wasn't powered, a known sore point at home. I would use that. It was a lot better to let her think I was concerned about not having powers rather than concerned about losing my mind. I could let her think what she wanted and still find out what I needed to know.

"What would my DNA look like under the analysis program?"

"Genes for enhanced powers are shown in bright colors. You would have an indigo one, for your intelligence. But other than that, it would look essentially like a Regular's DNA."

"And any diseases that a person is wired to have—those show up in the genome map?"

"Like what?" she asked.

Oh, just stop asking these questions. There's no point. A voice again.

"What about mental illness? Does that show up?"

"Of course."

"How does that look?"

"Depends on what the illness is."

"Let's say, I don't know, schizophrenia."

"Like any other nonpowered gene. It's coded in white and carries a number."

"And that kind of marker would be there from birth, right?"

"Well, from before birth, yes. From just after fertilization, when the blastomere is forming. Why would you ask about mental illness genes?"

Better back off on that. If I asked whether she had seen that on my DNA, I was going to pull the conversation in a direction that would be hard to redirect. "No real reason. I'm just trying to get a full picture of how all this works."

"Why?"

"Just wondering about it, I guess."

There was a longer silence than I liked, but she took a breath and broke it. "You know I completely understand how it feels, not having powers . . . or not having the powers you want."

It was time to get out of the conversation. "I get that. But it's still uncomfortable to talk about."

She took in a breath. "Well, I've been thinking. If you believe it'll help, we can discuss getting you myo-augmentation."

"What?"

"It's true that I don't usually approve of cosmetic enhancement, but if you would feel better about yourself by having a mesomorphic muscular body, I could look into getting you a consultation."

An instant bodybuilder physique was not about to change me in the way I really needed. "Thanks, but I don't think that'll make any difference."

"Well, give it some thought. If you decide it's something you want . . ." Mom said. I started to wonder if maybe it was something *she* wanted me to get. I would fit in with the family image a whole lot better with great big biceps, pecs, and delts. But without true power behind it, it would all be just a facade.

"I'll keep it in mind," I said. Yeah, that was a good place to keep it. In my mind, where all the voices were. Right in the middle of the crazy.

CHAPTER 4

Battle Broadcast

On my first day back in school, ten minutes into third period, there was an announcement over the PA. It was our principal, the Colonel, as he still liked to be called, years after his retirement from the Quad Squad. "Pardon the interruption. We have just learned that members of the Justice Force have located and engaged the Gorgon Corps in battle. Teachers, please turn on your monitors and tune in to channel 221. Students, watch this carefully. It's likely to be a truly historic event."

Miss Connelly switched the channel on the monitor at the front of the room and turned off the lights. The camera work was very shaky. Whoever was shooting the battle was doing it using a long telephoto lens. Obviously, it wouldn't be a great idea to be too close to the action, unless your desire to document the event was greater than your desire to remain alive.

The image had that green glow of a night-vision camera, which meant the battle had to be happening somewhere in mountainous terrain on the other side of the earth—Asia, maybe, or the Middle East.

It was a pretty good fight, probably the best I'd seen in months. There were flares shooting through the darkness on the screen, which could have been mistaken for artillery, but were actually firebombs hurled at the Justice Force by Inferno. With the darkness, the distance, and the angle, it was hard to make out much detail, but you could see Phaeton[3] bodies falling on the battlefield. There was a blur of red, gold, and blue.

"Hey, Baron! Wasn't that your brother right there?" Dean DeStefano shouted.

"Looks like him," I said. A hand-to-hand fight had begun, and it was hard to tell who was winning.[4] The only way to see the guys from the Gorgon Corps was from the glints of light reflected off their dark uniforms. Of course, everyone in the Justice Force could be seen, even in the darkness. They wore bright uniforms exactly for this reason.

---

[3] In case you never bothered to learn about Phaetons, I'll give you the so-called official explanation about these public enemies. Pronounced "FITE-onz," they're the wretches who tried to enhance themselves through second-rate mutation splicing or bionics jobs that were botched up. They ended up as walking mutations gone wrong. And given their history of vicious attacks, they've come to be considered the lowest, most savage tier of villains.

[4] Why hand-to-hand? Why not bring out some heavy artillery and just blow the Gorgon Corps into oblivion? Here's why: It was never made public— pretty embarrassing, obviously—but a few years ago, when the Regulators tried to take down the GC, they came armed to the teeth with major firepower. They found out the hard way that several Gorgon Corpsmen had the power to remotely cause explosives to detonate. So if it wasn't made public, how do I know? Because Blake told me. He had been friends with Bob "Ish" Ishkatel, who was finished off when a 90mm shell in his bazooka exploded in the barrel, blasting back, right in his face. Bad ending for him, but it meant that Blake could warn his team not to go in armed with anything explosive.

The view switched to another shot, closer and from an angle that looked like it was being taken by someone lying on the ground. There was a crawl on the bottom of the screen that read, LIVE! JUSTICE FORCE (USA) ROUTS GORGON CORPS AT CHITWAN VALLEY IN NEPAL. FIVE MEMBERS OF GC CONFIRMED KIA, INCLUDING LEADER TOXICON, WITH NO CASUALTIES TO JUSTICE FORCE.

My classmates burst into applause and cheers. Even Miss Connelly clapped her hands. I joined in with everybody else.

On the screen, I could see the silhouette of my brother kicking ass and taking names.

And all around the classroom, I could feel eyes stealing glances at me. No doubt, several kids had to be thinking, How can one brother be such a star hero and the other one be such a complete nothing?

And truth be told, I was wondering the same thing myself.

CHAPTER 5

Blur

A t lunch on that first day back in school, I sat in the cafeteria with Virginia, Shameka, and Travis at our usual table. Shameka wasn't talking much, because her voice modulator had to be repaired. It was giving off a buzzing tone when she spoke, and occasionally squealed with reverb. If she spoke without it, she wouldn't be able to control her amplitude and could make a whole lot of people go deaf. She didn't have to worry about getting on a hero team; she already had a written offer from the Supersonics, and she had preregistered her hero name—Deci Belle.

The girls and I were watching Travis eat. It was amazing; you'd think he had the power of Matter Ingestion. Though there were obvious benefits to MI, like being able to eat fire and then become blazing hot, or to eat acid and then spit caustic lye, there probably weren't a lot of useful powers to get from eating crazy amounts of pasta salad.

I couldn't eat. I was too angry. "Can you believe that they didn't do anything to Rick Randall after what he did to me? I mean, not even a single day of detention."

Virginia and Shameka looked at each other, then at me. Obviously they were thinking, Bad topic.

"I mean, seriously," I said. "The kid broke my neck, almost crippled me, and now I've got half a hardware store implanted in my spine, all because he wanted to show off. And the school does nothing to punish him. Nothing at all. I mean, doesn't that make you sick?"

Shameka suddenly became very interested in the texture of the croissant still on her plate. Virginia was looking at me, and I could see it on her face: *Boy, I really don't want to talk about this with him now.*

"Hello?" I said. "No opinions at all? You're fine with the fact that they did nothing?"

Virginia took on a casual tone of voice. "Well, actually, he was given fifty points for a good sack. 'Perfect form' was what Mr. M had said. That kind of put Randall in the top position for accrued PT valor points."

Valor? "Whoa, whoa. Wait a minute. Rick Randall damn near kills a guy in PT class, the most blatant example of unnecessary roughness possible, and he gets rewarded with extra points and the top honor position?"

"Well, that pretty much hits it on the head," Virginia said, trying to sound lighthearted.

Wow. I wasn't sure which was more disturbing: that the school did nothing to discipline a violent scumbag just because he's got the so-called hero thing happening, or that my supposed friends didn't even care.

CHAPTER 6

My Own Worst Enemy

The events of seventh period didn't do much to increase my sense of belonging. Even though I was wearing the same navy uniform as everyone else in the class, I wasn't like them. Not looking the way most of them did—that is, being a whole lot smaller than the average guy in the hero track—wasn't the worst part. Lots of people had powers that weren't obvious from looking at them. For me, though, physically speaking, it was more or less what you see is what you get.

I'm pretty sure I wasn't the only one who ever zoned out in class, and it wasn't as if I'd been sending death beams from my eyes to the teacher. But for some reason, Mr. Q decided it was time to make an example of me.

"Hello, there, Brad! Mr. Baron? I do hope I'm not boring you with this lesson."

"Huh?" I said, sitting up in my chair and blinking. Most of the kids had too much honor to turn around and watch another student get disciplined. They faced forward or turned their gazes away. Except for the few who wanted to see me get verbally throttled.

The left corner of Mr. Q's mouth curled upward. "Certainly, it isn't as if the fate of civilization will absolutely depend on your knowing this material."

"Well, no. Probably not," I said.

"But it *is* possible. Wouldn't you agree it's *possible?*" Mr. Q was expecting me to admit I was wrong and apologize for arguing, and then pay rapt attention for the rest of the period. Which, I admit, I should have done.

"The thing is, Mr. Q, I really don't get why we *all* need to take aeronautics when not all of us can fly."

Mr. Q nodded his big head a few times. "Ah. I understand now. So what you're saying is, you don't see the value in your classmates learning principles of flight because you feel it doesn't benefit *you*, due to your own abilities. Or lack thereof."

I knew that Mr. Q had a reputation for being a great teacher, but I thought he was an arrogant, elitist bastard.

I was of no interest to him. He only really paid attention to the high fliers.

"You know, that's not a bad idea," he went on. "Let's change the curriculum. We'll get rid of any classes Brad Baron doesn't like. We'll only keep the ones that he's good at. It'll make for a pretty short school day, won't it?" He grinned, looking for laughter from his favorites, the few toadies who were all too happy to oblige.

Still, I felt like I had a legitimate argument. "I totally understand how anyone who's able to fly would find this really useful. But I don't see how it'll make any difference in life for the rest of us."

Virginia turned back toward me and glared. I knew her well enough to read from her face exactly what she was thinking: *He's going to blast you any second. Stop being an idiot!* And, of course, she was right.

And that might have been the end of the issue, but Mr. Q felt the need to discuss it some more. "You don't see how the study of aeronautics would make any difference to you," he said. "So pursuit of excellence is not something that matters to you. Is that it? And we shouldn't study powers that you don't have. Which doesn't leave much to study. But I suppose not everyone can live up to the legacy of your father. Or your brother."

So there it was. I'd figured he was headed in that direction. *Your brother is such a hero; your brother was so wonderful when I taught him; your brother stepped up when tragedy befell your poor father; your brother is an idol for kids and adults around the world . . . blah, blah, blah.* And then the inevitable— spoken or unspoken: *So what went wrong with* you?

I was tempted to point out that Mr. Q himself didn't exactly compare to Blake or my dad, either, so he might not want to go down that road. But I kept my mouth shut.

"So, Brad," Mr. Q said in his most reasonable voice, "whatever shortcomings you may have, you don't think knowledge of aeronautics would be helpful to you if you're, say, fighting someone who *is* able to fly? Let's say you're up against a Phaeton. Now—"

"It's pretty unlikely that I would ever find myself up against a real Phaeton," I said. I wasn't trying to be a smart-ass, but I was aware that I was sounding like one.

"Fine, then. Say you're fighting—oh, wait. Why fight anyway, right? Maybe you think it would be better to *debate* an enemy into submission instead."

"Well, there. That would be great, wouldn't it?"

Because of the injuries he'd sustained in the Battle of Des Moines, the left side of Mr. Q's face was made of FerroAlloy. And when he got mad, it would lose shape, going liquid metal. I could feel the floor vibrating a tiny bit and the room getting warmer. All signs that he was losing his temper.

If I could have gone back in time then, I probably would have said something different.

No more than a few seconds later, the trembling and shimmering in the room faded away, returned to normal, as his face went back to its usual form.

I glanced at Virginia. She was shaking her head at me, like, *You don't even* need *enemies. You're your own worst one.*

I couldn't argue with that.

Mr. Q cleared his throat. His cheeks were flesh again, but they were bright red with embarrassment. "Well, once again, you got us completely derailed from our lesson."

I was about to point out that he was the one who'd engaged me in conversation that was off topic, but there was no point. He worked some keys on his computer, and I knew I was about to get a demerit on my record.

When I heard three tiny clicks in my IDent card, I looked over to Mr. Q, confused. Disrespect is a one-demerit offense, two at the most for multiple infractions. He wasn't allowed to give me three. But that was what he'd done, and he was smiling at me, waiting for me to object.

The truth was, it wasn't just getting the demerits that bothered me. What really pissed me off was the fact that Mr. Q gave them to me just because he *could* and he knew that I wasn't in much of a position to object.

"Anything else you want to say?" Mr. Q asked.

Like that he was a washed-up old hack whose powers were never that great anyway? Or maybe that he was just like all the others who took advantage of their powers to subjugate anyone in a weaker position? It took every bit of self-control to keep my mouth shut.

"I'm inferring that you have something you want to say to me," he said with a grin. "If you do, then let's hear it." He folded his thick arms across his chest.

"I have nothing to say." I hated that I didn't have the guts to stand up to him. It really got to me that he'd imposed such a strong punishment when what I'd done hadn't even been so bad.

"Good. Then let's just get back to—"

"Oh, except the fact that you hit me with three demerits instead of one, which is kind of a violation of my rights."

"Your rights?"

"Well, yes. I mean, we *are* supposed to be about justice here, aren't we?"

The skin part of his face started to go red again, and

I wondered if the metal would turn fluid, too. "Okay, I'm done with you. You can go discuss your rights—and your wrongs—with the principal."

"Seriously?"

"Serious as a heartbeat.[5] Get up and go to the main office. Now."

He started typing my transgression into the computer system even before I'd closed the classroom door behind me.

---

[5] Of course he meant "Serious as a heart attack." The guy couldn't even use a cliché the right way.

CHAPTER 7

By Any Other Name

I walked down the hall to the main office, not even setting off the power suppressors on the walls. My enhanced intelligence barely registered unless I passed right next to them, and even then it was only a very faint hum that could have just been residue from being around kids with powers.

Mrs. Kolczyk, the principal's secretary, was a Regular, but she never seemed like someone who resented people with powers. I always figured she liked being around in the learning period of the students at the Academy, some of whom would eventually become famous heroes. *Oh, Velocity? I knew him when he was a little ninth grader,* she could say. *And let me tell you, he may be able to run a hundred miles per hour now, but back* then? *That boy was late for school every other day!* From the few times I met her, I figured she was basically a nice enough woman. "Bradley Baron, right? Mr. Q just sent a message that you'd be in. The principal will be with you in just a moment."

I went to the bench and sat down. On the other end was a girl I vaguely recognized. Colleen something. She was either a junior or a senior—that's about all I knew. I hadn't heard anything else. Nothing about breaking speed records, feats of strength, invulnerability, invisibility. Not a thing I could remember.

She was slouched down low on the bench, legs stretched out and crossed at the ankles. She wasn't wearing the requisite dark blue uniform for Academy Hitters. The jeans she was wearing, not to mention the holes in them, were strictly against school rules. And on top, she had on a gray jacket, which she had completely unbuttoned and open, showing a light green shirt underneath. Then it came to me: she wasn't in the Academy; she was in the alternative program, the A-program. No wonder I didn't know her.

She slowly turned my way and took me in with a bored look. Whether it was her sleepy gaze, her slightly-too-big lips, or her light brown hair and green eyes, I couldn't say, but I immediately got that nervous and clumsy feeling that I got whenever I was alone with really good-looking or cool girls. (Which wasn't often, I'll admit.) She wasn't classically pretty or perfect-looking, as were just about all the other girls at the Academy, but there was something about her, something I couldn't put my finger on, that made her really attractive.

She looked over at the IDent tag hanging from the lanyard around my neck, noticing (no doubt) the terrible hologram portrait (maybe the dorkiest one in the whole school) above my name.

"You're Brad Baron. I heard about you."

What could she possibly have heard? There was no significant crossover between kids in the A-program and the rest of us. "Really?"

"Your brother is Blake Baron, right?"

Of course. What else? "Yep, he's my brother." Let's change the subject. "You're Colleen . . ." I tried to get a look at her IDent tag to find out her last name, but she had put small ANARCHY NOW! stickers over her name and face on the tag. Strictly against the rules. Then I remembered. "Colleen Keating, right?"

"For better or worse. Hopefully worse. Anyway, I go by Layla, not Colleen."

"Layla," I repeated. "How does that come from *Colleen?*"

"It doesn't. But Colleen Keating? I'm just not into the whole hero-name-alliteration thing. My friends call me Layla."

And then I remembered the one thing I'd heard about her, the only reason I even knew her name. If I had it right, there was a rumor that she had been the prime suspect when the biochemistry lab was blown up one night last year. No evidence, no charges, but her name had definitely been mentioned.

She squinted at me. "So what did the younger brother of a big-shot hero do to get sent to the principal's office?" She made *hero* sound like a slur. Like *loser.*

Sarcasm wasn't something you heard much at school. It was considered unseemly and disrespectful. And that might have been what was getting to me. Even though what she'd said was a slam on me—intentional or not—that attitude she had, well, it made her totally hot.

Mrs. Kolczyk cleared her throat. "Colleen, stop bothering Brad."

"What do you mean? I'm not bothering him. I'm not bothering you, am I, Brad?"

"Bothering me? No. Not at all." Trying to play it cool. As cool as Kelvin, as they used to say. (Before he got melted by Inferno, that is.)

"See?" she said to Mrs. Kolczyk. Layla turned back to me and rolled her eyes. "Anyway, so, like I was saying, why would a good little scout like you—"

"I'm really not so good." Ha.

"Yeah, right. What did you do to get sent here? Return a library book a day late?"

She thought I was a total stiff. And from her point of view, as a student in the A-program, I could see how she would. But I didn't like it. "I pretty much went off on Mr. Q in aeronautics class."

She raised an eyebrow. I couldn't tell if it meant she was impressed or that she didn't believe me. "Really. What'd you say to him?"

I shrugged like it was no big deal. Still, I kept my voice low, not wanting Mrs. Kolczyk to overhear. "He was just going on and on about flight vectors and updrafts, and I let him know that I thought aeronautics class was a waste of time for anyone who's not a Flier."

She grinned. "Yeah? Nice job." She didn't make any effort at all to keep her voice down. "I can't *stand* that dickhead."

Mrs. Kolczyk shook her head and typed on her keyboard. I heard two demerit clicks register on Layla's IDent card.

She toyed with the ID and then shrugged, apparently not bothered in the least.

"How do you know him?" I asked. "He doesn't teach in the A-program."

"He comes over to lecture us A-holes sometimes, saying that we should still be ambitious and try to adopt hero values. But you can tell he thinks we're just scum. He's been retired for, like, twenty years now. All he knows about flying in battle is what he's seen looking up from the ground."

"That's pretty much what I told him." Not even close, but hey . . .

"Good! That . . ." She paused and glanced over at Mrs. Kolczyk, then went on. "That *fine example of a teacher* needs to be taken down a few pegs every so often. You did a public service by calling him out. If he got run over by a bus, the world would be a better place."

"Oh, Colleen," Mrs. Kolczyk said. "Don't you ever get tired of saying mean things about people?"

"Oh, Mrs. Kolczyk. No, I don't. Not when they deserve it."

The office door opened and our principal, the Colonel, came out. He looked at me with his craggy stone face. "I saw you out here, Mr. Baron. Seems like you crossed the line with Mr. Q, eh?" He turned his gaze on Layla, then back to me. "And now, consorting with Ms. Keating? Hm. Very ill-advised."

"What's *that* supposed to mean?" she said, taking mock offense.

The Colonel adjusted the tie around his 38-inch collar. His big, blocky finger scraped his jaw, granite on granite. "Oh, I'm sure you can interpret my comment accurately."

"Probably," she said. She smiled at me with a conspiratorial look.

The Colonel shook his head and said, "All right, Brad. You first. This young lady can wait a little longer."

I got up and turned to Layla.

"See you around," she said.

"Yeah. See ya later." But I knew that, just like we hadn't really crossed paths before, I would probably never actually talk to her again.

CHAPTER 8

Principal Concern

The wall behind the Colonel's desk was covered with framed pictures of heroes who had been students. Most of them showed the heroes next to the Colonel, either with their arms around his shoulders or in a handshake.

One of the pictures that didn't have the Colonel in it showed the Justice Force from about twenty years ago. Just to the left of center was Dad, in his twenties, probably, dressed in his full uniform as Artillery.

Next to that picture was another one showing the Justice Force but with a few personnel changes. Dad was gone by the time this was taken. And Blake had grown and come of age. He'd stepped up to become Artillery. The uniform had been retired when our Dad died, but when Blake was ready, the Justice Force modernized it a little. Sleeker and slicker, but the same colors and basic look.

Most important was that Artillery was still a Baron. The public loved the whole idea of the son taking on the role of the fallen father.

"Quite a bunch of alumni, isn't it," the Colonel said.

"Impressive." Which was the truth. Probably close to half

of the heroes from America who were in the big leagues were on that wall.

"Your father, there. He was a student here before I was principal, but I did get a chance to meet him the one time. You never met him, though, right? He was killed before you were born?"

"Yes, he was."

"Tragic. A real loss. I don't care what the conspiracy theorists say. I believe the Justice Force was ambushed and your father died a true hero. I remember where I was when I heard about it. I was in this coffee shop and . . . well, that's another story. Just a real shame. Your brother, though, of course I know him well. And he did a great job today. Very impressive."

"Yes, it was."

"*Very* impressive," he repeated. "I love when I can show students footage of our alumni in the act of doing something heroic, in real time. Just love it." He glanced at me and then cleared his throat with a rumble that made the pens on his desk buzz. "And now, here you are. Sent to me for disrupting a class." His stony brows furrowed. "Not exactly what one would expect from a Baron, is it?"

"I wouldn't say that I was 'disrupting the class,' really."

"Well, that's what I read in his message."

I could have explained that it was Mr. Q who had started the argument and he had been the one who'd kept it going, but I felt that saying *He started it* was lame and would only make me seem like a little kid. So, once again, I did what I always do when I feel like I'm in a losing battle: I shut up and shut down.

"Look," he said. He leaned forward in his chair and rested his massive elbows on the desk, which creaked in protest. "Whatever happened in Mr. Q's class happened, and I'm going to trust you—on your family honor—not to be disrespectful to teachers again, and we'll just leave it at that. I have other worries about you."

"You do?"

"I do. This whole incident that happened on the flash-bang field. That's a real concern."

Finally, a school official was addressing it. "Yeah, it was pretty bad. But I'm mostly okay now."

"Well, that's good, of course. But I'm still concerned about you being reckless on the field."

I wondered if I'd heard him right. Or maybe he was kidding. He had to be kidding. I waited for a smile, but it didn't come. "I'm not sure I get what you mean when you say I was reckless."

"No offense meant, but it's not too great an idea for someone your size and strength to try to take on someone like Rick Randall."

"I didn't try to take him on. He came after me. Why would I go after him? I'm not suicidal."

This conversation needs to end. It was a terrible time to hear voices.

"Well, I'm not saying you 'went after him,' exactly. But let's face it: you really shouldn't be playing with the big guys like him, should you?"

"Are you saying I'm going to be excused from PT class?"

"Oh, no. Not at all. I can't do that. What I'm saying is that this could have had a terrible outcome."

"I know. But like I said, I'm pretty much okay. The doctors did a good job fixing up my neck."

"That's good. Because it would have been awful if they couldn't. It could have destroyed any chances of getting brought into the Sentinels."

I laughed. "I really don't think there's too much likelihood that I'd get drafted into the Sentinels."

Now it was the Colonel's turn to laugh. "No, I meant Rick Randall's chances, of course. He's on their short list, and, well, if he had injured someone, even if it wasn't his fault, they might have second thoughts."

"Um, Colonel, I don't think I'm understanding what you mean."

He leaned back in his chair. "Well, now. If you had gotten seriously hurt—"

"I *did* get seriously hurt."

"I mean, if you had gotten more seriously hurt, like permanently, then it would have looked horrible, and I'm sure you would agree, being from a family of heroes and having a strong sense of patriotism and justice, that it would be a terrible loss if, due to your actions, Rick Randall were for any reason unable to serve."

"A terrible loss . . ." I repeated. I couldn't believe what I was hearing.

"Yes, so I want to make sure we don't have any other close calls like that. When your PT class is playing any physical games, like flashbang, for instance, I hope you'll be more careful about jeopardizing any other student's career."

Stunning. Totally stunning. If I hadn't seen his stony lips moving, I would have had to wonder if I was hearing things again. "So what exactly am I supposed to do?"

"I think the best thing you could do for all concerned is to stand by the sidelines and just watch."

"Just stand by and watch."

"Well, yes, Brad. That's certainly the best place you can be. Don't you think the safest thing for you to do is just keep your distance from any heavy action?"

What could I say? "Yes, sir. I'd have to agree you're right." I knew he was talking specifically about PT class, but it made me wonder if I was ever going to see action—action of any kind—at all.

A newspaper clipping I keep in my desk drawer even though it was written before I was born:

MASSACRE AT HOOVER DAM

The Justice Force was ambushed by an unidentified group of Phaetons while trying to repair a potentially disastrous fissure in the Hoover Dam in Arizona. As members of the Justice Force worked to prevent a more serious rupture, an event that could have cost inestimable loss of human life and extensive property damage, the Phaetons attacked and killed Artillery (Buckminster "Buck" Baron) who had been in a temporarily weakened state due to his exertions to hold the crack in the dam shut while it was being repaired. Also assassinated was the newest JF member, Marguerite "Aguafemme" Mendez. She is believed to have been crushed by falling debris. As of the present time, her remains have not yet been recovered.

CHAPTER 9

Oh, Brother

A week later, when I got home from school, I found Blake sitting on the couch, feet up on the coffee table, and looking like he owned the world. Which wasn't too far from the truth.

He still had on his red, blue, and gold flight suit, though the front was unzipped down to his waist. Custom-made to fit him perfectly, of course, it was some kind of top secret material the Justice Force team had designed just for them. Impervious to friction from air resistance, highly resistant to extremes in temperature, and tough enough to withstand medium-caliber gunfire. (Not that he *needed* that particular feature, but still . . .)

"Look who's home from school," he said in that rich baritone.

"How's it going?" I put my books down and went over to the couch. He stood and we did the sideways man-hug thing. "Mom didn't mention you were coming in."

"Well, things seemed to be pretty under control with that mud slide in Peru, so I thought I'd drop by."

Since he moved out of the house to join the Justice Force four years ago, I always was kind of shocked when I saw him.

Not that he wasn't on TV all the time. Seeing him in the flesh when I wasn't used to it every day was different. About six foot three and built like . . . well, like a superhero: strong, square jaw; shiny, friendly eyes; and a bright white smile. It was incomprehensible that we were brothers. Or even related in any way.

And of course, it wasn't just his looks. He was brave. He was strong. He was loved by all. He was a leader. He was thoughtful and caring. He gave his time, his effort—devoted his life—to helping people according to the tenets of the Justice Force. And he was one of the most powerful heroes in the JF, which was in accordance with his hero name: Artillery. Big guns.

"Aren't there Peruvian rescue teams who can handle their own natural disasters?"

He laughed. *Hearty* was the word for it. "Well, sure there are, but if I can help, why wouldn't I?"

Everything about him was perfect.

He was so . . . so not me.

The one main flaw? He wasn't super-bright. But he had so much charm that very few people ever really noticed this about him. They viewed him as a regular guy, if you can be that and a world-famous hero at the same time. He could really do no wrong.

"I would've thought, after your battle with the Gorgon Corps last week, you'd want to take it easy."

"You know what they say. 'No rest for the weary,' right?"

"Who says that?"

"I'm just saying. That's what 'they' say. I don't know who."

Mom came into the living room from the kitchen, carrying three glasses of iced lemonade. "And besides, the Justice Force isn't just about fighting crime and terrorism," she said.

"And villain alliances," Blake added. "Phaeton and human."

"Of course," Mom said. She handed one glass to Blake and another to me. "They helped divert water during the drought just last month. And wasn't it Lynn Levy who helped kill off that livestock contagion in Guyana?"

"That was Lynn and Deena Delaney. They've been doing great work since they started teaming up," Blake said.

"So? What's the story with you and Deena?" Mom asked.

"No story. That's all just gossip tabloids. She's interested in someone else anyway."

Mom shrugged. "She's a terrific gal, Blake."

"Yeah, she is terrific, but we're just coworkers. And besides, I'm kind of back with Janet."

"Oh, right, right. I forgot. Sorry."

Blake turned on the two-thousand-megawatt smile. I didn't need any more details about Blake Baron's Love Life.

"I'm going to go up and take a shower," I said.

"Okay," Mom said. "Then, we're going to go out to dinner."

"Sounds good." I headed for the stairs.

"Hey," Blake called. I turned. "Looks like you filled out some since the last time I was home. Shoulders are broader, right?"

You didn't need to have voice-modulation-detection powers to tell that he didn't really believe that I had changed at all.

"Maybe. I'm a growing boy, after all," I said, trying to sound easygoing.

We went out to dinner at McClellan's, and when people weren't coming over to the table to ask for Blake's autograph, Mom and I were listening to details of the last two or three battles—blow by blow—that Blake and the JF had been in over the last couple of months.

The manager brought over complimentary champagne flutes of chocolate mousse and didn't leave before getting a photo with Blake, their arms around each other's shoulders. That one would go up on the wall, no doubt.

"Did you hear about the Phaeton the Power Division took care of in New York today?" I asked Blake.

Blake squinted for a couple of seconds, like he was deep in thought.

"This was the one who was smashing up all the elevators in the Empire State Building," I added.

"Right. Until Plastique dropped her special blend down the shaft. That left Phaeton stew splattered all over the place."

"Brad," Mom said, making a face. She was never what I would call a squeamish person, but she seemed to get a little bit upset whenever conversation turned to Phaetons getting wiped out. "Can we keep this a little more appropriate for dinner conversation?"

"Sure. Sorry, Mom." I turned to Blake. "So are you guys going to get Mutagion, or what?"

"He's the big prize. He would definitely be the one to get," Blake said, nodding. "Did you see that coverage of Meganova and the Vindication Squad today?"

"I saw that," I answered. "The way he just—"

"Didn't Dad team with him back in the day, Ma?" Blake asked.

"He sure did. For about seven years, I think. But I haven't seen him in ages."

Blake answered. "Yeah, Mega-N mentioned it when we worked together a few weeks ago. The bridge collapse?"

"Right, right." Mom nodded. "I saw that one on a monitor at work. He's looking a little thicker around the middle, I have to say."

"He's still got it, though," Blake said. "Strong as all get-out, and nowhere near past his prime."

I shook my head. "I don't see what's so great about him, to be honest."

They turned to me, each of them with a look as if I had just said that I didn't understand the point of justice and humanitarianism. Which, I'll admit, was basically what I *had* said.

They stared at me for probably five solid seconds before Blake slowly smiled and then laughed. "Ah, good one. You had us going there."

They started to talk about the relative merits of various hero teams like Night Patrol, Power 11, and the Vindication

Squad—who was leaving where, which ones had become free agents, and so on. I had heard the conversation (or a basically identical conversation) at least a thousand times in the past.

I woke up suddenly. It was dark, but I could see Blake's silhouette. He was standing silently in front of my closet, looking toward me.

"Didn't mean to scare you," he said.

"You didn't. I don't scare that easy."[6]

He nodded, then grabbed a chair against the wall. He was noticeably being careful not to make any scratching sound as he pulled it closer to the bed.

He cleared his throat, then spoke in a whisper. "Listen, I need to talk. Are you awake enough to have a conversation or should we wait until morning?"

"I'm fine. What's up?"

"How's that neck doing?"

"It hurts now and then. Weather changes don't feel especially great."

He came closer and touched the back of my neck. "Wow. That's a serious scar, huh? And there's a whole lot of metal in there, too, right?"

"Half a hardware store, about. I have three prosthetic vertebrae, some hydraulic crap, nanotech smart system, the works."

"Bro, I'm sorry I didn't get to come in to see you when

---

[6]Pure bravado. I probably heard it in a movie and liked how it sounded.

it happened. Real busy with Justice Force business."

"No big deal. Don't worry about it."

"It is a big deal, and I do worry about it. I also worry about you getting mixed up in flashbang games with powered kids. You can't handle that. You should know better."

"It's not like I had a choice. PT isn't optional. From now on, though, I'm going to keep my distance from games or whatever where I could get hurt. I'll hang around the sidelines."

Blake frowned slightly, almost recoiled. *A Baron on the sidelines. Pathetic.* "People do know you're my brother, right?"

I had the urge to punch him, but all it would have done was gotten me a broken hand. So instead, I shook my head, turned away from him, and lay back on my pillow. "I'm going to sleep now."

"I don't think so." He reached over and easily lifted me into a sitting position, using just one hand. I could have resisted, but that would only have made me feel weaker. I was glad, though, that he didn't have any telepathic powers, because if he had read my mind, well . . .

"Okay, so you got intelligence. But I can't believe you have nothing good." He held his arm out in front of me. "Squeeze my forearm."

"I'm not doing this."

"I got lots of patience," he said. "You can cooperate now or we can do this dance. In the end, you're going to do what I say, so why not just do it and save—"

I grabbed hold of his huge forearm and squeezed.

"Come on," he said. "Harder. Put some muscle into it."

I tightened my grip, but it was like trying to squeeze a tree. Solid oak. I let go. I knew that he wasn't deliberately *trying* to humiliate me. Well, maybe he was.

He nodded. I could see he had his lips pursed, thinking. "Okay, so maybe strength isn't your strength." A white flash of teeth, the smile that was loved around the world. "No flying, huh?"

What could I do but shake my head? Was he actually going to run down the list of all the things I couldn't do?

"No thermokinesis? No tracking, no duplication, no molecular manipulation." Well, it seemed like he *was* going to list all the ways I fell short. I just looked at him, pointlessly trying to will him into feeling rotten.

Blake sighed. "Look, I know exactly how you feel."

"You do?"

"Well, no. I don't, but it's, like, a saying. I'm trying to be understanding." He shrugged. "I'm not worried about this," he said.

He shook his head and stretched his left leg out in front of him, then twisted his neck. He didn't say anything, but I got the feeling something was hurting him.

"What's wrong with you?" I asked.

"With *me*? We were talking about *you*," he whispered.

"No, I mean, are you in pain or something?"

"Not at all." He was lying. I had no doubt. "And anyway, I came here to talk about this other . . ." He trailed off, but

I knew he was just trying to change the subject, away from himself.

"Other what?"

"An opportunity. I'm gonna help you. I want to take you to meet a friend of mine from the JF. You never met Rotor, did you? I'm pretty sure you didn't. He's working in our sub-terranean lab right in the city this month, so we're gonna go talk to him. He's a real idea man. He'll help us out."

"Well, I have school tomorrow."

"No big rush. I'm back now, staying home for a little bit."

"Staying home? Why? What's wrong?"

"Nothing's wrong. I just . . . I'm way overdue for vacation or a leave or whatever, and now's as good a time as any."

He was absolutely lying. His smile was fake. It seemed like he was stuck between thoughts—or emotions—and he wasn't clear about what to say.

"Why don't you just tell me?" I said.

He glanced at me, and I saw something in him that I never saw before. In fact, I don't believe *any*one had ever seen it in him.

"What are you scared about?" I asked.

It was written all over his face: *Should I tell him? Will he be able—or willing—to keep the secret? Better to keep it quiet. I* could read him like a storybook.

"Just say it."

Blake shut his eyes for a second. "Okay. You know about the Battle of Chitwan Valley? In Nepal?"

"The one last week? You'd have to live under a rock not to know about it. We watched it at school."

"Well, the thing is, I think I got injured."

There was almost nothing in the world he could have been less likely to say, and somehow, it didn't surprise me at all. "Injured? You don't *get* injured."

"I know. I know that. But I think . . . well, I am now."

"How?"

"I'm pretty sure it was Vilify, but it could've been one of the others. Four of those damned Phaetons got me in a ravine. The TV cameras didn't catch it. I fought my way out, but I'm guessing that was when it happened."

"So what's wrong?" It was astonishing that *I* was asking *him* how he was hurt.

"Some small things. Ligaments in my left knee. Spleen, maybe, something in my guts—I don't know what. But the real problem is . . . my internal gyroscope system is way off. Can't fly straight, not easily. My pitch and yaw are screwed. So I have some trouble with what's up and what's down when I'm airborne."

"That's kind of serious."

"No kidding. And I have to go so slow, I'm like a what-do-you-call-it."

"A sitting duck?"

"Right. Exactly. And the vision in my right eye is off. Blurry. Triple vision."

I thought for a few seconds. "Well, you have to get it all checked out."

"Hell, no!" It wasn't loud, but it was strong. The glass of water on my night table hummed from the powerful low frequencies in his voice. "Nobody—not a soul—knows this. And nobody *can* know. You understand?"

Oh, I understood, all right. If word got out that Blake Baron was not in top fighting form? The Justice Force would become the targets of every major villain—solo or team, human or Phaeton. When the strongest link suddenly became the weakest, lots of people would want to break that chain.

"But you can't go around injured indefinitely."

"Oh, no. It's definite. I'm injured.[7] But I'll figure out how to deal with it. I mean, I've punched through granite walls to rescue hostages. I've pulled sinking cars out of rushing rivers. You think I can't handle this?"

"I get it. But this is pretty different. You need to—"

"No! Nobody. Especially not Mom. Nobody. I probably shouldn't've even told you, but, hey—you're my brother. I'm going to have to trust that you have enough . . . discreetness—"

"Discretion?"

"Whatever, yeah. Enough discretion to understand how dangerous and serious and important it is that you don't breathe a word of this to anybody."

"I won't say a thing."

"Okay. I trust you on that."

Blake gave me what, for him, was no doubt a light bump

---

[7] Yes, he really said that.

on my upper arm with his fist. I thought he might have broken my humerus.

"Ha. No, but seriously. Just in case anybody gets the idea to check out what's in that mysterioso mind of yours for some reason, just make sure you don't, like, think about it at all."

Sure. Not even for a second.

One thing struck me as pretty funny. After he spent the last twenty minutes running down the list of all the ways I was inferior, he undid all that in a few seconds. When he told me about his injuries, little did he know that the knowledge gave me an insane amount of power.

CHAPTER 10

Misguidance

While we were walking out of linear calc, Ms. Matthews put a hand on my shoulder and stopped me. "I got a message on my computer that you're needed in the guidance office."

"Me? What for?"

"It didn't say. Guidance, I would guess."

I barely had the chance to sit down when Miss Davenport came out of her office. I didn't know for sure if she was a Regular or if she just had really low-level powers. Either way, she looked like a normal person and never gave a hint about any powers she might have. She smiled at me in a way that seemed practiced and held the door open.

I stopped dead in the doorway. There were three chairs facing her desk.

One was empty.

My mom was sitting in the second.

And Blake was sitting in the third, by the window.

I had no idea what was going on, but I knew one thing for sure: it wasn't good.

"Hi?" I said.

Mom's "hi" was falsely cheerful.

"What's wrong?" I asked.

"Nothing," Mom said, none too convincingly.

"We've just been talking with Miss Davenport for a little while," Blake said.

Really. How long had they been there? "So, what's going on, then?"

"Have a seat," Miss Davenport said, putting what was obviously meant to be a reassuring hand on my shoulder. "Nothing to worry about."

Nothing to worry about offers the same amount of reassurance as *This won't hurt a bit.*

I took the empty chair and she sat down behind her desk.

"So," she said, "I know you're wondering what could be going on that would cause me to ask your family to come in for a meeting."

All I did was nod. I didn't trust my voice. I honestly couldn't think of anything I had done that was so bad or so weird that the school would have to call in my mom and Blake for a guidance meeting.

Miss Davenport took a breath. "Well, I'll tell you straight, Brad. We have some concerns about how you've been doing in school."

"My grades are mostly okay."

She had my school transcript right there in front of her. "Well, yes. Yes and no. Sure, you do fine in things like history, English, and math. But, well, why don't you have a look for yourself?"

She slid the paper across her desk. It wouldn't show

anything I didn't already know. I pretended to examine it even though I knew where the conversation was heading.

"I think you'll see a pattern there," Miss Davenport said. "Straight academics are fine, but you didn't do too great in Practical Combat Techniques, Aeronautics I, Physical Training, Speed Optimization, to name a few. In terms of classes that require application of powers? Well, you do fall a bit short there—I'm sure you would agree."

"Okay, true," I said. "No argument: physical-powered stuff isn't my strength."

Miss Davenport chuckled politely, like, *Kid, you won't find this so funny when we're done here—believe me.* Blake shifted in his seat and looked at his thumbnails.

Miss Davenport continued. "It's a bigger issue than it not being your strength. Learning about powers and how to be a hero is, to be blunt, what the Academy is all about. It's our whole reason for being, as they say."

"Are you kicking me out of school?"

Mom turned to me. Blake looked at Miss Davenport. Miss Davenport went pale.

"No, no, of course not. No. What we want to do is find a way to make things better for you here. And we think we have a good solution."

I already got the feeling that *their* idea of how to make things better for me was pretty different from *my* idea about it. "Okay . . ." I said, drawing it out.

Miss Davenport reclined in her chair. She seemed to feel she was back in comfortable territory. "Brad, you see, it's like this: you're sixteen, a junior, and, well, looking at your transcript and your profile, it's clear you're lagging behind in your development." She glanced at another paper on her desk. "Your strength factors all average out to 25.5, which is . . . well, it *is* higher than a Regular's strength. But let's be direct: it's nowhere near the strength of a true powered person. I mean, don't take this the wrong way, but there are powered students in elementary school with higher strength scores than yours."

Blake didn't say anything, either, but by the way he turned his head away, it was pretty clear he was embarrassed.

"No significant powers have manifested yet, and again, at sixteen, we expect to see most powers at least *start* to bud. Of course, I don't know what your genome map shows, but at this point, it's highly unlikely that you're going to develop any powers that you don't already have. I don't imagine I'm telling you anything you haven't probably thought about quite a bit yourself. I know this may sound harsh, but I really think it's time to face the music: it just doesn't look like you're ever going to get strength, flight, invulnerability, or any of the other major physical powers. And, given the incident that happened in PT class, well, we're lucky you didn't get hurt even worse. Overall, it seems clear that you shouldn't be in classes with the more highly powered students."

"If I'm not being kicked out, I'm not sure where this is going. Are you asking me to try harder?"

"Well, there's nothing you can do if you don't have powers. It's not your fault. Here's what I'm getting at: you do have intelligence. You're really quite smart. And, Brad, I want you to believe me when I say this: there is nothing wrong with being smart. I mean that sincerely. Granted, it's not like being able to punch through stone walls and rescue trapped people. And no, it's not quite as exciting as flying. But still: it can be useful. Even coming from your family, these things happen. Not everyone can be a hero. The world needs *all kinds* of people, including really intelligent ones. Some Regulars truly value intelligence. You can make a good life for yourself, make a good living. There's no shame in that."

However much she might have been trying to make me feel better, it was having the exact opposite effect.

"What do you want me to do?"

Her already big eyes went wide with what I guessed was concern. But her voice had an edge of impatience. Or maybe condescension. "There is nothing you *can* do. That's my point. Look. You're terrific just the way you are. But you're not truly suited for the powered program here. And since we would never want to see you leave, we have a great solution for you. You'll be switched over to the alternative program."

"Wait, *what*?" There was no way I had heard her right. "What did you say?"

"Now, don't you worry. You'll get an excellent education in the A-program. There will be lots of classes that you'll feel much more comfortable taking. Advanced Dual Variable Calculus. Quantum Mechanics. Let's see, what else?" She looked at a school handbook. Obviously she didn't do a whole lot of work with the A-program. "Oh, right. There's Theory and Practice of Dimensional Transmutation. Concepts in Genetics and Power Enhancement. Anatomy, physiology, pathology. So many. And you can still take electives in theoretical aspects of powers, if you'd like."

"You want me to switch over to the A-program? For all my classes? Even the ones I'm good at?"

She nodded. "It's kind of an all-or-nothing program."

"You're saying you think I'm really an A-hole."

"Brad!" Mom said.

"No, Mom, that's what they call themselves. These are the kids who don't have cool powers, but the Academy won't throw them out, because they're from high-powered families."

Blake shifted in his chair. His face was red. "Maybe if he, you know, applies himself more . . . maybe then he can stay where he is."

"Honey," Mom said, "we need to listen to what Miss Davenport recommends."

"Yeah, well, that's easy for *you* to say. You're not—" Blake stopped himself. Which was a good move. Last time he pulled that one, he ended up getting the cold shoulder from Mom for almost a week. "Sorry," he said.

"This is what we've been discussing, and it's what we agreed would be best for him," Miss Davenport said. I figured Blake wanted to smack that understanding smile right off her face. I sure did.

Wait a minute. "Wait a minute. You all have been discussing this? For how long?"

"That's not important," Miss Davenport said. "What's important—"

"Hold on. Not important? It's kind of important to me that you've been plotting to wreck my life by dumping me into the A-program and nobody told me a thing."

"Brad, every single one of our graduates has gone on to live a perfectly fine, productive life. I know that, in time, you'll see that this is best."

Mom finally touched my arm. "Are you really, truly opposed to doing this? Are you *happy* in the Academy?"

As always, Mom made a good point.

By no reasonable definition of the word could I honestly say I was "happy" as things were. But, still: the A-program? Really?

"Whatever," I said.

Miss Davenport smiled again. I wondered if her teeth were false. They were too big and white for someone who wasn't a natural hero. Cosmetic dentistry, definitely. "Listen, Brad, it may not feel like it now, but we're all doing what we know is best for you. You'll be so much more comfortable in the A-program, being with kids who are more like you. You'll see. But I want you to go in with a good attitude."

I had an idea of what I wanted *her* to do, but saying it wasn't going to help anything. So instead, I just said, "I will."

"You don't want to sabotage yourself, right? I mean, you

have to be part of making your own happiness. Embrace this opportunity. Let yourself grow into the person you were always meant to be."

Well. I didn't know then, but I can say it now. In spite of all her obnoxious and trite little platitudes, and my firm belief that she was more interested in getting me away from the stars in the Academy and tucked quietly away with the rejects, she did have one thing right: I found my people in the A-program. And without that, I might never have come to understand who, or what, I really am.

Over the past five decades, the Monroe Academy has molded boys and girls into young men and women who demonstrate the hallmark values of heroes the world over.

We help students develop their powers and abilities so they can be put to use in only the most noble and heroic ways.

With the emphasis on virtue and honor, we guide our students to develop their bodies, powers, and civic pride, enabling them to become leaders in the American and international ranks of heroes.

Monroe Academy for Powered Teens:
We accept only the best . . . we produce only the best.

Excerpt from
Monroe Academy brochure

CHAPTER 11

Silent Treatment

There wasn't much talk on the ride home from school. I was still taking in the news that I was being yanked out of the mainstream Academy program. And the fact that it had been in the works for a while and Mom hadn't told me a thing about it felt like a total betrayal.

Before we left school, I asked when the change was going to happen. Because it was almost the end of Friday, Miss Davenport said, it would be "just perfect" to start on Monday. And over the weekend, I would have a chance to go buy the A-program uniform. Couldn't be better timing, she said.

When we got home, I headed upstairs. Blake called to me when he reached the living room. I stopped midway.

"You know, Brad, I'm not any happier about this than you are."

"Yeah, well, at least you knew it was coming. Thanks for letting me know."

Well, it's not my fault you don't have any decent powers. Even my psycho voices were against me.

Over the weekend, I met Virginia, Travis, and Shameka at Ducky's Diner, a place that serves mainly Regulars. I didn't especially want to have the conversation anyplace where we might run into kids from school. I told them about my getting dumped into the A-program.

"Hold on. Can they *do* that?" Travis asked. He took a big bite of his Ducky burger. I'm pretty sure that news of an impending attack by the Phantom Legion wouldn't get him to take a break from eating. "Can they just do that to you?" he said, barely intelligible with his mouth full of food.

"They can do whatever they want," Shameka said. A few people turned around. She adjusted the volume on her voice modulator. "It's a private school."

Virginia poked at her Greek salad, not saying a word.

Travis squeezed his eyes shut as he swallowed what was probably way too big a gulp of food, making his face go red. "The thing is, if they didn't want you to stay in our program, why not just tell you that you have to find another school?"

"Two guesses," I said.

"I don't know," Travis said with a shrug.

Shameka shook her head. Virginia pursed her lips.

"Um, my brother? And my parents?" I said. "Why do they even *have* the A-program? For kids who can't hack it in the regular program but come from families that the Academy doesn't want to piss off."

Nobody said anything for a while. Finally, Shameka cleared her throat, which made her voice modulator give a high squeal of feedback. "Well. You know, we'll still see each other all the time, right? I mean, it's not like you're moving to, like, Alaska, right?"

"No, it's definitely not," I said, probably not sounding too convincing.

"And we'll still eat lunch together," Travis said. "You'll probably have the same lunch period, won't you? Don't they have the same lunch period as us?"

"I'm sure," I said. Lie. I had no idea.

I looked over at Virginia, who still hadn't said a word. She didn't have to. Ever since we first met—in fourth grade at Shameka's swimming pool party, when, even though I couldn't swim, I jumped into the deep end, which just ended with me sinking to the bottom of the pool. Virginia dove in and pulled me out, all this before she had even developed her power of aqua-respiration. We turned into close-enough friends that we could leave some things unsaid. Which, fortunately, was what she did at Ducky's. Saying it out loud would have been too rough.

Nothing would ever be the same again.

CHAPTER 12

Bad Good Kid

As I walked down the corridor toward A-wing, I realized that I had never even been in this part of the building. It was empty, not a student in sight, most likely because I was an hour and a half late to school. Mom had tried to wake me up at the regular time, but I fell back asleep. The truth is, I had barely slept all night, so, yes, I was tired in the morning.

And so there I was, walking down the A-wing hall in my new gray jacket, looking like a true A-hole.

I checked the schedule Miss Davenport had e-mailed me[8] and found the room for my third-period class. I opened the door and went in.

My first thought was, This is a room full of sick people.

It wasn't that the kids in room A-301 actually looked unhealthy. But not one of them—not a single one—had the perfect muscular build that I was so used to seeing fill every classroom I had been in since elementary school.

---

[8] "Your new teachers have been notified that you'll be joining their classes! They're all very excited to have you!! Have a terrific first day!!!" We have heroes for just about every supposedly good cause, and yet we don't have a single one who has taken on the mission of apprehending and punishing all the people who use cute little emoticons and/or more than one exclamation point per sentence.

They just looked like Regulars. Like ordinary people.

The ones who wore the uniform gray jackets had them totally unbuttoned, with T-shirts underneath. Some didn't even wear the jackets; they were hanging over the backs of chairs or stuffed partway into backpacks.

All told, there were only eleven students in the whole class. I couldn't see their faces, because they were sitting with their backs to the door, watching something on the video monitor. It wasn't footage of battles they were analyzing. It wasn't newsreel of hero demonstrations or parades or anything like that.

It looked like a normal movie you'd watch at home or in the theater. It sure wasn't the kind of movie I had ever seen in school.

"Can I help you?" a voice asked. It was a thin, middle-aged guy with a goatee and a ponytail. I hadn't even noticed him when I came in, because he was leaning back in his chair, his feet up on the teacher's desk, which was off to the side of the door. "You look a little lost," he said.

"Um, well, I think I'm supposed to be new in this class. In the program." I took a look at my schedule and then walked toward him. "Are you Mr. Wittman?"

"I'm afraid so," he said. He looked over my schedule. "Yup, you're in this English class now. How's it going, Brad?"

"Okay. Thanks."

"Yeah, we're about halfway through this movie. Have you seen it?"

I looked at the screen a moment. "I don't think so."

"Ah, it's great. See, the guy who just got wiped out—"

"Wittman," a kid called out. "We're trying to watch here. Why do you have to talk during all the good parts, man? It totally ruins it!"

"Hey, Jack. Stop your bitching and just watch."

"You suck."

"So do you. Relax."

The kid hadn't turned around. He shook his head and held his arm up, one extended finger sending a clear message to the teacher.

Who totally ignored it. No demerit clicks. No throwing the kid out. Nothing. Mr. Wittman turned back to me. "Don't mind him. He gets a little intense during movies."

"Wait," I said. "This is the one about the crime family? Where the police are crooked and the one good son turns out to be the most vicious guy around?"

"You got it. You want a great story about good and evil, one that'll turn your head around? Have a seat. You've come to the right place."

The end-of-period bell rang, but nobody moved from their seats. I started to get up, but Mr. Wittman waved me back.

"Relax." He took a cell phone out of his pocket and speed-dialed a number. "Hey, can you hold on to your crew for, like, fifteen minutes? We're watching something here, and I just want to get to the end of this sequence. . . . Thanks. Yeah, that would be perfect."

The teacher didn't take his gaze off the screen or his feet

off his desk the whole time. And he was going to ignore the bells and send us to our next class late, just to watch a movie? It didn't look to me like they ran too tight a ship over in the A-wing.

We watched for about twenty minutes more when he took out his phone, dialed again, and said, "Yeah, I'm sending them over in a minute."

He swung his legs off the desk, stood up, and turned on the lights. "All right, that's it for today. Get lost."

The students stretched, talked to one another, and grabbed their bags as they got ready to go.

"Oh, right. We have a new student in class," Mr. Wittman said. "Brad. He'll be on you guys' schedule. Help him out. Make him feel welcome. See you later."

A few kids murmured "hi" to me, a few more nodded, and the rest didn't pay me any mind at all. I started to shuffle out with them. This was going to suck, big time.

A strong hand grabbed my shoulder. "Hey, new guy," a female voice said.

I turned. It was that girl, Layla Keating. The one I'd met in the principal's office the week before. "I remember you," she said. "The bad good kid."

"So does that mean you're the good bad kid?"

"Babe, around here, we're all bad bad kids. Welcome to the club."

CHAPTER 13

Out of My Mind

My next class was Integrated Science. *Great.* Sounded to me like one of those courses for the students who couldn't hack the real thing—like how earth science is sometimes called Rocks for Jocks.

Well, it turned out to be pretty different from what I'd expected. Half the room had a regular lab setup, and the rest seemed to have stations with all kinds of projects in progress. I approached the teacher, who was a tiny lady, maybe forty or so, with a long skirt to the tops of her sandals and a Jet Lag band T-shirt.

"Hi," I said, handing over my schedule. "I'm Brad Baron. You're Miss Franks?"

"Hiya. And it's Tricia," she said in a rich Texas accent.

"Miss Tricia? It says—"

"Nope. Just plain old Tricia. Welcome, Brad. How're you doing?"

"Okay, I guess. It's my first day, so I haven't really—"

"Tricia!" one of the guys in the class called out. "Someone from the other class messed with my project. It's all screwed up."

"Oh, boy," the teacher said to me before turning back to

the kid. "You're getting riled up already? I'll be right over there, Choke," she called. Then, to me, "That boy needs to work on his frustration tolerance a mite. I'll tell you what, Brad. Why don't you take a look at what the other kids are doing and just as soon as I get all of them up and running, I'll sit with you and we can talk about what you want to work on in here."

She gave me a big smile and went off to help the sallow-faced kid named Choke.

Everyone was involved in something or other: a couple were on computers, others were performing what looked to be physics experiments with steel balls. One guy was holding a metal bar in his bare hand, heating it over a Bunsen burner flame.[9] In a corner was what looked like a big playpen, with straw on the floor and a large white rabbit that hopped around, constantly changing direction. A girl stood nearby, watching the rabbit and making hissing and humming sounds.[10]

Back then, I was basically shy. Or maybe insecure. Whatever you want to call it, I wasn't great at mingling with people. So I stood around by myself for a couple of minutes, which felt awkward, too.

---

[9] Turned out that this kid took on the name Inflammable, not knowing that the word actually means "flammable." Two minutes with a dictionary would have saved him from years of embarrassment.

[10] This was, I later found out, Melanie Krone, who could emit subsonic sound waves that were inaudible to humans but were *extremely* audible— and irritating—to different types of animals. She could whip them up into a frenzy, I suppose making them useful as angry (if unpredictable) weapons.

I went over to that girl Layla. She was sitting on a lab stool, her hands on either side of a desktop power computer, watching the screen. Something was wrong with the computer: it was flashing through different Web sites, then bringing up documents and scrolling through them, then switching over to a video game, and starting all over again. Her hands weren't on the keyboard, so I couldn't tell if she somehow thought she could fix the computer by placing healing hands on it. If that was the case, she wasn't doing a very good job.

"*So* frustrating," she said. She frowned and shook her hands out, then turned to me. "What are you going to work on?"

"Uh, I don't know. What are the choices?"

"Depends." She checked out my IDent tag again, looking at my colored power squares, of which there were pitifully few. And they were all pale in hue, meaning the few abilities I did have were pretty weak in strength. "Whatta you got?" she asked, pointing her chin at my IDent tag. "Blue 255-M. That's intelligence, right?"

"Well, yeah, but it's nothing incredible. It's just M-level."[11]

"Hey, that's a lot more than I have. I'm just a G.[12] What else do you have going on?" She reached forward and pulled

---

[11] Of course, I wasn't actually an M-level. That's just how I tested for the level evaluator. In all likelihood, at that point I was probably either an R-level or S-level, at least. Not even a year later, the court psychologist measured me as a T-level just before the trial, and I wasn't even trying.

[12] G-level isn't too bad. A summa cum laude graduate of Harvard would look like a dope next to a G-level.

my tag closer to her. "You can unbutton that jacket, you know. We're pretty casual down this way. Let's see. Flight? Nope. Strength? Not much. Durability? Uh, no. So . . . what'd you do to get sent to the A-program at such a late date in your academic career?"

I wasn't sure how to answer that. Not in any way that didn't make me look like a complete loser. *Well, it's like this: as you see, I have no worthwhile physical powers, I can't do anything exciting, and—oh, yeah—I got badly injured in PT class because I'm such a weakling.* Uh, no, not the way I wanted to come across to her.

Not that I really believed I could have a chance with a girl like her, but still, I didn't need to humiliate myself, either. "Let's just say I wasn't conforming to the standards of the Academy." Suitably mysterious, I figured.

"Well, duh. Nobody in here conforms to the Academy's standards. That's why we're A-holes in the first place. But okay, fine. Don't tell me. I'll find out my own way."

Not having a whole lot of experience, I couldn't be certain, but it almost seemed as if she was flirting with me. I felt my face get hot, and I worried that I was turning red. "Is that right? And how will you do that?"

"I have my ways. And why are you blushing? Worried that I'm flirting with you and you don't know how to handle it?"

My face felt even hotter. And the more I tried to control it, the worse it got.

"Nice color," she said. "You just keep trying not to be embarrassed. See how that works out for you." She leaned back, her elbows resting on the table behind her, chest out. I tried to get a look at her tag, but she had dropped it down the front of her shirt, out of sight.

I was sure she had other squares on her tag. I just wanted to get a quick look at it.

"Ahem," Layla said. I blinked and realized I had been looking for her tag a bit too long. She gave me a crooked smile. "Don't you know that nice boys aren't supposed to use their intersight to look through a girl's shirt?"

"I wasn't looking at your . . . no, I was just . . ." I shook my head. Better to just let it go.

She laughed. "Oh, I know what you wanted to see. Relax. You're a guy. It's cool."

I couldn't help but notice that her bra strap[13] wasn't made of shiny ViewStopper quartzlon fiber. Point being that she clearly didn't even care if kids with intersight looked through her clothes.

"Hey, if you want to know what I have, just ask," she said.

"What do you mean, what you have?"

"Powers. You're wondering. Instead of being embarrassed and worrying that you're striking out with me, go ahead and ask. Or just say it. You know what it is."

And it dawned on me: *Ah. Wow. She's a telepath.*

"Finally," she said.

"What?"

---

[13] Which, I just want to make clear, was *overtly exposed* and *entirely visible* to the naked eye. I may be a lot of things, but one thing I'm *not* is a creep.

"Took you long enough."

And that was why my face felt warm. It wasn't because I was embarrassed (or not totally that); it was because she had gotten into my head.

"Right," she said. "And I pushed just a little harder than I needed to. Sorry. But it was funny. You were so flustered!"

"Thanks. Thanks a lot. That's a riot. So can you tell what I'm thinking right now?"

She squinted, and my face got hot again. "Now, now," she said. "There's no need for that kind of language. I was just playing."

"Okay, fine." It was hard to be mad at her. "And you can actually read and write?"[14] I had never met a telepath before.

"Some, yeah."

Given how severely illegal the power of telepathy is, I was stunned that she would let me know she had it.

"No big deal," she said. "I'm not exactly worried that you're going to turn me in to the authorities." She laughed, and these crinkles showed up at the corners of her eyes, and she was just . . . better to think about something else, given that she had free rein of my mind.

"Listen . . . Layla, can you do me a big favor? Please? Don't go into my head without at least telling me. It's kind of a total invasion. If you want to know anything, just ask me.

---

[14] Reading is being able to know someone's thoughts. Writing is being able to tell another person something using telepathy by putting the words or ideas directly in his or her mind.

I'll tell you, as long as you promise not to go strolling around in my mind whenever you feel like it."

"Okay. Fair enough," she said.

"Thanks." I looked around at the other kids working. "Does anyone else know?" I asked, keeping my voice quiet.

"The trustworthy few, yeah, but it's not like I advertise it. I don't exactly want to go to jail."

"So why tell me?"

"Because I can tell you're trustworthy."

"How?"

"By reading you," she said.

"I can't believe you actually use it."

"Hell, yeah, I use it. One thing I should tell you, though." She leaned close enough that I could smell pomegranate shampoo or something in her hair. "I didn't look around much, I swear, but there are some things in your mind that'll change everything for you."

The voices. She found the source. I figured she probably found some mental illness, maybe one that was about to bust loose and completely take me over.

"Okay, fine. If I decide I want to know about whatever this mystery is, I'll tell you. But right now, I'm asking you: don't go in my mind and look around. It feels like a—you know—like an invasion."

"Fine. I promise. But trust me: this is something you'll want to know. And when you *do* want to know, tell me. I'll help you with it. Until then, I'll stay out of your head."

I could see she meant it sincerely. It was weird to me,

how we had practically just met and yet it felt as if we were suddenly on close terms. Maybe too close for so soon. Time to change the subject. "So, what? You were trying to fix this computer?" I asked.

"What, this? No, there's nothing wrong with it. I can interact with software and machines. Biomech merge."

The teacher came over. "Brad, you've made a friend. Good."

"We met before," I said.

"Yeah, and he got himself transferred to the A-program just so he could be closer to me," Layla said.

"Of course he did," Miss Franks said with a big smile. "*All* the boys in here came just to be near you. Didn't you know that, Layla?"

"Tricia? Is sarcasm a requirement to get hired as a teacher in the A-program?"

"It's a requirement to be here as a teacher *and* as a student, Layla." She smiled again, gave Layla's shoulder a squeeze, then pointed at the computer screen and moved on to check with another student.

"She is so annoying," Layla said.

"You should see the teachers on the other side. This one seems kind of cool."

"She's cool, yeah, but in an annoying way. She sees right into you. And not with intersight or telepathy. I checked."

"She's pretty smart?"

"Like you wouldn't believe. Anyways, I have to get back

to this or she'll come over and give me a hard time."

"Or demerits."

"We don't do demerits. A-holes barely have any merit to start with."

She turned back to the computer and put her hands on both sides of it. The screen started flashing again, changing from Web sites to blogs to movie clips. I wasn't watching the screen, though. I was watching the reflection of all the changes shining in her eyes.

Mom had been on an early shift at the lab that day, so she picked me up from school.

"Well? How was your first day?" she asked when I got into the car.

"It was fine."

"Were the teachers okay?"

"They seemed fine." There was actually no way to tell how they were as teachers, but I liked the way they talked to us.

"And what were the other students like?"

"They were fine."

"I mean, do they seem different from the ones in—"

"Mom, I don't know. They're kids. What else am I supposed to say?" I hated getting interrogated about school, but I couldn't really blame her for wanting to know how I was doing. "Sorry. I'm tired."

Which was true. I went up to bed right after dinner.

In the dark, I thought about Layla Keating. I'd never met a telepath before. Not one I was aware of, anyway.

She had gone into my mind, easy as could be. I thought about how she'd said she had found out something about me that I didn't even know.

I had claimed not to care, that I didn't want to hear about it, but the truth was I couldn't get it—or her—out of my mind.

In accordance with Article XIV of the Oslo Conventions Agreement, any and all forms of telepathy, including psionics, psi powers, latent telepathy (delayed response telepathy), retrocognitive (past thoughts) telepathy, precognition, emotive telepathy (remote influence or emotional transfer), or transfer of kinesthetic sensations, or Psionically Induced Altered States of Consciousness, are considered crimes against psychological privacy and integrity, and, as such, are forbidden by all sovereign nations belonging to the Union of Nations, Eurasian Alliance, Unified African Nations, et al.

Article XIV of the Oslo Conventions
SECOND TREATY
Protocol 2, Section 11
Ratified 24 May 1963

CHAPTER 14

Force

English class. We were in a horseshoe shape—no desks, just chairs—and Mr. Wittman was sitting on one end. "Yes, Barry, I'm well aware that justice is part of the team name. But that has nothing to do with the question. Do you have some kind of answer, or do you want to argue in circles some more?"

Barry Brown[15] tilted his head back, eyes to the ceiling, and groaned. "Damn, Wittman, why you gotta twist everything around? I'm just saying: they got the word *justice* right in their name. *Justice* Force. That's got to mean *some*thing."

"So if I introduce myself as Mike 'the Hottest Guy Teacher in the World' Wittman, does that mean that I *am* the hottest guy teacher in the world?"

A bunch of us laughed.

"Dude, you're not even the hottest guy teacher in the A-program!" said a kid named Wade Wexler. More laughter.

---

[15] Yes, *that* Barry Brown. And no, I don't believe they'll ever catch him. Hell, I don't believe they'll ever even figure out where he's hiding. But this conversation in class, of course, was before he became famous for the Fort Knox thing.

"He's the *only* male teacher in the A-program," Brenda Brubaker said.

"That's what I'm saying," Wexler said. Laughter all around.

"Easy, now," Mr. Wittman said. "You guys are going to pump up my ego too much." I tried to imagine any of my teachers in the Academy running class like this. Couldn't even begin to picture it. Mr. Wittman went on. "But you see? My point is that just because they have the word *justice* in their team name doesn't mean that, ipso facto, they're all about justice. Or maybe they are. But the name is just a name, right? Isn't that kind of obvious?"

A lean and tall guy, long legs stretched out in front of him and crossed at the ankles, shook his head. "But they picked it for a reason. They didn't call themselves 'the Light and Fluffy Doughnuts' or, I don't know, 'the Lazy Cows' or something. The word *justice* didn't just appear in their team name by accident."

"Duh," said Barry. "They want everyone to automatically associate them with justice. Advertising. Obvious."

Layla shook her head. "Well, there's a problem, though. Is it an accident that they used the word *force*, too? Or did they not get how that could totally undermine the impression they wanted to make?"

"Meaning what?" Mr. Wittman asked.

"Meaning *force* can be a noun, like something that's powerful, or *force* can be a verb, like to make someone do something against his will."

"They didn't mean that they force people to do things," Wade said. "That's stupid. Why would they want anyone to think that?"

"I'm just saying that maybe they weren't even aware of it, but it's in there. It's telling."

"You think they're that dumb?" the lean guy asked.

"Hey," Layla said, "heroes aren't necessarily known for being geniuses."

This was *not* the way you talked in school. Even though Wittman wasn't himself saying anything blatantly against the JF, it was still pretty subversive.

I turned and saw that Layla was watching me.

"So what're you telling us, then?" one of the girls asked Mr. Wittman. "That the Justice Force wasn't in the right when they took down the Gorgon Corps?"

Mr. Wittman shook his head. "Uh-uh. I'm not telling you anything. I'm just asking you. What do *you* think? Look at all the factors and make up your mind for yourself."

There was silence in the room. I looked from person to person. Each one of them was deep in thought. Then one started talking, and the comments started flying.

"They killed what's-his-name. Toxicon. They didn't have to do that."

"He was the Gorgon Corps leader. They wouldn't have won if they didn't get him out of the picture."

"They could have captured him. They didn't have to murder him."

"That's exactly the point about force. Justice Force killed him, and that made it much easier to get the rest of the Gorgon Corps under control so they could be captured."

"Well, this isn't a game. Yeah, the stakes are high. And they'd been after the Gorgon Corps—everyone has been after the Gorgon Corps—for a long time."

"Was there any real proof that the GC was the bunch who sabotaged the Tokyo train?"

"They *did* break laws. Don't we have laws for reasons?"

"Maybe some laws are wrong."

"What about telepathy?" I heard myself say. I wouldn't have predicted that I'd get in on the discussion. But I was very aware that Layla—a telepath—was watching me. This wouldn't be a bad way to maybe score a few points with her. "Why is that power illegal but others aren't?"

"Because it's considered immoral and unethical," Barry said.

"Why?" I asked.

"It's invasive," another kid said. "It's, like, dishonest and deceitful. A violation of privacy."

By this point, what started out as a way for me to impress a girl had somehow turned into a real point I wanted to make. "So it's immoral to use your powers to read minds, but it's totally fine to use your powered strength or speed or flight to kill people?"

"Phaetons, not people," a guy said.

"In this case, but still. Whatever," I said. "I don't care if we're talking about a house cat. I just don't get that it's illegal to use telepathy, but it's fine for heroes to use their powers to kill people."

"The heroes you're talking about are killing *villains*," one girl said.

"How about trying to capture them and put them on trial instead of just wiping them out?" Layla said. "Isn't that justice?"

It went on like that for a while. And through the whole heated discussion, Mr. Wittman just listened. Occasionally, he would make comments like, "No, go ahead and finish what you were saying," or "Okay, we got it. Now let *her* talk," but he didn't really steer the conversation much at all. The main thing he said was that he wanted us to think and to speak our minds.

The truth is, I couldn't even remember the last time I had been told to say what I really thought. I might not have been totally sure about what I believed, but maybe being in a place with people who had different points of view would help me figure it all out.

CHAPTER 15

Totally Subversive

At lunch in the caf next period, I was getting interrogated by Virginia, Shameka, and Travis.

"So, what? Are they all, like, total freak shows?" Travis asked. He was not known for his sense of tact, which was about as subtle as a sledgehammer.

"Not really. That's not the impression I get."

"Ah, you're just being nice," he said.

"Well, they were put in the program for *some* reason," Shameka said. "They can't be like us."

Us. Something about it hit me funny. "Does that make them worse?" I asked.

Virginia gave me a harsh look. "She didn't say they were worse. She just said they're probably not like us. Which I'm sure is true. What's up with you?"

"Right, well, I was put in there, too. So you're saying I'm not like us, too." I wasn't sure if I was being a jerk on purpose. Or if I was being a jerk at all. I just knew I was getting frustrated with the conversation.

"Hey, take it easy, chief," Travis said. "No offense meant."

I was trying to be patient. "It sounded like there was a

little bit of judgment in there. It isn't a 'better' or 'worse' thing. It's not a winning game."

Travis shook his head and wiped the crime scene of sauce off his face with a napkin. "Everything is a winning game, son. Are they going to be heroes? I don't think so. They're in that program because there's something not special about them."

"Um, how many of them have you actually met?"

Shameka shook her head. "Come on. Get real. Maybe they're too weak, no powers. Maybe they have a bad attitude. Maybe all they got is brains or whatnot. But whatever the reason, they're in the A-program because they didn't have what it takes to be in the Academy."

"Really. Okay. And so why am I in there, then? What's my big personality failure?"

Well, that shut the three of them up pretty fast. Looking at each of them, I could see it in their faces.

Oops.

Didn't think of that.

Better just shut up now.

Ugh. The voices again. But not one of my friends, or so-called friends, could look me in the eye. "Right," I said. "I'm in there now."

Virginia cut in. "Yeah, but we all know you shouldn't be. You belong with us, not them."

I wasn't so sure. Especially not after this conversation.

I turned away, and I noticed Layla talking with a few

other kids from the A-program by the wall. I got up from my seat.

"Where are you going?" Virginia asked.

"I need to talk to someone."

Before I even got within a few yards, Layla turned around and looked right at me while the others kept talking. I suspected that she had enhanced proximity awareness, or maybe remote sight.

"Look who's here," she said. I couldn't tell if her crooked smile was friendly or mocking. I was hoping it was the former.

"Hey," I said. "I have a question for you. That discussion in class today?"

"Yeah? What about it?"

"It's just that I'm not used to hearing that . . . kind of talk. Not in school, anyway."

Layla shrugged. "Wittman's cool. He just wants us to think for ourselves."

"And so how many people in the A-program are, um, antihero?"

Layla shrugged and shook her head. "Some. The smarter ones." She looked at me slyly. "You want to go out for lunch?" she asked.

"What do you mean, go out? We can't."

"We're gonna ditch and grab something to eat. If you want to come along, we can explain all this, but we're not going to talk about it in here."

Leaving school grounds. Getting caught meant an immediate suspension and a parent conference. Not what I needed at the moment. I nodded toward the sensors by the cafeteria door. "How are you planning to get past them?"

"Don't worry about it. We have everything covered. You coming or not?"

I looked over at Virginia, Shameka, and Travis at our table, all of them laughing about something. No doubt assuming I would be back right away for more conversation about some TV show that was on the night before.

I turned to Layla and her friends. "Well?" I said. "What are we waiting for?"

It wasn't easy to fight the urge to look over my shoulder at the school as we crossed to the parking lot after slipping out a side door. "I don't get how we can leave without being picked up by the monitors," I said.

"You can ask Deirdre, more commonly known as Boots," she said, nodding to the girl walking to her left. The girl turned our way. Eurasian, she looked, and very beautiful. She had Maori facial tattoos, which were only allowed as cultural exceptions. She was wearing dark brown leather boots, laced up to her knees, with the very top cuffs reaching midthigh. Hence her nickname. I had seen her in the A-wing; she was in the other class section and we passed in the hallway during class changes. She looked me up and down with a smile, and I felt totally naked. Which might as well have been the case if she had intersight.

She reached into her jacket pocket and held up a device that looked like a small cell phone, but with only a few buttons and two blinking blue lights. "Blocks out our video images, neutralizes our heat signatures, transmits reverse ultrasound and microwave signals, and scrambles the tomographic waves. Easy."

"Boots is pretty good with anything electronic," Layla said to me. "Detectors, computer, video. She's amazing with all of that. You should see what she can do with an ATM."

I stopped walking, not sure I heard her right.

Layla took my elbow and pulled me along. "I'm kidding, of course," she said.

"Really?"

"No, not really. And you know the other guys, right?"

She nodded with her chin toward two kids walking ahead of us. I knew them from class, but we had never actually met. "Not by name."

"That one is Peanut," she said, pointing at an enormous guy with dreadlocks. He had to be six-five at least, and he was built like a professional bodybuilder. Obviously he was juicing with Myomegamorpherone.[16] Not surprisingly, he was one of the louder ones in class.

---

[16] Which meant his muscles were mainly for show. Sure, he was as strong as any Regular who was built like him—could probably bench or squat several hundred pounds—but he didn't have genetically enhanced strength. Anyone with actual powered strength, even someone half his size, could easily bounce him around like a rag doll. And the Myomeg had all the great side effects of any anabolic steroid, including 'roid rage and testicular atrophy. This latter affliction, I figured, was the reason for his nickname Peanut.

"That one is Javier," she said, pointing to a second tall guy with a loping stride. He wore pegged jeans and a tight, expensive-looking shirt under his gray A-program jacket. He turned when he heard his name. I thought of that line from Shakespeare's *Julius Caesar*: "lean and hungry look." He gave Layla a smile and a wink that made me think this was a guy who was used to getting his way.

"Javier is very pleased with himself," Layla said. "Not only is he from a hero family—his father is Le Grand Épée—but he claims he's descended from royalty. He has microvision and micromyocontrol.[17] He's really good at designing and building things."

"What, like bookshelves?"

"No, like microexplosive devices, toxin delivery devices, stuff like that," she said, not breaking her stride.

I stopped walking. "Seriously?"

"Well, in theory. You coming with us or what?"

If I had stopped there, turned around, and gone back into school, maybe things would have turned out to be different. Maybe. Maybe not.

---

[17] A metahuman ability to control muscle movements to an extraordinarily high degree. A great power for microsurgeons . . . or bombmakers.

CHAPTER 16

That Kind of Talk

We went in Peanut's truck. He was driving and Javier was the only other person in the front, so the rest of us were in the backseat.[18] I was between Layla and Boots. The conversation between the boys was dominated by a debate about the relative quality of the bands Fight for Fight's Sake and Sandwiches There.

"Sandwiches There," Boots said. She sang from their latest hit. *"Try to call me, babe. I won't answer. Find yourself another dancer. 'Cause I don't do that two-step anymore."* She had an amazing singing voice. A lot more pleasant-sounding than the argument up front.

We ended up at Napoli's Pizza downtown. It was pretty packed with the lunchtime crowd—mostly Regulars, I figured. (Though, of course, you can't always be sure.) We stood at the counter and ate our slices.

The music debate from the car expanded and continued. Javier had a weird accent, something I couldn't place. It

---

[18] When we first squeezed in, Layla whispered to me that Javier needed space and couldn't have direct physical contact with people without going temporarily insane.

sounded like a combination of French, Spanish, and maybe a hint of German. Layla stayed out of the conversation, watching something on the TV mounted above the cash register. I was mainly trying to keep a balance between my eagerness to eat and the repeated blazing-hot cheese burns that were scalding the roof of my mouth. This was one of those times when I really wished I had the power of heat resistance.

Layla nudged her elbow into my arm. I felt a tiny charge, making me wonder if maybe she had electro-generative powers. "Look at this guy. Think he loves himself at all?" She nodded up at the TV.

It was a news interview with Meganova. He was wearing his team uniform and even had a cape on. All flash, showboating. The TV volume was off, so we couldn't hear what he was saying, but there was a crawl running across the bottom of the screen:

MEGANOVA BACK ON U.S. SOIL AFTER APPREHENDING
ARGENTO "NIGHT TERROR" HAMILTON IN BOLIVIA.
MEGANOVA UNHURT. NIGHT TERROR TO BE ARRAIGNED
BY INTERNATIONAL TRIBUNAL.

Meganova smiled as he craned his neck to listen to the interviewer's question. He laughed and looked into the camera. He smiled and shook his head with the *Aw, shucks, just doing my job* grin he always used.

"What an asshole," Layla said. Her expression looked

like she'd just tasted sour milk. "Meganova," she grunted. "Mega-Blowhard."

I looked over my shoulder to see if anyone had heard her. Not that I totally disagreed with her; Meganova was not my favorite. There was something about him that always struck me as kind of fake, or maybe self-promoting. Still, what Layla said, calling one of the premier American heroes names in public, could lead to trouble. Like, riot-type of trouble.

"They've been after NT for a long time," I said. "Whatever you think of Meganova, this *is* news."

She shook her head, all the while eyeing the screen with disgust. "I don't have a problem with it being news. I have a problem stomaching this guy's phony heroics."

"Hey, what's that?" said the guy on the other side of the counter, the one who made the pizza. Napoli, presumably. "Whatta you mean, 'phony heroics,' kid?" He wiped his brow with the back of his hand, leaving a smudge of flour on his forehead.

"He's all show. If there's no media covering a battle or so-called rescue or whatever, you don't see a sign of the guy."

"Whoa, hang on there, girlie," said a brawny construction worker standing to Layla's left. "You're talking about Meganova, the guy who dropped into the Battle of Ardelach in Lamazistan with Mr. Mystic? Them and the Vindication Squad helped the army push back the rebel scumbags."

"And wiped out a whole bunch of Lamazistani civilians," Layla said.

To my right, Peanut, Boots, and Javier started wiping pizza grease off their hands. Javier's face darkened, like a cloud was passing behind it. Boots shook her head slowly, eyes on the counter. It was obvious; they were getting ready for a fight. I happened to agree with what Layla was saying, but if this turned into a brawl or something and we got arrested, well, I figured Mom wouldn't exactly be thrilled.

"Maybe we should get out of here?" I suggested. "We can still get back for seventh period."

The construction guy's buddy chimed in. "Them that you're calling 'civilians' was just a bunch of rebel scumbags who don't wanna work a real job."

"Hold on," I heard myself saying. "They couldn't get jobs. The Lamazistani president ordered—"

"Yeah, yeah, yeah," said the first construction worker. "Look, far as I care, all of them people can kill each other. Good riddance." A bunch of other people standing around the pizza joint cheered the construction worker. He went on: "But once they have their protest marches and start talking crap about the Vindicators, blaming them for protecting the president or whatever, then I say our guys go in there and clean house. A few of them others, the locals, get wiped out, tough luck. Cost of doing business."

Now *I* was getting pissed off. "A *few* of them? Try a few *thousand*." I could feel Layla's eyes on me.

"Same difference," Construction Worker 2 said. "You wanna mess with Meganova and the Vindicators, ya gotta take your lumps. Life's a bitch."

"Yeah, and so is Meganova," Layla said.

There was a hushed second or two before people started shouting. Layla, her friends, and I slid off our stools and stood with bent knees, hands up, ready to take on the fifty or so offended Regulars.

I wondered how long I would stay conscious while being ripped apart by an angry mob.

There was a loud mechanical crack. "All right, nobody move!" someone shouted. A cop? No. It was Napoli. He was standing on the counter with a Shocker Shotgun leveled down at all of us. "I can't be having no more fights in my place. I had to put in a whole new front window last week, and I ain't doing it again today." He gestured to Layla and the rest of us. "Get the hell out of here. I don't need that kind of talk in my joint. Beat it. The rest of you, make room and let them out. All I wanna do is just get this lunch crowd fed and go on with my day."

With the business end of a Shocker Shotgun aimed at them, you can bet the people moved out of our way nice and fast.

Out on the sidewalk, I exhaled heavily. I hadn't realized I'd been holding my breath for a long time.

We started walking.

"Last time I go into *that* shite-hole," Javier said.[19]

---

[19] I knew *shite* was either British or Irish, which didn't fit with Javier's accent. Odd.

Peanut shook his head. "Yeah, it's too bad. That was an awesome slice."

Layla shoulder-checked me. "And look who turned out to be a tough guy. See? To think you could've stayed back for an exciting lunch in the caf with your Academy friends."

"Well, thanks for inviting me along, but I wasn't exactly looking to get murdered today."

In the truck, to my astonishment, the others returned again to their stupid argument about the bands. I was thinking about how close we had come to getting our asses beaten.

Back at school, they all stayed in the truck as I got out the left rear door. I looked at my watch. "Seventh period just started. What are you doing?"

"Getting a little advance on vacation time," Peanut said out the driver's window.

"Wanna ditch the rest of the day? Hang with us?" Boots said. Layla was watching me from the backseat. I did kind of want to go with them, but I figured I'd narrowly escaped getting into trouble and it was better not to push my luck.

"I think I'll just finish out the day."

"That's a good boy," Layla said. I crossed behind the truck and headed for the front door. I wasn't sure how I was going to sneak back into school.

"Hey," Layla called to me. "Tell the truth: how's it feel to misbehave?"

"You think you know me," I said.

"I think I do, yeah."

I said, "Well, think again, Layla." Cooler than I knew I had in me. I turned away and started up the steps.

"Hey, you can't get past the sensors. You should come with us. Friends don't let friends get scanned and yelled at by dictatorial principals."

Hm. "Is that what I am? I'm actually good enough to be your friend?"

She gave me that grin, the one that made me crazy. "It's not whether you're good enough. It's whether you're bad enough."

"And?"

"Well, are you?"

I did my best to duplicate her evil little smile. It came a lot more easily to me than I would have imagined. "You just wait and see."

"One would think the scientists and policymakers had learned something from the uncontrollable beast called the atomic bomb that their colleagues had created less than a decade prior. Rather, their arrogance caused them to believe they would be able to contain the powers they had unleashed. The potential destruction in terms of loss of human life made the Black Plague seem like seasonal allergies."

DAVID MARKS,
A Deal with the Devil: The Rise of Superhumans and the Fall of Humanity, 1975

CHAPTER 17

Show-Off

Blake was holding me prisoner. I sat on one end of the couch, Blake sat in the middle. His size-fourteens were up on the coffee table and he held the remote in his hand. He paused the image when he wanted to, or slowed the video down to point things out.

"Okay, so this here is when we brought down Troika and got Guillotine as a bonus. Watch this, watch . . . there!" He froze the image. "Look at Guillotine's face when we bust in. Is that great or what? He pretended to be trying to negotiate a deal; then he made a run for it. He shouldn't've fought. If he had just surrendered peacefully, he would've made it out of the whole thing. Oh, well."

Oh, well? It hit me weird when he said that. Yes, Guillotine was a villain. Yes, he had committed a bunch of high-end burglaries. Yes, he had kidnapped the president of France and held her for ransom. But he was a human being. It's not like he was even a Phaeton. To hear Blake—America's Favorite Hero—say "Oh, well" about a person whose death he caused—well, it totally rubbed me the wrong way.

"Oh, hey," he said. "Don't forget I want to take you to meet Rotor this week. The work he does may not be as high-profile as what the rest of the Justice Force does, but support staff is still important. It's the kind of thing you might be able to do. Oh, watch this one. It's great."

On the screen, a green image from a night-vision camera showed a bunch of Justice Force heroes gathered on either side of the wide doorway of what looked like an abandoned tenement. Thunderclap, in a shock-absorbent version of the JF uniform, kicked in the front door and walked in. Either the camera or the building or both shuddered as a pressure pulse traveled throughout the building. A few loose bricks dropped through the video frame and exploded against the sidewalk. The members of the Justice Force descended on the dozen or so Phaetons who came running out the front door, hands covering ears[20] with shattered eardrums. The Phaetons fought back viciously, and it got ugly as the JF fought back even more viciously. This wasn't the part they'd shown on the news a couple of months ago. In fact, it couldn't even be found on the Internet. This was strictly confidential.

"Look over there on the left. That guy is about to escape, and . . . here . . . I . . . come." On the screen, Artillery (Blake) whipped around the corner, either in low flight or long leap, and hit the Phaeton solid in the chest. In our living room, Blake shouted, "Woo-hoo! Yeah!" as the Phaeton on the screen went rigid and fell over like a petrified tree.[21]

---

[20] That is, those who had them. (Ears. Or hands.)

[21] Dead, it turned out. Its—or his—heart literally exploded inside the chest.

Phaeton or not, I got queasy about Blake's excitement at having killed the guy.

Mom came into the living room. "Dinner. Time to turn this show off."

"It's not a show," Blake said. "It's Justice Force battle footage."

"Well, I'll certainly want to have a look, but after we're done eating. Come into the dining room."

Mom was indulging Blake as he gushed details about the battles he'd made me watch on TV. After just having seen all this, it was kind of irritating to have to listen to a replay of it.

He shoveled a heaping forkful of steak and mashed potatoes into his mouth. He chewed mightily, looked over at me, and swallowed big. "What's with you?"

"What do you mean?"

"What's that face mean?" he asked.

"I don't know what you're talking about."

"You made, like, a sneery face."[22]

"No, I didn't."

"Uh-huh. What's the problem?"

"I didn't make a face."

"Mom?"

"You made a face."

---

[22] No such word as *sneery*, of course, but actually it's pretty expressive. I'll give him credit for that.

"Well, I didn't mean to."

Blake sat back in his chair and wiped his mouth with a napkin. "It looked like you had some kind of problem."

"I just don't see why you guys outright kill whatever Phaetons you come across."

Blake laughed. "What are we supposed to do, take 'em out to dinner? These are the bad guys, Brad. Getting rid of them is what we do."

"Why can't they be arrested? Or maybe they could get some kind of gene therapy and reverse the effects of what they did to their chromosomes."

"That's not possible," Mom said. "Gene therapy can't undo what they did, even if we could capture and hold Phaetons to administer it."

"Well, still. Maybe they could be, like, rehabilitated or something. I don't really see why they have to be murdered."

"Whoa, slow down there, pal," Blake said. "*Murder* is a word we use when we talk about humans, not Phaetons."

"Some people consider Phaetons to be human."

"Well, those people are wrong. Phaetons are not human anymore, not really."

"Well, so they don't have typical Regular DNA. But then again, neither do you. Right?"

A tiny, tiny twitch started by Blake's left eye. Most people probably wouldn't even notice it, but over my life, I had come to recognize it as a sign that he was either angry or frustrated or both.

"Okay, you really don't know what you're talking about." He put his fork down and leaned on the table. "Have you ever even seen a Phaeton in real life? Ever been up close?"

"All right," Mom said. "This is nothing to fight about."

"Nah, Mom," Blake said. "If Brad is man enough to make these statements or whatever, then he should make sure he knows what he's talking about. So, you didn't answer, Brad. Have you ever even seen a Phaeton up close and personal?"

"Well, no, but I'm just saying that—"

"You never had one charging at you full speed. Never had one leap at you, get its hands on your neck, breathe its foul stench right in your face. Am I right?"

There was a long, uncomfortable silence. "You're right," I said.

"You're damned right I am," Blake said. "So I don't think you're in a spot to be passing judgment on how the Justice Force, or any other hero team, does its job."

This was a side of Blake the public never got a chance to see. Angry Artillery.

Snot-nose little pissant loser. A voice again. Was that really what I thought of myself?

I nodded.

"Okay, then," Mom said. "I'd really prefer we talk about something else and have a peaceful dinner."

But Blake was looking at me coldly. He wasn't done. "When you get powers and join a team, when you've been on the front lines of the war against villains and Phaetons, then you can talk about this kind of thing. Until then, you should stick to doing your homework and living under the safety of the people who protect you."

It's rare that I have trouble finding words to express my thoughts, but at that time, I had nothing to say. Maybe it was because I wasn't sure what I actually thought anymore.

PART 2

That is what I'm here for: to protect and serve the needs of the people. I don't like having to kill criminals; believe me, I don't. But if they're going to commit crimes—if they're going to kill civilians, well, then that's really a risk they've chosen to take, isn't it?"

ARTILLERY (BLAKE BARON)
Address to United States Senate
when awarded the Congressional
Medal of Honor
July 4, 2016

Hell, no, I don't regret it. None of it. I'd do it again, too. He beat me fair and square. That is, if you consider ten against one fair. But yeah, he was the one who got in the so-called deathblow. Fine. He wins. For now.

"I'll be dead in a few hours, maybe sooner. But listen here: once I'm gone, twenty more Phaetons will rise up in my place. This here thing ain't over. Not by a long [*expletive deleted*] shot."

BLOODBATH
Deathbed statement,
Radcliff, Kentucky
June 29, 2016

CHAPTER 18

Lurking

I was about to step out the classroom door after English when something made me stop. Right outside the door, I heard a conversation among Layla, Javier, Boots, and Peanut.

Layla said, "Because I think he has a lot to offer."

"I just don't think he's vital," Javier answered.

"He's got all the right ideas," Boots said. "Politically, Brad is cool."

"He does not sound too cool to me," Javier said. "He sounds like a hero-worshiper to me."

Layla defended me. "He may seem that way, but underneath, he's not. He just hasn't woken up yet."

"*Ach, Gott in himmel!* We are supposed to be his teachers? When, or if, he shows he is like us—then, I think, is when we talk about bringing him in."

"I'm okay with letting him in, if he wants to be," Boots said.

"Yes, but I am not," Javier said. "He could be a danger."

"He wouldn't hurt us," Layla said. "I can tell."

Javier made a *harrumph* sound. "And so how do you know this?"

"You know how I know."

There was a silence between them, and the regular noise from other people continued in the hallway.

"I'll vouch for him," Layla said.

"What reason have you to say that?" Javier said. "You hardly know him. You are not using your head."

Layla was getting heated. "You're the only one against it—"

"I'm against it, too," Peanut said, sounding tentative.

"Oh, please," Layla said. "You're only following Javier's lead. Use your own mind and you'll realize that Javier has no basis for his position. At all."

"It is called being careful," Javier said.

"It's called being paranoid. Look. He's just right for us. I know he is. And I want him in."

"Only if he can prove that he is vital material."

The second bell rang and they moved off to the next class. I missed the rest of the conversation.

"I know something you don't know."

Layla said it in a teasing voice, quietly, as she passed behind me in science class. I'd been in the A-program for almost a week, and practically every time we had Integrated Science, Layla had sung to me, *"I know something you don't know."* At first, I tried to get her to tell me what she was talking about, but it became obvious that she had more fun when I played her game, so I stopped asking.

I was sitting alone at one of the desktop computers. I could have paired up with someone for a while to work on a project, but that really only made sense for people who had complementary powers: heat formation and freezing ability, invisibility[23] and thermovision,[24] telekinesis[25] and telestasis.[26] I didn't have any powers I needed to develop.

I did, however, have a few ideas I needed to develop. Miss Franks, or rather, Tricia (I still wasn't used to calling a teacher by her first name) had given me a few days to find something I wanted to work on. So now, half a week later, she came my way and had a look at my computer screen.

"Ah. Doing a little reading on the Kraden Project," she said.

"Do you know much about it?"

"I wrote part of a master's thesis on it, so yes, I know a little bit. What aspect are you looking at?"

I had a decision to make. My ideas were pretty easy to

---

[23] Yes, I know there's no such thing as true invisibility, and yes, I'm well aware that the correct term is *sub*visibility, but it amounts to basically the same thing, right? They can control and expand the space between atoms in their body, and blah, blah, blah. The point is, you can't see them. In my book, that's called *invisibility*.

[24] The ability to see changes in temperature, which allows the lucky person with this power to see where people have recently been, based on slight variations in ambient temperature.

[25] Moving stuff using only your mind.

[26] Kind of the other side of telekinesis: making something immovable, making it "freeze" in place. Pretty helpful when you want to apprehend someone who's trying to run away.

dismiss as crackpot nonsense. Except, maybe, to someone with an open mind. I could float the ideas out to Tricia, but it would be taking a chance.

"I have this idea that the Kraden Project scientists in the 1950s were wrong."

"About what?"

"Well, about pretty much everything." I kept my voice low. "They thought they had *created* 'powered genes' and, by using an early version of genetic engineering, grafted the powered genes onto regular human DNA."

"It's pretty well documented. The Kraden Project was where the first metahuman genes—and the first metahumans—were created. But you have a different theory?"

There was something in her voice. It wasn't mocking or skeptical. This was the very first person I had ever gotten up the nerve to say my theory out loud to.

"I think the powered genes were *always* there. The first heroes were not actually *created* during the 1950s; that was just when the scientists inadvertently activated dormant genes, genes that had been there all along. The geneticists and government agencies thought they were building new genetic material, but it would never have worked if the base genes hadn't already been present."

Tricia nodded, thinking. "And you believe this why?"

"Because I think you can't create a hero. You're either born one or not."

"Destiny?"

"Science. I don't believe you can graft powered genes onto

regular ones. I think the powered genes became activated by accident during the Kraden Project in the U.S., and the other ones in Russia and China, and then those genes were passed down."

"Then how do you explain why your brother has powered genes and you don't?"

Ah, the core of my theory—that is, the huge hole in my theory. "I can't."

Pretty interesting. Oh, great. Should I tell her that I got psychosis instead of strength? I glanced over at Layla. She was looking at her computer screen, but I would have sworn she had been watching me until I turned her way.

"Okay, Brad. So this is an intriguing hypothesis. Scientific method, though. Do you have any evidence to support it?"

"Well, not a lot. None, really. Nothing you'd call hard scientific evidence. But they shut down the Kraden Project in—what? 1983? And that was because they had no success creating metahumans through gene grafting. Since then, Phaetons are really the only ones who have gotten anywhere at all with trying to graft genes, and we know how that turned out. If I'm wrong, why can't scientists re-create what they did way back when?"

"That's a good question. There's a theory that it had to do with the atomic tests the Americans and the Soviets were conducting in the Aleutian Islands."

I nodded. "Right, and the unusual, once-in-a-century weather conditions."

"You've done your research."

"As much as I could."

Tricia nodded and smiled. "All very interesting, Brad."

"You don't think it's ridiculous?"

"I think there are a lot of things I can't explain, so I'm open to ideas. Original thinking is what causes us to move forward. If the ideas can be supported. Keep at it. And keep me posted."

I felt Layla's eyes on me. I looked over, and sure enough, she was watching me. I smiled, and she smiled back before turning to her computer. I wondered again what that argument right before class had been about. I knew it had something to do with me, but I didn't know exactly what it was about.

I was happy about the conversation with Tricia. I'd gone out on a limb a little bit to test the waters, and she didn't think my ideas were idiotic. There were still a few ideas, though, that I'd held back. One was that Kolvasz-Zimmermann's life—or death—might somehow help me understand why Blake was powered and I wasn't.

I looked up the scientist. His death in prison, specifically. The autopsy report, made public by a Freedom of Information Law request, confirmed that he had an astonishing amount of barbiturates and alcohol in his system, enough to kill a silverback gorilla. The report, however, also noted that five of his front teeth—two top, three bottom—were cracked off halfway. Much as one would expect if something like, say, a bourbon bottle had been forced into his mouth.

And then, with no warning, the screen went black and a

message came up in red letters. It had the FBI-AVID[27] logo, and below that, this message:

User: Bradley Baron
Reason for surveillance and intervention:
keyword search triggers 8450485-B, 384948-A(3), 9338288-J § 2, 5, 6, 8, 11, 42

Dear Mr. Bradley Baron:
You are hereby instructed to report to the local FBI-AVID Unit at 335 Federal Plaza within the next 12 hours. You will be interviewed by two agents of AVID regarding questionable Internet activity and suspicious subject searches. This appointment is mandatory, and you must attend. Please type in the time in the box below that you intend to attend. You do not need to bring legal representation with you, as it is not needed.

I typed into the box:

I will attend the interview tonight. But just for my own information: is this in any way connected to the hours of homemade porn made by—and of—Layla Keating that I watched? I mean, that stuff is *sick*!

---

[27] If you live under a rock and don't know, AVID is the Anti-Villain Investigation Division. I'd say the FBI gets, let's see, *zero* points for creativity on that one.

My screen flickered and then there was an image of yellow smiley face almost filling the screen. And then a big boot appeared at the side and kicked the face repeatedly. It became a frowny face, with one eye closed and a big dent in its head.

Layla came over and sat next to me. "Good one. What tipped you off?"

"How it was written. 'You *do not need* to bring representation with you, as it is *not needed*.' Although, I guess, with the FBI, that redundancy could've actually been confirmation that it was legit."

She smiled. "That's true." She nodded at the computer. "I heard your conversation with Tricia. Pretty interesting."

"And you think I'm crazy."

"Not exactly. Just because you're crazy about *me* doesn't mean you're crazy."

"Who said I'm crazy about you?"

"Are you denying it?"

I didn't answer.

"Turn *more* red, why don't you?"

"You really like trying to embarrass me, huh?"

"Kind of. And I'm not just trying, I'm succeeding, if you ask me. Anyways, here *you* are, doing plain old research, like a Regular, when instead you could be sharpening up those skills."

"I don't have powers with skills that need sharpening."

"Ah, but that's where you're wrong," she said.

"Really? And how would you know?"

She gave me that evil grin. "Because *I know something you don't know.* Want me to tell you?"

I didn't like the idea of letting her think she was manipulating me. But the truth is that I was pretty damned curious. Maybe I didn't have good reason, but I believed her—I believed she knew something important to me. "You seem so desperate to tell me, fine. What?"

It was written on her face so clearly I could practically hear her: *Desperate, huh? Trying to turn the tables on me. Slick.*

"Finally, you admit that you really want to know."

"No, I'm humoring you." I didn't know if I could win this little power game with her, but I wasn't about to go down without trying.

"Humoring me. Right. If that makes you feel better. Anyway, here's the thing." She lowered her voice to just above a whisper, which seemed a little melodramatic to me at the time. "You know we have our little group. But the part I never told you is that we're more than just school friends. It's more like sort of a club. . . ."

"What, like a club with a secret handshake and all that?"

"It's more serious than that. We're committed to fighting for justice."

"There are more than fifty hero teams—plus independents—who are already doing that."

"You know that's not what we mean by justice. We're talking about *real* justice."

I took a look around to see if anyone was close enough to hear. "Sounds pretty dissident and subversive to me."

"You have no idea," she said. Her eyes were locked on mine. "And I nominated you to join us."

"Is that right? Funny, I don't remember asking to join. Wouldn't it have been a good idea to ask me first?"

"I can tell, at heart, you're one of us."

"Hm. Really. Well, putting that aside for now, why would you even want me? I don't have useful powers."

"I have my reasons. I know what I'm doing. Look we can't get into it here, but you kind of need to prove yourself."

"How?"

"Well, what we're doing is the kind of stuff that someone who wanted to hurt our little crew could use to get us in a whole lot of trouble. So we—not me, really, I trust you—the group needs some sign of commitment from you."

"I'm not sure what you mean."

"I mean you need to show us that you're willing to put yourself at risk like the rest of us. We need a sign of good faith."

"How about a sign of good faith for me? Tell me what it is you claim to know about me that I don't know."

"Join up with us and I will."

I watched her. I hadn't noticed the flecks of violet in her eyes before. If I did this, I couldn't say how much of it was for the political agenda of this alleged group and how much was just a way to get closer to Layla.

"I'll give it a try," I said.

"But first—"

"Yeah, I heard. A sign of good faith. I have an idea for that."

CHAPTER 19

Passing Muster

emembering the address wouldn't be a problem. Neither would recognizing the building. But I was watching Blake's every move, counting every step, scanning the entrance hallway for cameras or detectors.

I didn't see anything remotely suspicious. From the outside and inside, the place looked like any other slightly run-down, small residential building in the city.

Except I didn't hear a single sound from any of the apartments above us: not music, not voices, not footsteps. Not a peep.

"Why is it so quiet?" I asked.

"No tenants. The Justice Force owns this building. It's just a front. Or, I guess, a top."

"What?"

"You'll see."

At the back of the ground-floor hallway, there was an elevator. Blake pushed the button, and when the doors opened, I saw that it was in such bad condition I wondered if the elevator was even safe to use.

"Go on," he said.

I went in, my stomach a little twitchy. The doors closed

heavily, and Blake pushed the button marked B. The elevator lurched and descended.

"You guys seriously have a lab in the basement of a crummy apartment building?"

Blake gave me what he must have believed was a sly smile.

The elevator stopped and the door opened, but Blake didn't step out. Instead, he turned to the emergency-stop button, twisted it, and flipped it up. I could see the glint of glass. He leaned forward so his eye was a few inches away. Obviously, a retinal scanner.

And the back wall of the elevator slid away. Behind it was a cubicle about the same size as the elevator, but the walls were made of a bright, shiny metal. Blake led and I followed. A steel door closed and he pushed the single button, holding his thumb on it longer than I would think was necessary. Most likely, a thumbprint key.

It became clear that we were in another elevator once it started descending fast enough to make my stomach lurch.

"Pretty cool, huh?" Blake said.

"Wow," I said. "I thought we were already in the basement. How far down does this go?"

"Pretty far. We had to get G-Force to dig out the shaft. It goes way down into the bedrock."

The elevator slowed, flattening my stomach up against my diaphragm in a less-than-pleasant way. When we came to a stop, the door opened with a fast *whoosh*.

We stepped out into an enormous room. Video monitors covered every bit of the wall in front of us. Sitting at a huge desk was a middle-aged guy who looked vaguely familiar.

"Hey, Rotes. How's it going?" Blake said to the guy.

"It's going. Going and going and going."

I glanced at the monitors. They were all showing different things: aerial views of streets, low-level shots of nuclear reactors, people walking on streets in cities and small towns, shots of airport runways, international monuments, and countless highways and bridges. Also, it looked like there were hookups to surveillance cameras in just about every type of business, hospital, and outdoor environment.

"Keeping an eye on things?" Blake said, and laughed.

The older guy said, "Yeah, I haven't heard that one yet. Today."

"Ha. So, Rotor, this here's my kid brother, Brad. Brad, Rotor."

The guy half turned in his swivel chair and looked up at me with tired and red basset hound eyes.

"So, like I said when I called," Blake started, "I was hoping you might talk to my brother. See, Brad, Rotor doesn't have any significant powers, really. The best thing he can do is watch a bunch of things at once and process information faster than most computers. But just because he didn't have great abilities, that didn't stop him. Right, Rotor?"

"Right," he said, entirely without enthusiasm.

"Nope, old Rotor here still got a job with the Justice Force as one of our status surveillance experts. We're tied into every surveillance system in the country, including personal home systems. You see how the images keep changing?

The computer chooses what to show based on . . . Rotor-oo, what it's called?"

"An actuarial algorithm."

"That's right. And all Rotor here has to do is watch them and report anything that looks suspicious. It's not a bad gig, is it, Rotor? Low risk of danger. Don't have to worry about staying fit. And you get to travel. We have twelve different surveillance labs all over the country, and more in our international bases. So Rotor gets to rotate with a bunch of other guys. Nice benefit of the job, having the opportunity to see all those places, right, Rotor?"

"I see them on TV screens, sitting by myself in a subterranean room for weeks at a time. It's not exactly sightseeing."

"Ha! Good one, Rotes. Anyway, I thought that since you don't really have powers—I mean, not the big ones—you might tell my little brother how there are still important things to do as support for the teams."

"It's just wonderful," Rotor said with not the slightest hint of emotion in his voice.

Rotor was not much of a motormouth, so we didn't stay long.

On that elevator ride up, I got the sense that Blake was disappointed, feeling that his mission had failed.

But it wasn't a total loss. Not at all. *My* mission had turned out to be a smashing success.

"And you know where this is?" Javier asked.

"I know exactly where it is. I was there."

We were in Javier's car, parked in the lot of a fast-food place, taking our lunch period off school premises as usual. Javier turned to Peanut, who was in the passenger seat, then looked back to us.

"That is interesting, but what has it to do with us? How do we use it?"

Boots shrugged. "I can't say. But it's definitely worth knowing about."

"That's some pretty serious intel," Layla said. "Not something we could ever have gotten on our own."

She looked steadily at Javier. Finally he nodded, then turned to me. His gaze was steady, cold, and deadly serious. "So, do you have any big plans for tonight?"

CHAPTER 20

Hideout

I didn't go into the city too often. It wasn't that I was nervous about the higher rate of crime there, despite hero patrols augmenting the police force. For some reason, that didn't worry me. I just didn't much like the noise, the dirt, and the ruins of historical, financial, and political buildings that had been targets over the years.

I had no idea that Layla and some of the other kids lived in the city. I told Mom I was going to a movie with Virginia and Travis.[28] She dropped me off at the theater, and I walked the four blocks to the train station. In less than half an hour, I was in midtown.

It took a little while for me to find the neighborhood of the address that Layla gave me. It was in a seedy part of town: the buildings were run-down, a lot of the cars had boots on their wheels and were obviously abandoned, and the stores in the neighborhood were the kind where half the shelves were

---

[28] I had been thinking about calling Virginia, Travis, and Shameka for a week, but I kept putting it off. It may sound cold, but I just didn't have a huge desire to talk to them anymore. With me in the A-program, we didn't have that much in common. I figured that if we were really and truly deeply close, we would have stayed friends and I would have wanted to call them. I guess sometimes friendships just fade.

empty and the guys at the cash registers sat behind bulletproof/laserproof glass. Was this really where Layla lived?

I found the low-rise apartment building and called the dummy number from my phone. It connected, and there was a click and then I was disconnected. There was a buzzer sound and then the solid *thunk* of a heavy metal bar inside the door being electronically unlocked. The door opened a few inches. As I reached for the knob, I heard Boots inside, calling down the stairway, "Don't touch the knob. Just use your foot to push it open. It'll close by itself."

Weird, but I did what she told me to. A single bare bulb lit the hallway. It cast just enough light for me to see what looked like decades of grime on the floor.

"Come on back," Boots said. "Don't touch anything."

She didn't have to tell me twice. I barely wanted to breathe the air in there, much less touch anything. "Oh, you'll want to skip this second-to-last step," she called again.

"Broken?"

"Wired to blow."

I laughed. She didn't. I skipped the second-to-last step.

Boots opened a door near the end of the filthy hall. I followed her inside, hoping somehow it would be less dilapidated.

No major difference on the other side of the doorway: water stains on the ceiling, buckled wood flooring, and so many gigantic cracks on the walls they looked like road maps.

Javier was at the far end of the room, hunched over a worktable. Against one wall was a row of desks, each with at least one computer on top of it—some had three. Peanut was watching something on a computer screen. It looked like a cartoon.

Layla walked across the room to me. "So. Welcome to our lair."

"Your *lair*? Seriously? Well, I love what you've done with the place."

Boots walked over to Javier, sat on a wheeled stool behind him, and watched him work.

"Um, what exactly is this?" I asked Layla. "Please tell me this isn't where you live."

"It's where we come to hang out."

"What, you rent it? And nobody even lives here?"

"We don't exactly rent it. We have an arrangement with the old guy who owns the building."

"An arrangement."

"Well, yeah. He does his thing in other parts of the building, that thing that may not be totally legal, and we do our thing in here. Nobody asks any questions, and everyone stays happy."

"And what is the 'thing' you guys do in here?"

"Lots of stuff. That's one of the reasons I had you come here. We'll tell you, but you have to understand that this is all seriously secret. High stakes. No joke."

"I get you."

Layla sat at the table. I pulled out a chair and sat, too. She called out, "Hey, can you guys come on over? We need to have that talk."

Javier put down the tools he was using and headed toward us with Boots. On the way, Javier leaned over and murmured something to Peanut, who looked in my direction and laughed.

Everyone sat down at the table. There was a long, awkward silence. Finally, Javier spoke. "Go ahead, Miss Keating. This was your idea. So talk."[29]

"Okay, then. Brad, you ever hear us—or anyone in the class—use the word *vital?*"

"I guess, maybe."

"Do you know what it means?"

"*Vital?* Other than 'crucially important'? That's the way I know it."

"For us, it stands for 'Villains-in-Training: A-hole Legion.'"

I laughed. Layla and Boots smiled, but the guys looked serious. Layla went on. "Well, it's kind of funny, but it's not totally a joke. We got together because we're like-minded about some issues. Mainly, the roles the supposed heroes play, the role our government plays—"

"The military/Industrialists'[30] connection to the heroes," Javier added.

Layla nodded. "The whole deal. Really, like what we talk

---

[29] ("Go ahead, Meeze Kitting. Zeese vas your idea. So tock.")

[30] The Industrialists, often in league with the military, were the businesspeople—usually phenomenally wealthy—who sponsored or otherwise invested in heroes, ensuring a way to make heroes' work a money-making endeavor. I believe Karl Marx referred to these folks as "capitalist pigs," or something to that effect.

about in Wittman's class. Now, there's talk and there's action. The first doesn't do any good without the second."

"So what kind of action are you taking?" I asked.

Javier leaned forward. "Let us just say that we are working to build a relationship with someone very big."

"And who's that?"

Now Javier leaned back in his chair and put his hands behind his head. "That is for us to know and for you to learn."

"Villains-in-training, you said. Are you serious?"

"Do we *look* serious?" Peanut said.

Given that Peanut was wearing a tank top that revealed the notes he wrote to himself in ballpoint pen all over his body (*Work triceps* and *More upright rows for lats*, each with an arrow pointing to the designated body part), I decided not to answer that one directly. "You want to be bad guys and go up against the heroes?" I asked instead.

"Heroes," Javier said. He didn't spit on the floor, but he might as well have. "And 'bad guys'? What are you, twelve years old?"[31]

Layla shot him a look but then turned back to me. "From stuff we've talked about, and the few things you've said in class—"

"Assuming it's not all total bool-sheet," Javier said, leaning on that accent hard.

---

[31] When he said *heroes* this time, the *H* came from the back of his throat and the *W* in *twelve* was more like a *V*, all of which sounded more Russian than French/Italian/Spanish. I was starting to wonder if his accent was just an affectation to go with the Eurotrash image.

Layla reamed him out with a string of curses, ending with, "So if you're not going to cooperate, just keep your trap shut. Okay? You're pissing me off."

"Everybody needs to just calm down," Boots said. "Fighting is not going to help anything."

Javier still glared at Layla, but he didn't say another word.

Layla ignored him and kept her attention on me. "We want you to be a part of our group."

"I don't really get it. I'm not sure what it is you want me to do. I mean, I totally agree with you about how there's a mixed-up view of what the so-called heroes do, but how do you plan to go up against them? I mean, *us*? Seriously? Unless there's something you haven't told me, none of you— none of us—have any incredibly impressive powers."

Boots put the heel of one boot against the edge of the table and tilted her chair backward, rocking it. "Oh, some of us have powers. Just not the ones most people find exciting. But there's lots we can do to start righting all the wrongs."

"Like what?"

Javier's head turned to me like it was on a swivel. "Like we shall tell you when we're ready and good. You have not even said you would commit to the group. All you are doing is questioning us, as if to say we must answer to you."

Layla turned to Javier and looked at him. His face went a tiny bit slack; then he made eye contact with her. "Okay, fine," he said. "I get the message. I'll be quiet. But just . . . *okay*."

"We have lots of plans," Boots said. "We believe in preparation, not rushing into bad situations."

"We're talking espionage, sabotage . . . *cam*ouflage," Peanut said. He looked around at all of us staring at him. "I don't know. I couldn't think of another rhyme."

I shrugged. "It's great that you trust me, but I don't have . . . I don't see what I could bring to the table. I really don't have decent powers."

Layla looked deep in my eyes. "Never mind about that right now. We brought you here because we trust you. We sense a kindred spirit. Someone who believes that the heroes need to be stopped. That there are better ways to run the world. And we think you care about those things, too, and you would be willing to fight for them. Are we right?"

I looked at all of them, then at the walls, the bright light shining down on Javier's bench, then again at their faces. I thought about Blake's offensive comments about killing villains, especially Phaetons, as the duty of heroes.

"It sounds good, yeah," I said. "But I just don't think I have anything to offer."

"That's where you're wrong," Layla said.

And then I said four of the most important words I've ever spoken.

"Okay. Tell me everything."

CHAPTER 21

Vital

D o I have to take some kind of blood oath or something first?"

"This is not necessary," Javier said, pushing his chair back. "The blood will come fast enough if you ever betray us." He turned to Layla. "Are we finished here?"

"For now. I still have some things to talk about with Brad. If you don't want to stick around, feel free to leave."

Everyone except Layla and me got up and went back to where they had been before the little talk we had. "So," I said to Layla, "I still don't get what I have to offer."

"That's what I wanted to tell you. Come on."

"What's the deal, Layla?"

"What I'm going to tell you is pretty personal, and I just thought you might want to hear it in private."

She grabbed my wrist and pulled me up. Layla led me past the windows and into a side room. She closed the door behind us.

The room was very small with a single mattress on the floor, a tiny night table with a lamp that was on, and two wooden straight-backed chairs. That's it. Not exactly luxurious.

My heart was beating just a little faster and harder than usual. It was the first time I could remember being alone in a room with Layla, and, lack of romantic surroundings notwithstanding, this had a feel of, well, intimacy coming soon.

She moved me over to one of the chairs and pushed down on my shoulders so I would sit. She pulled the other chair over and sat down. Our knees were touching. She wasn't a girl I would usually have a chance to have any physical connection to at all, so this felt like something. I wondered if it meant anything to her.

"You're a telepath," she said.

I laughed.

"That's funny?" she asked.

"It's ridiculous. I am *not* a telepath."

"Yeah, you are. Trust me. You just don't know it, because you haven't learned how to use the power."

"Uh-huh." I decided to humor her. "And you know this how?"

"That one time I went into your mind in school? I saw it. I could tell it was dormant, or latent, or whatever. But it was definitely in there. I'm telling you: you're a telepath, and a powerful one, too."

She was crazy. "Right. Okay, since you're a telepath yourself, can you read what I'm thinking right now?"

"That's really funny. I'm not kidding, though." She shook her head, thinking. "Look. Have you noticed that you sometimes can tell pretty much what a person is thinking? Has that ever happened?"

"That's called being observant, reading body language. Being intuitive. Everyone can do that."

"Brad, I know what I'm talking about. What you think is natural is more than just interpreting physical signs or simple deduction. That's the very outer edge of your ability."

Two things I knew for sure: she wasn't just kidding around, and she happened to be wrong. "Then why can't I do serious reading and writing? The real telepathy stuff?"

"Did you ever try?"

"I never tried to fly, either. Because I know I can't."

"Any idiot born with the power of aerotransvection can fly. Every bozo born with extra strength can lift or bend or punch holes in things. Great. Telepathy is totally different. It takes training and practice." She squared her shoulders. "Let me ask you this: does it ever seem like you're hearing voices?"

That pretty much stopped me dead.

"You have. I don't have to read you to see I hit a nerve. Now, here's the thing: I'm a level B telepath, at best. I can do basic stuff. Reading, a little writing. But you—I think you're like a level H. And the scale only goes up to level I. If I'm right—"

I laughed again. "Okay, sorry, but I think you're just a little delusional here."

"No, you're the one who's delusional. But the voices have

nothing to do with it. You're not crazy. The voices you hear are highly emotional thoughts that float to you just because you have the ability to read. Unfocused telepathy. You just don't know how to control it yet."

"Yeah? Okay, so who's going to train *me?*"

It was right there in her eyes. I didn't need telepathy to know exactly what she was thinking.

CHAPTER 22

Going In

etting frustrated isn't going to help, Layla thought to me.

"I can't help it," I said out loud. "It's been almost an hour and nothing's happening."

You really have to be patient. When she thought to me (writing), it was not exactly in her voice, but it had the feeling of her voice. Very hard to articulate.

"And to tell you the truth," I said, "it would be less frustrating for me if you would talk out loud instead of writing."

She sighed. "Okay, that's fine. I just thought that if I kept writing, it might activate or, like, jump-start your telepathy. It's there. I saw it. Let's try again."

"You know, it's getting late. My mom's going to murder me. I still have to take the train back."

Layla shook her head. "I'll have Peanut give you a ride. Come on, let's go. One more try." She slapped the side of my thigh. "Wake up. Concentrate."

By that point, I knew better than to argue with Layla. I would make one last attempt, just to shut her down, and then I had to get home.

"Make it count," she said. "Focus."

I let out a long breath and closed my eyes. I put all my mental energy on Layla. I did the meditative breathing she taught me so I wouldn't be distracted by other thoughts. I started to feel warm in the middle of my abdomen.

"Are you in?" I asked.

Shhh. Don't talk out loud. It'll distract you. Yeah, I'm in. Concentrate on where you feel my thoughts coming from. Stop! You were about to talk. Just focus.

It was weird. The words she was writing to me—well, they weren't even really words. They were more like abstract ideas that somehow became words in my mind.

But I couldn't answer them. I could *think* an answer, but that's not writing. That's thinking thoughts that go nowhere outside my head. And I sure couldn't read her. All I saw in my mind's eye was darkness. I didn't even know where "she" was. It was starting to feel like a total waste of time.

Don't stop. Don't answer me. Just hold on. I follow what you're thinking, and you're thinking too much. I can tell you feel that heat deep down. That's good. I'm going to try something that might help you find me. Clear everything.

I worked to keep other thoughts out of my head.

Breathe. Breathe. Breathe. Good. Now you're going to feel a light—don't ask me—yes, I mean feel. It's not like seeing, exactly. When you feel the light, follow it in your mind. Keep breathing just like you are. That's good. Okay. Look out for that light.

I had no idea what she was talking about, "feeling" a light, but I tried to concentrate on my breathing. Breathe in, hold, breathe out. Breathe in, hold, breathe out.

And there it was. There was no other way to explain it other than how Layla did. I felt a light. It felt pale green, whatever that means.

That's it. Focus on that light. Focus. And follow.

I had no rational idea of what I was doing, but I just put all my thoughts and energy on that light.

That's it. Follow. Follow. Follow.

And that's when it happened.

I fell

Fell in to her

    electrified water hot cold alive

And then I was out of it, ripped out, when I heard a shrieking sound.

I was aware again, back in the room, and I could still hear the last reverberations of Layla's shout. I opened my eyes and saw—first in slow motion, then speeding up to regular time—Layla falling backward in her chair, and she was twisting and putting her hands out to break her fall, and the chair hit the wood floor.

I dropped to my knees and turned her head to face me. "Are you okay? What happened?"

Her eyelids fluttered a few times before they opened. She looked at me. And she smiled.

"We just did it," she said.

CHAPTER 23

Powered

The door slammed open, and the others rushed in.

"What happened?" Boots said.

Layla took a deep breath and blinked a few times. "Just some intense reading and writing, is all."

"Oh, is that what you call it?" Javier said.

"Don't be rude," Boots said to him. Then, to Layla: "Are you okay?"

Layla nodded and smiled. "Seriously. I'm fine. We have to drive him home in a few minutes. Peanut, can you get your truck ready? We'll meet you downstairs in five."

After the others left, I helped Layla up and righted the chair. "What happened?"

"What happened was you came through like a . . . a . . . I don't know. It was like getting hit by a train."

"I'm sorry. I had no idea. Are you all right now?"

"Yeah, yeah. It was just for a second. But you did it. What was it like for you?"

"It was weird. I followed, I guess, the light, and then it just happened. I felt—*felt* is the wrong word, but I just can't do any better. My mind felt . . . like I was plunging into electrified water, icy water, but not icy in an uncomfortable way.

I don't know. It happened really fast, and then I was pulled out when you yelled."

"Yeah, well. We're going to have to do a lot of work so you can control it. But I knew it. I knew that you have strong telepathy. You may have other psi[32] powers we don't even know about yet."

"It's hard to believe."

"Well, believe it, because it's true."

"I'm a telepath."

"Yup."

"By definition a criminal."

"Congratulations."

Layla stayed back while Peanut drove me home. I had a hard time coming up with anything to say.

"Hey. You know you can't talk about the Vitals and our lair and all that. It's top secret," Peanut said.

"Of course."

"You don't think your brother'll figure it out, do you?"

"Not too likely. He's not what I'd call a genius."

"Yeah, mine neither."

Peanut wasn't a brain trust himself. "Hey," I said. "Look at that. We have something in common, then."

"What's that?"

---

[32] *Psi*, if you don't know, is standard shorthand for *psionics*, which refers to psychic abilities, most commonly telepathy. As such, use of any psi powers is illegal in most countries. Psi, of course, is often represented by the Greek letter psi, Ψ.

Seriously? "We both have brothers who are dim bulbs."

"I don't know what 'dim bulb' is, but mine doesn't have that. He's got autism."

Oh. Ugh. "I didn't mean to be a jerk. Autism, huh? That's . . . tough."

Peanut shrugged. "Well, you know. It's what it is, right? Actually, he might be a genius. He doesn't really talk, so who knows, right? The good thing is I can tell him stuff and he listens, and I know he won't say nothing. Eddie likes when I hold him by the wrists and spin him around. Makes him laugh. We got a pretty good relationship."

I didn't say anything else for the rest of the trip home.

Blake was still up when I got in. His gaze moved up from the documentary about World War I he was watching to the clock on the mantel. "A little late, aren't you?"

"I guess, yeah. I ran into some kids from school, and we were hanging out, so I kind of lost track of time."

"Academy kids or A-program kids?"

"Mostly Academy," I said. I figured that answer was less likely to turn into some kind of confrontation."

"All right, well, it's getting late. You should probably hit the sack."

"Yeah, I'm pretty tired." It was only when I got up to my room that I realized how totally wiped out I was. Completely drained.

I was physically exhausted, but my mind was racing. I felt like I had discovered an awesome weapon in the basement—a combination grenade launcher/50-cal. machine gun/katana sword/nuclear bomb—that only I could control.

Telepathy? Of all things, *telepathy?* Sure, it was an illegal power and I wouldn't be able to brag about it. Anyone who found out was obliged to report it, like learning the whereabouts of a public enemy. But aside from the small issue of being against the law, telepathy was an incredibly powerful and valuable power to have. Having telepathy wasn't going to get me back into the Academy. But then again, I wasn't so sure I even wanted to go back to the Academy. I was just starting to feel as if I had found my people. I was feeling like a genuine A-hole.

CHAPTER 24

Practice

During the week after Layla first showed me my telepathic powers, she and I agreed that we shouldn't work on developing my telepathy skills on a deep level during Integrated Science class until I had enough control not to blast right into her mind, as I had done that first time. We would work on that at the lair.[33]

"For now, during class," she said, "you just sit next to me, close, and you concentrate. I mean, really focus, on sensing my mind."

"Sensing you."

"Try to locate my mind. Don't try to connect with me. First just try to feel where I am."

I was glad she was concentrating on directing some software rather than maybe sneaking a quick look into what I was thinking.

Because one thing was for sure, and it was always on my mind: I was falling hard for her.

---

[33] The only way I could say or think *lair* with a straight face was to look at it as being an entirely ironic usage of the word.

And that was something I knew for sure wouldn't sit too well with Blake, who had been home for a couple of weeks. There had been some stories in the press wondering where he was. I didn't know what exactly he told the leaders of the Justice Force, Flatliner and Miss Mistral, but their official comment was that Blake was taking a long-overdue and well-deserved vacation. So I guess to avoid any questions about why he was still hanging around at his childhood home, doing a whole lot of nothing, he went on a Hawaiian vacation with his on-again/off-again girlfriend, Janet "Radarette" Jeffries from the Justice Force. But he couldn't leave without giving me some (completely unsolicited) advice.

"So I'm heading out in the morning," he told me at night. He always seemed to want to have heavy conversations when I was going to sleep. "But there's something we need to talk about."

"I don't want to switch back to the Academy."

"No, it's not that. It's something else you're doing that's a big problem."

I still didn't have quite enough control of my telepathy to get into someone's head without their knowing it.[34] Layla was just about to start teaching me that skill. And the last thing I needed was for Blake to know about my developing powers. So I decided just to stay out of his head, at least until I learned stealth.

"What am I doing that's so bad?"

---

[34] That is, by using the always preferred SMI: stealth mind incursion.

"It's nauseating that you got dumped out of the Academy. I mean, even if you don't have any powers, they could've let you stay in as a courtesy. Family legacy, after all. But there isn't too much we can do about that now. So, yeah. You don't get to pick your classmates. But you do get to pick your friends, and the ones you picked are no good."

"Who are you talking about?"

"You know who. That Keating kid and the lowlifes she hangs around with."

"Wait, have you been spying on me?"

"I don't need to. There are still people working at the school who I talk to. They keep me appraised[35] and tell me what's what."

Getting mad at Blake wouldn't do me a bit of good. Yes, I was pissed off. And yes, he was overstepping into my life. But I was pretty sure he couldn't stop me from hanging around with whomever I wanted. And anyway, if he really wanted to push me on it, well, I knew his little secret, which I figured would give me more than enough leverage to get him to back off.

Sure, he could kill me with one punch.

But I could destroy him with one sentence.

---

[35] Yep. He said "appraised."

CHAPTER 25

Easy

I followed Layla up the flight of stairs that led to the lair. As we walked down the decoy corridor, I hoped that maybe none of the others were at the lair. I had been alone with Layla in the small side room, but that was all about working on my telepathy skills. And with Javier, Boots, and Peanut just outside the door, well, it didn't feel too private.

Not that I had the nerve to make a move. But I was looking forward to the time—which I hoped would be soon—when I could read Layla and maybe find out how she actually felt about me. I wouldn't lie and pretend I wasn't interested in a physical relationship, but the truth was that being in her mind was probably way more intimate than sex could ever be. Being inside her, in her mind, was pretty thrilling. It was hard not to think about it, and I did practically all the time.

Anyway, as for my hopes of us being alone in the lair, no such luck. Boots was on the couch, watching a rerun of an old sitcom on TV. Javier, wearing a white tank top, was hunched over his worktable. A curlicue of blue smoke rose in front of him. He was using a soldering iron for something, probably to attach an impossibly small microprocessor to a ridiculously tiny device. Peanut was perched on a stool next to Javier. There was a computer monitor in front of them with some kind of nature show on, a stalker-and-prey scenario.

"We're going in to work on his telepathy," Layla said.

Javier turned to look over his shoulder at us. "You are teaching him lots of skills, are you?"

She looked at him for a moment or two, hard, before saying, "He's a fast learner. He's got a lot of talent."

"Oh, yah? Super."[36]

He turned back to his itty-bitty construction project. I turned to Layla. She just shook her head and nodded toward the side room. Just before we got to the door, Javier called out, "Hey, has any of you ever seen a video of a wild boar eating a cat? Anyone?"

"I can pass on that," Boots said, not looking away from her TV show.

"I thought you guys were working on making contact with some big players," Layla said.

"We are," Peanut said. "We're, like, this close to one of them."

"You know how they say: all work and no play, yes?" Javier said.

"And this is just so cool," Peanut said.

"What about you, Mr. Telepathy?" Javier said to me. "Want to see it? It's quite impressive. Have you ever seen a

---

[36] "Syoo-pair."

wild boar just take apart a scared little pussy, eat it all up, bones and all?"

Javier thought he was pretty slick. I wasn't going to be intimidated by his crap. "I don't know how I missed it, but it sounds just great. Maybe a little later."

I could feel him glaring at me while I walked into the room behind Layla.

"What's his deal? I don't think you need telepathy to read the aggression coming from that guy."

"He's pretty aggressive, yeah. Territorial, too. And he's . . . a little possessive about me."

Ugh. That was what I was afraid of. I wasn't sure I wanted to know exactly what she'd meant by that, but if I didn't ask, it was going to bother me all night. "Possessive. Why?"

"Because in his mind, we're going to get together one day. All fantasy, trust me. Anyway, don't worry about him. We have work to do now."

Evasive. But the good news was that the very work she was talking about doing would eventually give me the ability to find out all kinds of useful information.

We had been practicing for another couple of weeks, and we were making headway. Finding my way into Layla's mind was easy for me by that point. I knew how to go softly, so it wasn't startling or intrusive or uncomfortable for her. This was reading. It was easy to lose track of time when we read each other. The only limit was the exhaustion that finally set in from all the intense concentration. I still hadn't figured out how to do it undetected, though.

I know you're here, so don't worry about that for now, she thought. *Just get used to moving around, exploring.*

I felt like some kind of a cat burglar or something.

Stop thinking that way. It's just disconnecting you from this. And you need practice writing. Try to put some thoughts here, in my mind.

Right, right. I keep forgetting, I tried to write.

Not quite, but not terrible. Relax. You're learning really, really fast. You have a talent for this. Okay, now, stay with me. I'm going to open up some areas in my mind for you. See if you can find your way in. You're going to look for memories, emotions, or data.

I don't really know how to recognize that.

You'll know it when you're there. Try to . . . well, to feel it in your mind. Relax into it, and I think it'll happen.

Hey.

What?

We're having this whole conversation, this whole . . . interaction, just in our joined minds. Pretty amazing. Kind of brings a whole new meaning to "hooking up."[37]

---

[37] You know that awful feeling you get when you say something and you realize it's a mistake the second the words leave your mouth? It's even worse when it happens with TP thoughts instead of spoken words. Then if you think about what a jerk you are, the other person knows *exactly* how embarrassed you feel: that's because she knows your every thought and feeling, exactly when it takes shape.

I guess so. Anyway, concentrate on what you're doing here.
So I did.

Every day I worked on it, and every day I got better. Layla had been right about my having a talent for telepathy. I felt like I was getting more control over it all the time. I didn't have to look for the "light" anymore. I could enter her mind at will, with practically no effort.

I guess this is probably the best time to explain telepathy, at least the kind I have, in as clear a way as I can. Again, the only way I can do it is by using an analogy, but I think it'll make sense.

It's a lot like going into a house. Lots of rooms.

Now, this is a big house, the human mind, and there are lots and lots of rooms. Some of them connect, either directly or by passageways maybe behind the walls. Not all houses are built the same. Some people are easy to read: ranch houses, Colonials. Everything is laid out in a logical, pretty simple way. But some are much tougher: more individualized, maybe not any particular type, but a mysterious structure, with add-ons and confusing construction.

So sometimes you go in and you can pretty much tell exactly where to go to find what you're looking for. Sometimes it takes a lot of exploring.

In some cases the rooms are wide open; in some cases the doors are partly closed. Sometimes doors are closed but can be opened, and sometimes they're locked tight. The strength of the lock depends on how and why the host has closed off that part of the mind.

Some of these places are dark and require slow going. Others are brighter and you can move around pretty easily in them. The thing is, as your reading skills improve, it's kind of like having your own head-mounted light: you can see no matter how dark it is.

So what can you do in this house of the mind? Well, a lot. You can wander around and just get an idea of what the owner is like. You can look for a specific room (childhood memories, plans, hopes, dreams—like I said, most people have pretty big mind-houses) and see what's there. You can push open doors that the host wanted closed.[38] You can even kick in the locked doors, if you're skilled enough. All that is reading. Writing, of course, is more active. Take things—pull out memories or thoughts. Leave things in the house— messages, ideas. Disrupt things—break mental connections. Back then, it occurred to me that there might even be a way to burn the whole damn place down if you wanted to.

Which I eventually found was a lot easier for me to do than I ever would have guessed.

Whenever people were near me, I concentrated on reading them. I was getting better at writing—putting idea fragments into their minds. I couldn't do any actual commands yet, not

---

[38] A command projection is when you telepathically compel the target do something.

without it being obvious to them that something unnatural was going on, but I was still able to plant sensory impressions and have some fun with it.

One day it was warm, and we sat outside the deli we sometimes went to for lunch.

"Watch this," I said. I nodded toward the sidewalk across the street.

There was a lady walking and carrying a shopping bag from an expensive clothing store. I kept my eye on her, entered her mind, and did my thing.

She started waving her hand at the air next to her head. She stopped walking, looked around, then started again. And then she swatted at the air, her mouth pressed into an annoyed frown.

"What did you do?" Boots asked.

"I wrote the sound of a mosquito buzzing in her mind. Loud. Like one big-ass mosquito."

We laughed.

"That is very amusing," Javier said, his accent sounding especially German, or maybe Austrian, that day. "But imaginary mosquitoes are not likely to do much damage to heroes. If your telepathy is so strong as Layla says it is, then I hope we can expect more impressive uses of your powers."

The guy was starting to get on my nerves. "What kind of damage are you planning to do to heroes, Javier? Do you have any actual plans?"

"I am working on this," he said. His voice was low and he avoided eye contact.

"Okay, let's see how you like this," I said. "Watch the guy right by that mailbox."

I had zeroed in on a young man bobbing his head to the beat coming from his three-hundred-dollar headphones.

He abruptly stopped walking and looked up. He held both hands, palms out, in front of him and said something we couldn't hear. He shifted to take a step to his left, then did the same toward his right. He stopped, laughed, and said something as he pointed to his right. He laughed again and took a step in that direction before heading forward on his way.

"I made him think there was another guy, one that he bumped into, and then did that crazy shuffle people do when they don't know which way the other person is going to go."

"And what good will that do us?" Javier asked.

"I made the image completely detailed. He could give a specific description of the guy, just like if he'd been there in real life. Not easy, but I did it."

"Again, amusing, but what use does it serve for our purposes?" Javier asked. He was definitely getting on my nerves.

"Think about it, Javier. If I can project the image or idea of a person to block someone, I can project an army of Phaetons, or a building, or lightning, or fire. Imagine if Flatliner is coming our way to attack. I can make him think he's looking at trees instead of us, and he turns to go in another direction. Is that useful enough for you?"

That shut him down pretty tight. All he could do was nod and smile to disguise his embarrassment.

Looked to me like I'd won that round with him.

BRADLEY BARON: "There's a reason we call them powers rather than abilities. It's because that's how they make you feel."

PROSECUTOR 9: "And how is that?"

BRADLEY BARON: "Powerful."

The People of the United States v.
Defendant #5958375-Er/00-m
Trial transcript, p. 253

CHAPTER 26

Control

I was going to the lair a few times a week. I wasn't crazy about every person in the crew, but hey, you can't love everyone.[39] The truth was that I liked the subversive nature of what we were doing. They kept the lair mostly dark, which I figured was mainly for effect.

Some illumination came from Javier's halogen work light and several computer monitors. He and Peanut were often hunched over the computers, speaking in hushed tones. They wouldn't say what they were doing. Boots and Layla teased them, saying that they were looking at porn. The only reply they got, a nonsensical one at that, was Peanut calling back, "Yeah, you wish!" I figured Javier liked the idea that he was working on something secret from the rest of us. And Peanut liked the idea of doing anything Javier liked.

Boots watched more TV than any human being I've ever known. It didn't matter what was on; she would watch sitcoms, reality shows, nighttime soaps—anything. And she'd watch them over and over, and she could recite the dialogue while watching.

---

[39] Okay, let's just be honest: I didn't much like Javier. The others were fine.

Since the day outside when I showed the Vitals some of my skills, I had been concentrating on getting to the next step: writing specific commands or thoughts into someone's mind without it being known by the target. It wasn't the same as what I'd done outside; putting a sound or sensation in someone's mind was easy. Putting in more complicated thoughts was a much harder deal. This wasn't something Layla could do; when she wrote, you were aware that there was another presence in your consciousness. I wanted to be able to do it undetected. I wanted stealth.

It was during one of those times when we were developing my telepathy that we heard a litany of shouts and excited curses coming from Javier in the other room. He was definitely revved up, but it didn't sound like he was unhappy.

All his loud carrying-on made it pretty hard for Layla and me to concentrate on what we were doing, so we pulled ourselves together and went out into the living room. Javier was doing a victory strut around the space, hooting and hollering as he did.

"What the hell?" Layla said.

"We're in! He is willing to talk to us."

"Who?" I asked.

"Who? *Who?* Who have I been trying to make contact with for the past two months?"

Given that Javier never talked to me unless it was absolutely necessary, and also given that I had less than zero interest in reading whatever he was thinking, I had no idea what he had been doing for the last two months.

"The Big M, man!" he shouted. "He is interested in talking to us!"

Boots shook her head. "You've got to be kidding."

"Do I *look* like I'm kidding?"

"How did you find him?" Layla asked.

"Not easily, believe me," Javier said.

"Who are we talking about?" I asked.

Javier took a deep breath and very obviously relished the moment before he finally answered. "Mutagion."

Mutagion. *The* Mutagion. He had to be in the top ten domestic (or top twenty international) most hunted Phaetons. Not likely you could find a man, woman, or child in America who hadn't heard of Mutagion. His name was commonly invoked as a way to get children to behave, as in, "You keep playing with matches and Mutagion's gonna come and take you away." The funny part to me, though, was I couldn't say for sure exactly what it was he had done that was bad enough to earn his reputation. Anyway, whatever it was, he was one of the most hated villains in the country. Javier had to be lying. Layla seemed to agree.

"You're lying," she said.

"Why would I make this up? We tracked him down on the Underweb and kept making prefaces."

"Prefaces?"[40] [41]

"He says he'll meet with us," Peanut said.

---

[40] He meant *overtures.*

[41] No, I'm not kidding.

"About what?" Layla asked.

"Does it matter?"

She looked at him, astonished. "Does it *matter*? Um, yeah."

"Do you understand what this means?" Javier asked.

I couldn't help myself. "It sounds like it means you got an appointment with a guy hunted by every law enforcement agency and hero—individual and team—in this nation and several others, and, though there's a decent chance his reason for agreeing to meet with us very well could be to kill us and bury us in shallow graves, it probably isn't too important to know what exactly the purpose of the meeting is. Like, what could go wrong?"

"Oh, and there's one other thing," Peanut said. Javier shot him a look. Peanut shrugged and said, "Well, there is."

"What's that?" Layla said.

Peanut took a breath to speak, but Javier held up his hand and took the lead. "Mutagion will not have anything to do with us unless we first prove we are for real."

"Prove we're for real how?" Layla asked.

Javier took a deep breath. "He said we have to do something to show that we're serious."

Boots said, "Um, like what?"

Peanut shrugged. "He didn't say. It's just that we have to do something that'll prove to him that we're serious about being villains. He wants to know what we're about."

"Yeah, well, so do I," I said.

Javier glared at me, and I realized I should have kept my

mouth shut. But the guy was reckless and the fact that he apparently hadn't thought this out at all made me angry.

Javier was clearly angry, too. "What do you think we are all doing here? Hanging around in a little club? Fun and the games?"

"I'm not really sure, to be honest. Maybe you should tell me."

Javier stood up a little straighter, kind of like a dog raising its hackles.

"Okay, boys," Boots said. "Let's just keep cool. We're all on the same side, right?"

Back off, Layla thought to me. *You're making an enemy, which you don't need.*

I'm not trying *to make an enemy. Before we go off and do something to prove how badass we are, I just want to understand what he wants from this Mutagion guy,* I thought back to her.

Javier is arrogant and stubborn. And he holds a grudge. You need to be careful with him.

Why?

"Are you with us or not?" Javier asked me.

"If being with you means I'm supposed to blindly support every single thing you do and say—"

"And now I ask again: are with us or not?"

Discretion is the better part of valor, as they say, so I decided to back off and save my energy for whatever conflict with him was bound to come up next. "Yes, I'm with you."

"Then I thank you to stop arguing with me."

I wasn't arguing. I was asking questions, but if I said that, we'd start all over again, and in addition to making an enemy, I still wouldn't get the answers. *Why don't you ask him what this is about?* I thought to Layla.

"Okay, anyhow," she said, "what are we trying to do by contacting this guy?"

Boots chimed in. "You got to him on the Underweb? Phaetons can type? And read?"

"Some can, some cannot. It all depends on how damaged they are," Javier said.

I could feel Layla getting as impatient as I was. But she had a history with Javier that I didn't have, so she could get away with a more direct confrontation than I could. "So again: what is it we want to meet with him for? Other than possibly getting murdered by him, that is."

"That's something we will need to talk about. What can he do for us? He is a major person in the antihero movement. He's as good a connection as you can wish to get."

"Okay, yeah, but so what do we want this connection to do?" Boots asked.

"You know, I don't know," Javier said, now openly pissed off at everyone. "Here, me and Peanut went and made this amazing connection with a hero—and by that, I mean a villain—and instead of being impressed and excited about it, all you are doing is tearing it down."

This was my chance to maybe do some damage control. "Look, Javier. I'm sure I speak for everybody when I say we're both stunned and impressed that you could make real contact with a Phaeton at all, much less one of the most famous and feared ones. We're blown away, seriously. And yes, it's a big deal. But it's kind of like when you have an enormous destructive power: if you don't know how to handle it and what you want it to do, it can blow up in your face. None of us wants that. We're just trying to figure out how to make the most of the great work you did."

He glared at me. *Is this guy trying to make an idiot of me?*

No. It sounds like he means what he's saying, I sent his way.

"Okay, I guess you are right," Javier said. "We will have to talk about it. Maybe I overreacted or something." *But I am certainly not going to apologize to this kid. If he is waiting for that, he's going to have a long wait.*

I wasn't waiting for that. I couldn't care less if he apologized or not. What I did care about was what I had just done.

Without even trying, I'd put a thought in his head, and somehow I'd done it in his own mental voice.

I had just made my first stealth mind incursion. Not only did he not know I had been in his head, but he also thought the idea I'd planted was his own.

And that is what is commonly known as mind control.

CHAPTER 27

Who We Are

Half an hour later, we were all sitting on the couch and chairs, gathered around the low table loaded with snacks and drinks, continuing the Vital team meeting.

"I wonder what Mutagion looks like," Boots said. "There are no clear pictures of him. Not that I ever saw, anyway. And I can't believe he can use computers. They say he has claws instead of hands."

I shook my head. "There's no evidence that he actually has claws."

"There's no evidence that he doesn't!" Peanut said.

Layla said, "What the guy really looks like and what exactly his handicaps or whatever are is a whole other discussion. But we didn't come up with an answer: what's the goal of connecting with him?"

"Well, precisely that. A connection," Javier said.

"What do we *want* from an arrangement with—I can't believe I'm saying this—Mutagion?" Boots asked.

Javier didn't say anything. Nobody did.

I figured maybe I could get the conversation actually moving forward. "Okay, I don't mean this in a sarcastic way, but—forgetting about Mutagion for a minute—what exactly is it we want to do? I mean in the grand scheme of things?"

"What do you mean?" Peanut asked.

"I mean, like, do we have an actual manifesto or something? Anything that in any way documents what we stand for? What we're about?"

Peanut made a snorting sound. "Dude, we're not about writing books or pamphlets or whatever. If I want to write, I'll do it in English class."

"It's not about writing. It's about getting ideas together so you actually know what you believe, what you're trying to accomplish. Even anarchists have guiding principles."

Javier said, "We're not being philosophers. We are not talkers. We are doers."

I couldn't help but laugh. *"Doers?* Sorry, but I don't see too much getting *done* at all. Javier, you're probably the one who *does* the most around here—at least you build your little devices—but then nobody *does* anything with them. Planning and scheming may make us feel all badass and everything, and we don't like the heroes and we talk about changing things, but in the end, really: what are we actually *doing?"*

To tell the truth, I still don't know where all this came from. I was on my feet and even a little out of breath. I realized then that I had raised my voice, and weirdest of all: I had gotten kind of impassioned. Yes, I had some antihero feelings, and yes, I didn't much like the priorities or values a lot of people had—all that was true. But I never, ever would have viewed myself as political. And yet, there I was, in our secret lair, standing in front of these guys, these would-be villains, delivering this call to action, and they were all looking to me as if I had answers. Answers to questions I didn't even know.

Like a radio tuned to four different channels at the same time, I could hear thoughts from all of them, all at once.

Who does this guy think he is?

Hey, he's not bad. He's pretty smart.

Who died and put him in charge?

This kid has better ideas than Javier does. And he's smarter, too.

I knew there was more to him than it looked like.

He has a point.

"Yes, okay," Javier said. "Maybe you're right. Maybe we should have some type of statement saying exactly what we are all about."

I looked at him.

"No, I am being quite serious," he said. "It's not such a bad idea. Why don't you work on it?"

"Me."

"You. You're the smartest one here. You could make it sound good."

"But I don't really know what you guys want. I'm new. I wouldn't even know what to say."

"You seemed to have a pretty good idea two seconds ago. We'll let you know if we agree or not. What do you guys think?"

There was general assent all around.

"Okay, I can do that," I said. "But there's something we need to decide before I can even start."

"What's that?" Boots asked.

"If we're serious about wanting to be a villain team, we need to have a name."

"A name," Peanut repeated.

"We already have one: Vital," Javier said.

Layla shook her head. "Doesn't exactly compare to Troika, the Barbarian League, the Gorgon Corps. No, Brad is right. We need a new name. Any ideas?"

THE HELLIONS *Our Screed*

(first draft)

We are dedicated to righting the wrongs and injustices of the miscreants known the world over as "heroes," which we view as a ~~corruption~~ perversion of the word itself and all it should stand for.

Whether they work for nefarious government entities or are self-formed teams, corporate-sponsored or independent, national or international, we vow to stop them by whatever means and measures we deem necessary.

Should this require violation of existing "laws," we will do it.

Should this require theft, we will do it.

Should this require destruction of property, we will do it.

Should this require disruption of government agencies, we will do it.

Should this require takeover of corporate tentacles, we will do it.

Should this require loss of life or liberty, we will do it.

The Hellions will not rest or cease or desist from our mission until we have seen true justice reign or we are dead. ~~Whichever comes first~~.

The Hellions are:

?

?

?

?

?

(Hey: WE NEED TO PICK OUR VILLAIN NAMES ! ! !)

CHAPTER 28

Home Sweet

So I hear you've been spending a lot of time out of the house," Blake said. It was so great to have him home from Hawaii after a month without him. "Where you been?"

"Hanging out."

"Yeah? With who?"

"Some friends from school."

He cleared his throat. "I hope it's not with that girl."

I especially liked it when he came into my room un-invited and pried into my personal life. "Which girl is that?" I asked. I still hadn't looked up from the computer screen on my lap.

"You know which girl. The one we talked about before I left. Colleen Keating."

"Layla."

"Yeah, whatever."

"How was Hawaii?"

"You're changing the subject."

"That's right." I looked up from my computer. Of course he didn't look tan. His skin was totally protected from UV rays. Blake didn't know what a sunburn felt like. Or even a mosquito bite, for that matter.

"Why are you changing the subject?"

"Because. It's not up to you to decide who I hang out with."

He put on his smile, which only made me angrier. "I'm your brother," he said. "You really don't think I should look out for you?"

"This doesn't feel like 'looking out.' It feels like you trying to act like a parent. I already have a mother, and my father's gone. You're not him, and I don't need another, thanks."

He nodded. "That's debatable, but anyway." Blake folded his arms across his broad chest. He was going to wait me out. I just wanted the conversation to be over.

"I'm not sure where this is all coming from," I started, "but I don't know why you think you're in a position to tell me what to do. If I want to hang around with Layla Keating, that's *my* business, not yours."

He shook his head and then turned to shut the door. I wondered if he was actually going to try to physically intimidate me. Instead, he sat down in the desk chair, which creaked under his two hundred and twenty-plus pounds of muscle.

"Actually, it kind of is my business. Literally." He thought for a moment, then sighed.

"What?"

He looked at me for a few seconds, then started talking. "I'm going to trust you with something. This is important."

"Okay."

"The thing is, I found out yesterday after I got back that two oil companies pulled their sponsorship from me."

"Why?"

"They didn't say. Not the truth, anyway. Their explanation was something about prioritizing investments or something. The real reason, I'm pretty sure, is because I've been on leave from the JF and they don't want to back me anymore."

"Well, that sucks."

"Yeah, it does. Don't tell Mom. She'd be real disappointed."

"Won't she find out sooner or later?"

"Not if I can get myself back in fighting form and persuade the sponsors to stick with me. And that's kind of why I'm on your back about this Keating girl. Having a brother who associates with someone like that just isn't good for my image."

Blake should have quit while he was ahead. I'd actually started to feel a bit sorry for him. I did a little internal shrug and thought, Oh, well. Sucks to be you.

Everything was all about his hero status and his sense of superiority.

Heroes first. Always.

Which was exactly the attitude we—the Hellions—were planning to destroy.

CHAPTER 29

Financing

No need to remember to bring a debit card and no worries about having a big enough balance. Getting money from an ATM is no problem at all when you have biomechanical-merge abilities. It was pretty cool to see.

Layla moved her hand in front of the screen and then the buttons, eventually finding what she needed about a foot to the left and a foot below the screen.[42] Boots was running an interference generator to mess up the recording from the camera.

A bunch of weird icons scrolled over the screen, then froze. The cash door snapped open and twenty-dollar bills started rolling out, dropping right into the backpack Peanut was holding open to receive them. When the machine ran out of twenties, tens and then fifties were dispensed.

By my count, that ATM gave up $12,520 without the slightest protest or hesitation.

---

[42] On this particular ATM, that spot was the closest to the computer interface. Later, Layla explained that any mechanical or computer device has a way in for her; it's just a matter of finding it. Which, she said, is usually pretty easy: it's as if that access point glows bright green for her.

"Whose account did we just rob?" I asked while we walked away.

"Nobody's," she said. "The bank's. And it would take a team of accountants months to figure out where the numbers don't match. Not even worth the effort."

"Cost of doing business," Boots said.

"They probably lose track of ten times that amount every day of the year," Peanut said.

Did I feel guilty? Even though it was a multinational bank with assets I could barely begin to imagine, it was still stealing. Right? Sure. Whatever.

That particular bank, I should note, was a major contributor to the Justice Force, funding its jets, headquarters, and training facility/summer retreat. Hitting the heroes in the money belt was just an added benefit of our robbery.

As we walked away from the ATM, I understood why it would be so tempting to use powers for personal gain. I wondered why more people didn't go that way.

We took down four more ATMs before the night was over.

It wasn't as if we were stealing the money just for fun or to buy ourselves expensive electronics or anything like that. No, our plans for the money were all strictly business.

First off, Layla and Boots needed supplies to make our lair truly secret: secret from prying eyes, ears, and electronic surveillance. We were stepping up our operation, and we needed to act professional. That included having a real state-of-the-art lair.

The other thing was that we were about to go on our first official mission and we just didn't have a thing to wear.

Not long before, we had agreed that we didn't want anything as cheesy as team uniforms or matching logos. We decided we each wanted to pick or design our own costumes, based on whatever abilities we had or images we wanted to project.

One big issue I had to consider for my so-called costume was physical protection. This, of course, was a concern for all of us if we seriously expected to tangle with powered heroes. It turned into another heated discussion in the lair.

"The thing is," I said, "if we go up against someone like Myoman or Diesel or Iron Justice, it doesn't matter what we're wearing. Any one of them could rip any of us to little pieces without breaking a sweat."

Javier wouldn't sit still for that kind of talk. "Speak for yourself. I have a twenty-two strength level."

Peanut laughed. "Yeah, dream on. You don't have a quarter of that."

Boots chimed in. "Easy, now. No need for hostility here.[43] Look, Javier. Even if you do have S-twenty-two, Meganova and Gammarama have levels in the eighties, probably, and they're not even close to being the strongest heroes. No way

---

[43] At first, I thought that Boots was always making peace because she was really uncomfortable with conflict, which was at odds with the idea of her fighting heroes. I eventually figured out that it was because conflict didn't shake her up at all and she was totally comfortable addressing it. Very little seemed to get this girl agitated. Cool and calm, pretty much all the time.

any of us can stand up to that, no matter what kind of protection we put on."

Javier was quiet for a couple of seconds before he spoke. "Okay, yes, that's true. But what if we're against someone with lower-level powers? Then it probably wouldn't be bad to have some protection."

"As much as I can't believe I'm saying it," I said, "I kind of agree with Javier. We could be up against regular old police, for example."

Peanut laughed. "The cops? You're afraid of Regular cops? What kind of p—"

"Can you outrun a bullet?" I asked. "None of us are accelerates, so we can't dodge them, either. I can't think of a good reason not to wear KevFlex."

So for my outfit (I just can't bring myself to call it a costume), I knew that I needed some kind of mask if I wanted to keep Mom from being dragged into this.[44] The other thing I knew for sure: no way in hell was I going to wear spandex or anything old-school and tacky like that. I wanted to go as low-profile as possible. But I also did want some physical protection.

So I got a KevFlex shirt, and over that, I would wear a vest I had specially made. It was lined with pouches containing electro-rheological fluid. This meant that when an electric field was applied,[45] the fluid in the pouches would

---

[44] Yes, I know. Once someone is captured, it's not too hard to unmask him or her. My aim, though, was to *not* get captured. Best-laid plans and all that . . .

[45] Javier offered to set it up for me.

turn from soft gel to heat-resistant and largely bulletproof plates. I could turn the vest into armor at the flip of a small switch.

I got a dark-blue-and-maroon double-breasted leather jacket. I found a piece of black leather, cut it into the shape of the Greek letter *psi*, and sewed it onto the jacket, right over my heart:

$$\Psi$$

I added sap gloves: leather with sealed pockets filled with fine steel shot covering all the knuckles. I read that a punch delivered while wearing these gloves could bring an ox to its knees. I got pants made out of KevFlex. Boots with jointed titanium plates built into the soles finished off the outfit.[46]

The other big decision I needed to make was what I wanted to call myself. We didn't have our villain names right away, but that came very soon. We did have money. We had an undetectable lair. We had costumes. And within four days, we had completed all our preparations to execute the plan we had made for our very first mission.

We were ready for action. It was time for the world to meet the Hellions.

---

[46] Oh, and Justice Force boxer briefs, just for the necessary note of irony.

CHAPTER 30

Prep

E ven in the darkness of an alley, one block away from our target, I could see what we looked like, and it was almost impossible not to be embarrassed.

Five kids, wearing absurd costumes, standing in an alley at one in the morning, thinking we were pretty cool. We looked like a collective joke. Most likely, anyone who saw us would just laugh.

Of course, the main attraction of the costume that Boots picked was . . . boots. Up to midthigh and with hidden slash pockets for throwing knives and other stuff she wouldn't tell us, it was pretty hard not to look at them. Which, of course, was the plan: distract and attack. If you did have a chance to look up at her face, the zebra-stripes makeup covered her Maori tattoos and would probably make it hard to ID her. She picked the name Snakebyte, a fairly clever play on her computer skills.

Peanut went the bizarre route. He wore a red-and-black unitard (he couldn't resist showing off his physique) and antique steel gauntlets going from his first knuckles up to his elbows. The crowning part of his costume, though, was the mask. He bought himself two bison skulls from a creepy store called Bones-R-Us, and he had Javier affix the skulls with their long, curved horns to a hockey mask. It was very weird and undeniably disturbing, which, I guess, was the point. He took the name Baculum, which I told him meant a catastrophic plague causing a huge number of casualties.[47] He was very excited about that name.

Javier took the black leather approach, head to toe, including a creepy-looking mask he got at a fetish store. He named himself Black Dirk. I tried to explain that very few people would know that a dirk was a type of dagger, and his name sounded ridiculous. Not surprisingly, he wasn't interested in my opinion.

I had on my liquid-armor-and-KevFlex suit, topped off with the navy-and-maroon leather jacket and a standard-issue hero/villain black domino mask, which I lined with ViewStopper quartzlon. (Wearing a plain old mask would be pointless if going up against a hero with intersight.) I went with the name Mindfogger.[48]

Definitely the best-looking one of us, in my just slightly biased opinion, was Layla. I wasn't quite sure what the theme was, but she sure looked fantastic. She wore combat boots, flesh-colored KevFlex tights under fishnet stockings, some kind of biker shorts, and then this unbelievably hot

---

[47] Which is not at all what *baculum* means. Look it up, if you're curious. . . .

[48] I was actually going to use something similar, though stronger, which would have rhymed nicely with *mind-chucker*, but Layla said it wasn't good, because it wouldn't be printed in newspapers or spoken on the news, rendering it useless for publicity.

black-and-red top (she told me it was called a bustier or maybe a torsolette; I can't remember which and I don't quite get the difference) and sort of a modified Mardi Gras mask. It was something to see, if a little bit over the top.[49] She picked the name Bionica. She had no bionic parts, but she felt that her biomech-merge abilities made this a reasonable choice.

Boots was monitoring her interference generator. Layla had just gotten back to the alley with Peanut. They had big overcoats on and left their masks with us so they wouldn't attract attention in the critical part of the mission they had just completed.

"Everything is cool?" Javier said. "Any problems?"

"Not one. Worked like a dream," Layla said.

"Good. You happy now?" he asked me.

"Ecstatic," I said. This part had been my idea. In fact, it was done at my insistence. Layla and Peanut had gone down into the subway. When a train came to a stop at the station one block south of where we were, she put her hand on the lead car and did her biomech-merge thing, completely disabling the engine. They did the same thing at two other stations. This meant that there would be no trains—and no passengers—in the tunnels that wove around the area where we were pulling off our job. I said that if we didn't clear those tunnels, I wasn't going to be a part of the operation. Layla sided with me, much to Javier's annoyance.

---

[49] I know my description of how she looked sounds sexist and kind of like every adolescent geek-boy's objectifying dream-girl, but what can I say? *She* picked the costume.

"You are on?" Javier asked Boots.

"I'm on, they're off," she said, looking at the waveforms on her palm computer.

Javier nodded. "Okay, then. I think we should take a couple of moments to observe this moment, which is going to go down in history as the start of—"

"Can we just get on with this?" I said.

Javier sneered at me. "This is a big deal. I believe someone would want to say something . . . profound. Words that will be recorded in history e-books one day."

"I really should've taken a leak before we left," Peanut said, his voice muffled a bit by the bison-bone helmet. "It would be so sucky if Baculum had a pee spot on his pants during this whole thing."

"That's great," Javier said. "You just ruined this whole thing, you idiot."

"Why? Because I gotta whiz? It's natural!"

Stupid as the conversation was, it helped to make me less nervous. "Whatever you do, just don't think of a drippy faucet or rainwater running out of a gutter," I said.

"Oh, thanks! That's just great! Now I need to go *more*."

"No, no. I'm saying *don't* think of those things. The more you picture drops of water plopping into a bathtub, or that hissing sound when—"

"All right, stop this now," Javier said. "You boys are spoiling the moment." He gave a harsh look to Layla, who had been laughing during our childish exchange.

"We really should go," Boots said. "I can't keep up this interference too much longer before someone figures out there's a disruptor in the area."

We adjusted our masks. Javier slung a heavy rucksack over his shoulder. Peanut picked up one that was twice as heavy.

"This is it," Javier said.

I nodded and we moved out of the alley and to the soon-to-be scene of the crime.

CHAPTER 31

Depth Charge

Standing flattened against the wall on the staircase, three steps up, I wondered how things had come to this. I was looking down at the floor of the lobby where Boots lay, unmoving, facedown in a pool of blood. I glanced up to where Javier was crouched a few steps above me, a worried expression on his face.

I turned back to look again at Boots. The blood was soaking into the collar of her tan jacket. I'll admit it now: I was scared. But I didn't dare move, not one inch.

The elevator door opened, and Rotor hustled down the lobby hallway to crouch next to Boots. He reached to help her when Peanut's twenty-two-inch-circumference arms wrapped around him and lifted him right off the ground. Rotor craned his neck and saw a huge, horned bison-skull mask. The man looked like he was going to puke.

The elevator door started to close. Javier stepped out of the shadows next to the elevator and jammed in a steel pipe to hold it open.

"What are you doing?" Rotor asked in a choked voice, thanks to Peanut's bear hug. "I was just down in my workshop and I heard some noise. I came up to help the girl. What the hell are you doing?"

Boots sat up, took the towel that Layla handed her, and wiped the fake blood off her face. Layla repositioned some of the zebra stripes for Boots, making sure they were straight.

"You missed some there," Layla said. She took the towel and wiped more of the blood off Boots's neck.

"Down in your *workshop*, eh?" Javier said. "And you heard a noise? Or did you see something on one of your monitors?"

"I don't know what you're talking about," Rotor said.

"Let's take a look together, then. This sounds good?"

We dragged the bags and the rest of the stuff, and then we all squeezed into the elevator. I pushed the button for the basement. We went down and then the elevator stopped.

I thought to Rotor, *There's nobody else down there, correct?* He snapped his head to the right, then left, trying to figure out what he was hearing, or thinking. *I'm in your mind. We know you work alone. But is anyone else in the surveillance lab right now?*

His voice was high and choked with panic. "No. Nobody else is down there. How did you know . . . ?"

I motioned to Peanut, who was still holding Rotor, whose feet hadn't touched the floor of the hallway or the elevator since Peanut had first picked him up. I didn't want to take any chance that Rotor might recognize my voice, so I stayed silent when I flipped up the emergency stop switch to expose the retinal scanner. Peanut held Rotor's face close to the spot.

"Open up your eye," Javier said. "We know what we're doing. Unless you want Baculum here to tighten his grip, you had better let that reader check your retina." After Rotor opened his eye and the retinal scanner blinked red twice, then green once, Javier held up Rotor's hand and looked to me.

I held one thumb up.

As soon as Javier pressed Rotor's thumb against the reader, the back door opened up to the steel elevator.

"Let's do it," Layla said.

We began unpacking the bags. Javier affixed the charges he'd built against several spots in the steel elevator. He attached the detonators and timers.

"It's ready to go," he said.

You're sure? I wrote in his mind.

He glared at me. He didn't like me going in his head. "It should work," he said out loud.

I looked over at Layla. She had a smile of excitement on her face.

This is so cool! she thought.

If it works. I hope Javier knows what he's doing.

He does.

"Okay," Javier said to Rotor. "How do we send this elevator down to the surveillance lab?"

Rotor didn't say a word.

"Tell us now," Javier demanded.

Rotor stayed silent.

I took over and thought to him. *Either tell us how to send the elevator down automatically—and tell us now—or Snakebyte will figure it out, and if we have to go to that trouble, we'll send you along for the ride. It's your choice.*[50]

Rotor took a look at all the explosives that were loaded into the elevator, and he didn't waste any time telling us how to send it down remotely.

We had handcuffed Rotor to a park bench and we were in another alley four blocks away, changing out of our costumes, when we heard the muffled *BOOM* and felt the pavement vibrate as the timed detonator went off, destroying the surveillance lab.

When the fire department trucks arrived—along with any heroes who were summoned to the scene—they would find a message spray-painted on the sidewalk across the street.

A WARM HELLO FROM THE HELLIONS!

---

[50] Of course, I had no intention of letting Rotor get hurt. And I could have given him a command projection and made him tell us, but I felt like I wanted to keep that power in reserve for when we really needed it. Doing it this way seemed more badass.

CHAPTER 32

Aftermath

Blake had gotten the communication about the destruction of the Justice Force surveillance lab minutes after it happened. When I got home, he was still checking the online paper to find out how much of the location's actual purpose was known or revealed. "I cannot believe this!"

Mom was on the couch, flipping through the channels on the TV. Nothing at all about the incident; it was being covered up. "Well, at least there were no casualties, you said," she noted.

"No, and that's fine, but this was a *major* surveillance lab. It covered eight states and fifteen international airports. You know what it cost to build that place?"

Mom said, "And on the bright side, it's great that the papers didn't let on what was down there. What'd they call it again?"

Blake ran his finger over the computer screen. "They said it was, wait . . . right. Here: 'An underground steam-pipe explosion.' And they just left it at that."

"So, that's good. It won't be revealed what the place really was. The entire building was destroyed? All of it?"

"Yeah, well, it was like a sinkhole. Everything above the

lab collapsed, so the lab has probably been crushed to dust. That was a lot of expensive equipment. And we're even out the cost of what we paid for the building."

"Maybe the government, or one of your sponsors, will absorb the cost," Mom said.

"No, no. They won't, because we didn't get the purchase preapproved. They can't help."

"Where was it?" I asked. Blake said the address. I pretended to think for a second or two. "Wait, isn't that where we went the other day?"

"Yes, that's exactly it. Completely destroyed."

I did my best to approximate a look of shock. "We could have been there when it happened."

Blake grunted with disgust. "No, no. They lured the attendant, that sorry-ass loser Rotor, up before they sent the charge down. They weren't out to kill anyone. Just to kick the Justice Force in the nuts. Damn it!" He pushed the computer away.

Mom took another look at the screen. "You ever hear of this group? The Hellions?"

"No," Blake said. "They came out of nowhere." He shook his head. "I can't stand these upstart groups. Even though I haven't been on active duty for too long, I've already seen a change. When I started, the bad guys needed to have big ambitions, world domination and all that, if they wanted to play in the big leagues. Nowadays, you don't need to be so special to attack a group like the Justice Force. Makes me sick."

"Were they Phaetons?" Mom asked.

"Of course not," I said before I could stop myself. They both turned to me.

"How do you know?" Mom asked. "You didn't even read the article."

"Well, he's right," Blake said. "Most Phaetons don't have the brains to pull off something like this. They didn't attack us, not for real. They hit us in our money belt. They're not a real threat. We don't even know if they have any powers. They're nobodies."

Mom, ever reasonable, said, "Well, they made themselves *some*bodies. They got the public's attention. And yours."

It took a real effort not to smile.

It was equally hard to keep from smiling at school. Everyone— teachers, students, custodians—who talked to us or passed us in the halls or sat next to us in class had no idea at all of what we were capable of doing. What we *had* done. The five of us had a secret—a huge secret—that made us all feel pretty damned special.

After science, I was walking toward the cafeteria with Layla and Peanut when Travis called my name. He was across the hall, and he waved. I was in the middle of a sentence, so I smiled and nodded to him. Granted, it wasn't exactly an astonishingly enthusiastic response, but we didn't really even see each other outside of passing in the hallways once in a while. Other than a shared history, we just didn't have a thing in common anymore.

Without question, my old friends would have been astonished and horrified to find out what I had done. Not that I ever would have told them. Their little honor code would trump any nostalgia or loyalty they might have felt toward me, and they would have reported the five of us to the school administration and the civilian police, at the very least.

So did I feel guilty for not giving Travis a great big greeting? Nope. Should I have felt guilty? Whatever. It doesn't matter much now.

We were heading to meet up with Javier and Boots at the usual place near the caf where we would slip out the doors to escape for lunch.

"They're not here yet," I said.

"They're probably back there by the other door," she said. When I turned around, I bumped into someone. I practically bounced off him, he was so big.

Rick Randall. "Watch where you're walking, little man," he said. He was with his usual thick-necked pals. "Hey," he said, "I remember you. How you doing? Everything better?"

I nodded. His concern was not exactly overwhelming.

"Cool," he said. As he walked off, I heard him laugh. "That was the kid I busted up in PT class when we were playing flashbang that time."

"Yeah, he got hurt pretty bad, right?" one of the guys said.

"Hey, at least I didn't leave him crippled for real. Dude, he's lucky he just got a little rattled. That's what happens when a lightweight goes up against the big man."

A little rattled. It was a broken neck. Guys like Rick Randall, born with powers and strengths, feeling like they were the rightful rulers of the world—they always got to me.

And the way Randall had laughed about how I was *lucky* he hadn't hurt me worse in that flashbang game? It made me send some evil thoughts his way. I seriously wanted to take him down a peg or two.

I watched him and his boys head toward the caf, and then he suddenly stopped walking. "I'll catch up with you guys. Gotta make a pit stop." He turned and jogged the other way through the crowded hallway, not seeming to care if he bumped into people.

I shook my head and turned back to my friends.

"That's the dick who practically killed you, right?" Layla asked.

"Yeah, well. Don't worry," I said. "He'll get his."

We went to a deli nearby and ordered sandwiches. We ate in the car, parked a few blocks from school.

"I think I might lose my sanity," Javier said. "The waiting is horrible."

"Waiting for what?" Peanut asked.

"To hear from Mutagion. We did what was asked. We showed him that we are committed."

I shook my head. "Javier, I wouldn't hold my breath."

"Why do you say that?"

"Because I don't think that you should expect Mutagion to contact us. Even with what we did, he's . . . he's Mutagion. He's got better things to do than deal with a bunch of kids."

"We are a bunch of kids who destroyed a Justice Force surveillance lab. That is something."

Nobody said anything more about it. I thought that even if we all wanted to graduate to the big leagues and maybe hear from Mutagion, it really wasn't very likely to happen.

When we pulled into the school parking lot, there were two ambulances parked by the front entrance and a crowd of students gathered around. We headed over.

"What's going on?" Boots asked a kid.

"Totally crazy. From what I heard—and I'm an Audiate, so I hear pretty good—one of the PT teachers who was in the gym supervising flying drills ran up to the locker room to investigate these, like, unbelievably loud bangs. I heard them, too, even from here. I mean, how could I not?"

"So what was it?" Peanut asked.

"A teacher went up to the locker room and found this kid lying on the floor. He had four flashbangs, two in each hand, that he detonated right next to his head. You believe that? They're saying he won't be able to fly right for at least a year."

"I didn't think that he had flying powers," I said.

"Who?" Javier asked.

"Rick Randall," I said.

"How did you know that's who it was?" the excitable Audiate asked me.

"Lucky guess."

The front part of the crowd parted as four paramedics wheeled the oversize gurney, which was loaded up with a writhing and moaning and head-clutching Rick Randall, to the back of the ambulance, where they wrestled it inside.

The Audiate couldn't seem to stop talking. "Well, I heard he was starting to get flying powers, but that could just have been a rumor. I hear all kinds of things. Obviously. Anyways, even if he did get flight, four flashbangs at once? Who could fly after that?"

"Why'd he do it?" Boots asked him.

"Who knows?"

Well, I knew. Of course.

And Layla knew. I didn't have to read her thoughts. I could tell from the sly smile she gave me. "Very bad," she said.

"Yeah, well. What goes around comes around. Sounds to me like he went out with a bang *and* a whimper."

At eleven forty-eight that night, I got a text from Mary Sunshine. This was our code name for messages sent through the scrambler Boots used to keep our electronic communications hidden. It showed up on my screen in coded symbols. I ran the decoding program Boots had loaded up, and it turns out she was forwarding a message to us from Javier:

Our new pal made contact with us. Impressed with our winning shot. Willing to meet us. Tomorrow nite. Big score!

CHAPTER 33

Some Assembly Required

was tired in school the next day. I had been up most of the night. It's pretty hard to sleep when you're expecting to meet one of the biggest public enemies at large in less than twenty-four hours. Part of the excitement was knowing that Blake, the world-renowned Artillery, was sleeping like a baby down the hall from me, and he didn't have a clue.

So I was on the verge of dozing during the discussion of the bubonic plague in humanities class when there was an announcement over the PA system: "Teachers and students in the A-program eleventh and twelfth grades, we have a surprise visitor today who has taken time out of a very busy and highly important schedule to speak with you. A-program teachers, escort your classes to the small gym at this time."

From time to time, celebrity heroes who happened to be in the area and wanted some youthful admiration[51] for an ego pump dropped in to pontificate to students. As we walked down the hallway toward the small gym, there was

---

[51] Or adoration.

a buzz among all the A-holes. Usually these suck-up sessions happened in the Academy.

We made our way to the auxiliary gym and settled in on the wooden bleachers. It wasn't more than a couple of minutes before the Colonel came in with our special guest.

Layla put her hand on my knee as Blake waved to all of us, giving us his famous two-thousand-megawatt smile, as if the polite (but far from excited) applause was deafening. He called out "Hey!" and "No, thank *you*!" a few times and pointed at random people in the small crowd.

It made me want to puke.

Take it easy, Layla thought to me.

The Colonel glared at all of us and rolled his hands in a way to signal he wanted more gusto in the applause. The A-holes, of course, overdid it, clapping and cheering like we were thrilled to the point of delirium at being in the presence of such a luminary as Artillery, fan favorite of the Justice Force. Blake had such a big ego that it would never occur to him that he was being mocked. He soaked up what he thought was adoration.

After a couple of minutes, the Colonel and Blake began making "settle down" gestures as if they were trying to quiet down a stadium of British soccer fans.

"Thank you, thank you," Blake called. "Really, guys, thank you." He was wearing his casual uniform, looking more military than hero, except for the gold and red highlights.

When the applause died down, Blake bellowed, "I figure you guys can hear me, right? I don't need a microphone?"

The whole crew shouted[52] they could hear him just fine.

He's something, all right, Layla thought.

Just kill me now, I thought back.

"So I know all of you must be wondering what I'm doing here, talking to you guys instead of the kids in the Academy, which is where people like me usually go for visits."

I wondered if he appreciated the meaning of what he was saying.

"Well, I'll tell you," he said. "It's true, I'm a busy guy and usually if I have any time to give to young people,[53] I tend to spend it with the people who can get the most from it. And the truth is, those people are usually powered in all the best ways. So why, you're wondering, am I here today talking to you instead of doing Justice Force business?[54] Well, I'll tell you. I have a duty to serve the impoverished."[55]

I looked over at Layla. She was shaking her head. *He's a real charmer.*

Isn't he? If you're really nice to me, I can get you his autograph.

Really? Really and truly? Be still, my heart.

---

[52] Many with an overabundance of enthusiasm, which someone smart (that is, not Blake) would read as insincere and sarcastic.

[53] "Young people." Blake isn't even ten years older than me or my classmates.

[54] I predicted—correctly—that the answer was *not* going to be, "I'm not doing Justice Force business, because I have a few serious injuries that I'm not telling anyone about, and so this unexplained leave of absence I seem to be on is causing the rest of the Justice Force and all my corporate and government-agency sponsors to get frustrated with the fact that I'm not doing what I'm supposed to be doing."

[55] Not sure where he came across this word, but he clearly didn't look it up in the dictionary to find out the actual definition.

Blake took a big, deep breath that made his chest seem especially wide. "And that's why I'm talking to you today. Just because you don't have powers like others in your family doesn't mean that you're any less of a human being. It doesn't mean you need to live a worthless life. There are lots and lots of productive things you can do. I could stand here and rattle off a list of the literally hundreds of jobs and vocations and careers you could have, but that would really be a waste of my time. And yours. That's what you have guidance counselors for, anyway."

He paused a second for laughter that never came. "No, but seriously, there really are lots of things you can still do with your lives. Any career that's available to a Regular is available to you, probably. It's just that you have to accept who you are and maybe lower your expirations[56] a little. But not all the way. It's not that you have to sink to the bottom, no matter what anybody says. Find a decent middle level for yourself. If you don't, you're basically cutting off your nose despite your face."[57]

Blake's rallying pep talk went on for an incoherent twenty more minutes or so. It felt like half an eternity to me. I could have used my telepathy to find out if all the other kids thought he was as big a tool as I did, but I didn't really want to know. There was nothing he could possibly do or

---

[56] Did he mean to say *aspirations*? *Expectations*? I guess he decided just to split it down the middle.

[57] I'm not making this up: that's what he said, verbatim. He constantly . . . oh, what's the use. Forget it.

say that would have embarrassed me more than what he had already done. And every person in that gym knew that he was my brother. *Gah.*

"Well, I guess I should let you kids get back to your classes. I can stick around a little bit if any of you have questions for me or, you know, want autographs."

I waited until all the A-holes stomped off the bleachers and left the gym, laughing, no doubt at my brother. I couldn't blame them.

Blake was standing next to the principal, talking and trying to look like he wasn't disappointed that no one had stayed back to ask him questions.

Except for me.

"Colonel, is it okay if I talk to my brother for a couple of minutes before I go back to class?" I asked.

"Well, of course, sure you can." He smiled at Blake. "If you'd like to address the other students, the Academy students, come by my office and I'll set it right up."

"What was that all about?" I asked him once the metal gym door shut behind the Colonel.

"It was a pep talk."

"A what? Wow. I'd hate to see you when you're trying to be discouraging."

"Why would I be discouraging?"

"Why did you really come here? You don't give a damn about self-actualization in the alternative program."

"About . . . I don't even know what that . . . whatever."

"Why are you here?"

He lowered his eyes to meet my gaze. He had that steely look, the one that inspired so much confidence among Americans and citizens of our allied countries. "I'm here because I wanted to see what kind of people you've been fraternalizing with. I knew about the Keating girl, but I wanted to see for myself what the rest of your . . . peers look like. Very, very impressive."

I wasn't about to get into it with him right there in my school gym, so I turned to leave. He laid his big hand on my shoulder and stopped me. I wanted to shake him off, but it would have been frustrating and humiliating if I tried. That hand on my shoulder had the strength to crush solid rock into coarse sand.

"Let go," I said.

"I'll let go when I want. You're gonna listen to what I have to say."

"Let go of my shoulder, Blake."

"Just like I thought, the kids in the A-program are losers. They're going nowhere. And you're *not* going to be one of them. Not if I can help it."

"Blake?"

"You hear me? I'm going to talk to the Colonel—he thinks I'm the greatest thing going. I'm going to get him to put you back into the Academy. And you're going to do it, real powers or not."

I turned my head to look him in the eyes.

"Blake, get off me."

"You are not—I repeat, *not*—going to become one of those losers. You are not gonna bring dishonor on our family. You will *not*—"

Let go!

His hand came off my shoulder like he had touched a hot stove.[58] He blinked twice, totally confused.

Damn it. The last thing I wanted was for Blake to know I had telepathy. He stared at me. I was going to have to read him to find out how much he knew.

Whuh? Whuh?

His thoughts were totally disordered. He didn't get it, didn't understand that I'd gone into his mind. That had been close. I was going to have to remember to keep my emotions in check if I wanted to keep my power a secret.

I walked away from him, shoved open the gym doors harder than I had to, making them slam open, the sound reverberating through the gym.

It was all bravado, I know, but it felt necessary.

I wanted to make a point to Blake as I left.

There was no way to know what effect it really had. I didn't read him, and I didn't look back.

---

[58] Well, actually like a Regular would do after touching a hot stove. Heat didn't bother Blake much.

Student-Teacher Conference

Wittman and Tricia asked the bunch of us to stay after school for just a few minutes.

We were sitting in chairs and on desks, all of us trying to be casual.

"Thanks for sticking around," Wittman said. "We appreciate it."

"No problem. What's up?" Layla asked. She was good in tense situations, and I was glad that she was speaking up.

"Well," Tricia said, taking a deep breath, "we've been a bit concerned about you."

"Us?" Javier said. "Which of us?"

"All of you. This little crew," Wittman said. "We're going to be straight with you, all right?"

We made various sounds of assent.

"We talk freely in class and we want you to think expansively." Tricia cleared her throat.

"That's why we like your classes so much," I said.

"Good to hear," Wittman answered. "But here's the thing. We want to be clear on something: we're not suggesting you take any, well, irresponsible action."

"What do you mean?" Javier asked.

Tricia and Wittman looked at each other, apparently trying to decide who would speak next. Tricia did. "Well, it's like this. We really don't want y'all to be doing anything that would get you in trouble."

"Like what?" Boots asked.

I knew what, of course. They had suspicions. But nothing concrete.

"We don't know, exactly," Wittman said. "But we do get the idea that you have been . . . well, *plotting* might seem overdramatic. But let's just say, up to something."

We all looked at one another. I could read panic in Javier's mind. Peanut and even Boots weren't too much calmer.

"Yes, that's it," I said. "We're actually planning to overthrow every hero team we can find. Total destruction."

Wittman and Tricia laughed, but there was an uneasiness to their tone. "We don't mean to make this sound ridiculous, but we're worried."

"We're fine," Layla said.

"We talk a good game," I said, "but seriously. We couldn't find real trouble even if we wanted to." I laughed.

CHAPTER 35

Bluffs

W e're being watched," I said. Not that I could see anything. It was almost pitch-black where we were, by the abutment under the bridge. The bridge itself loomed huge above us, stretching out into the thick fog that rose off the river. The lights on the suspension cables several hundred feet above glowed like fireflies. They didn't drop any light, though, down to where we were. Which was both unnerving and a relief.

"How would you know we're being watched? I can't see a damned thing," Peanut said.

"I can feel it." I could sense thought patterns from a few different places. Not one was closer that twenty yards, but there were a few in front, a couple above and behind us on the rocky bluffs, and a few more up high, somewhere between us and the bottom deck of the bridge.

"Can you tell how many?" Layla asked.

"Not sure. Could be ten. Maybe more, fifteen or twenty."

"Sounds about right." It was a deep, gravelly voice, coming from the darkness to my left, about ten yards away, closer than I'd guessed.

Every one of us jumped. Javier bumped into me as he

whipped around to aim the proto-gun he'd built into the darkness. The rest of us just dropped into low crouches. Like that would do anything to help us if we were attacked.

"Yes, we are here for a meeting?" Javier said, making it sound more like a question than a statement. "A certain individual whose name begins with the letter *M*?"

"Mutagion ain't here," Gravel-Voice said. "You think he's stupid? You think he would walk into a trap?"

Layla cleared her throat. "No, we don't think he's stupid. And this isn't a trap. We came to see him. But we don't know who *you* are."

"Don't worry about who I am. What I gotta know is, who are you?"

I wasn't sure if I was seeing it right, but it looked like there were two narrow red eyes watching us. Occasionally they disappeared for a fraction of a second, which I took to be this guy blinking.

Javier somehow got up some nerve and said, "Look. We made an arrangement to meet Mutagion here. It was his choice of location. We are the Hellions, which is exactly who I told him we are. Now, if he is not coming, just tell us now and we will leave."

No response. Just more blinking of those red eyes, if that's what they were.

I could barely make out Gravel-Voice raising a hand to his mouth as he talked, apparently into a phone or transmitter. "I don't know, there's about ten of them . . . I'm guessing . . . Okay, hold on. . . ." I could just barely hear the guy counting us, very slowly, stuck after four, then louder, "Five! Five. That's what I was gonna say. There's five of them."

Of course, this was the first time any of us had been close to a Phaeton. Hell, it wasn't common for anyone at all to be this close to one of them and not be fighting or running or flying away. The fact that he had trouble counting wasn't surprising. Many of the Phaetons suffered from serious cognitive deterioration because of their black-market self-enhancements.

"Yeah, those are uniforms or costumes or something," Gravel-Voice said. "I know. They look like a pack of silly gooses. . . . Oh, right. Silly geeses."

Maybe this Phaeton didn't have too firm a grasp of arithmetic or grammar, but his sense of fashion was right on the money: we *did* look like a bunch of silly geeses.

"Okay," Gravel-Voice said. "I get it. I'll take care of it, just like you say." There was a beep as he disconnected whatever device he'd been talking into. "Yeah, so, it's like this," he said to us. Based on where his voice was coming from, I figured the guy to be close to seven feet tall. "Mutagion is gonna meet with you, but it's gotta be a certain way. Just so you get that you're outmanned, I should tell ya that we got fourteen Phaetons around here, all of them with weapons—hardware and bioware—aimed at the bunch of youse. One word from me or the boss and you guys is dust."

"How do we know that's true?" Javier said, making me immediately wish I had been reading him so I could have stopped him from essentially daring these Phaetons to kill us.

"That mean you're volunteering to become a demonstration?" came a slurred voice from the bluffs directly above us.

"Uh, no. I was only asking," Javier said.

That idiot is going to get us killed, I thought to Layla.

He's trying to establish a confident stance, she thought back.

Well, he's succeeding at establishing a moronic stance. Can you get him to act a little smarter?

He's not that good an actor.

"Everybody, stay exactly still," Gravel-Voice said, and almost immediately, a police patrol helicopter *thwack-thwack-thwack*ed overhead. Its searchlight beams swept the cliffs, but we were deep in the shadow of the bridge.

While the area near us was lit up for a second or so, I tried to get a look at Gravel-Voice, but I was too late. All I saw was a silhouette, and it—he—was big and tall.

I forced myself to calm down and concentrate. I tried to read him. All I got, though, were garbled words, out of order, almost like a recording of speech played backward.

His voice dropped several tones when he spoke. There was no mistaking it was directed straight toward me. "You try your telepathy on me again, little man, and it'll be the last thing you do."

I nodded, stupidly, given that it was dark.

"That's better," he said. He could see me nodding. Night vision? "I don't got psi powers, but I can feel when someone's tryin' to read me. I'm, whatdoyacall, sensitive to being read. Mutagion, too, so don't even think about it. We better get moving. He don't wanna wait all night."

The fact that he could feel me trying to read him kind of shook me up. I would have to be very careful.

Gravel-Voice directed us to go to the narrow service track we had walked down to get to the spot.[59] "There's a little concrete path. Follow it."

"You think we could get a light or something?" Peanut asked.

"No."

So we went single file, each one of us hanging on to some part of the outfit of the person directly in front. Javier led the way.

"We have some concrete here," he said, his voice hushed. Layla and Boots were between me and Javier, so it took a few steps before I felt the loam switch over to concrete under my feet. "Stone wall on the right," he said. "Use it to guide and keep balance." I couldn't say which bothered me more: that he was a pretty good leader or that Layla was hanging on to a leather strap on his jacket.

Don't be such a child, she thought to me. *Are you seriously going to get jealous in the middle of all this?*

What exactly are we in the middle of? Remind me.

I don't know anymore.

Maybe we're in the middle of our last hour alive?

I heard a stumble and Layla's hissed curse a few yards

---

[59] It was basically a steel gangplank, doing switchbacks down the cliffside. When we first set foot on it, the guide lights all went out, like someone had deliberately switched them off. We were able to make our way down by holding on to the railing.

in front of me. The whole line of us lurched and almost fell forward like dominos.

Sorry, I sent her way. *Maybe I should just keep my thoughts to myself for a while.*

Good idea.

I didn't know exactly where we were headed, but one thing was clear from what I could hear: we were walking to the edge of a wharf overlooking the river.

It was the perfect site for a mass execution.

CHAPTER 36

Stepping Off

Sometimes, when you're involved in something out of your ordinary routine, like a long night in the hospital emergency room or a vacation gone wrong, reality becomes distorted. It feels like you're in a weird semi-dream state.

Lined up at the edge of the pier, gazing across nearly a mile of black water to the lights on the other side of the river, while a Phaeton death squad was undoubtedly taking position to shoot us, sending our probably headless bodies toppling over and splashing into the garbage and oil slicks floating on the water—well, that wasn't exactly what I would call a sweet dream.

There was a dull snapping sound in front of us coming from out over the water. I couldn't quite figure out what the sound was.

Any idea what's going on? I thought to Layla.

Not a clue.

A nasal voice came from the same area as the snapping: "You coming in or what?"

"In where?" Peanut asked.

"Go to the edge of the pier," the nasal voice said. "Near me. Bend down and you'll feel the top of a ladder going over the side of the pier. Go down three steps and step forward."

"Like hell," Javier said.

"This was your idea," Layla said.

"My idea was to meet with Mutagion, not to drown myself."

"You ain't gonna drown, stupid," the nasal voice said.

"Well, I don't have aqua-respiration," Javier said. "And I don't have levitation. I'm not stepping out into water only to sink to the bottom of the river."

I didn't mean to read Layla, but her thoughts were so strong I couldn't help but hear her. *Javier, you got us into this, you jerk-off. Now you're backing out? What a little bitch.*

"Fine, move out of the way. I'll go." Yeah, that was me, and I was as surprised as everyone else to hear the words come out of my mouth. I pushed between Layla and Javier, bent down, and felt for the ladder. I found it: cold metal, hooked onto the wooden pier. I stepped down three rungs and felt the water lap against my boot.

"You gotta step off, there, tough guy. We're a few feet from the pier. Just one big step toward my voice."

It hadn't occurred to me to find out what my suit would be like if it got wet. My guess was that the KevFlex and all the rest would become really heavy. I wondered how long it would take to drown.

I knew that Layla and the rest of them were waiting for me to act, so one more second of hesitation was going to make me look even worse than Javier.

I stepped out.

My boot splashed in the water. And landed on something solid, maybe a few inches below the surface. I stepped with my other foot. I couldn't tell if it was emotion or reality, but whatever I was standing on felt like it was swaying and bobbing, just slightly.

"Here ya go," said the voice, to my left and down by my feet. "Right over here."

I took two steps, crouched down and felt around. My hand touched a metal lip. Some river water sloshed against it. I leaned over and felt a cold updraft.

I was leaning over a hatch. I was standing on some kind of submarine.

Five minutes later, we were crowded into a small nautical cabin. It was just Layla, Javier, Boots, and me. Peanut was too nervous to squeeze through the hatch, so he waited out on the wharf, under the watchful eyes of several Phaetons.

The cabin was exactly wide enough for the four of us to squish into and sit on a steel bench, shoulder to shoulder. There was a single red light on the low ceiling, which made it look like we were in some kind of hell. There were exposed pipes, cables, conduits, and flexible ducts running along the ceiling and all the walls. It smelled of diesel, sweat, and some other sharp organic scent—something pungent, like musk. I didn't hear a thrum of engines or anything else mechanical.

You think this thing is mobile? I thought to Layla.

Why? You looking to go on a cruise?

No, I was just thinking that we might be getting kidnapped.

You're really making me feel so much better.

Then again, we don't have to be kidnapped. They could just kill us in here and dump our bodies in the river.

You're a ray of sunshine, aren't you?

"What do you want?" The voice was deep and resonant, like a pipe organ. When he spoke, I felt a vibration in my sternum. And it just about made my heart stop.

I don't think any of us realized that there was someone sitting in front of us. He was on some kind of a chair, wedged into a narrow end of the cabin. It was too dark to tell for sure if any of the hoses and cables that looped all around his chair were actually connected *to* him, but it looked like some were.

And I realized I was sitting in front of someone very few people in the world had seen. There was a lot of conjecture, but nobody who ever got close enough to get a look at Mutagion had survived.

He seemed big, but he was sitting. There was a partial helmet or mask covering the left side of his head and face. The right side of his face was shiny and distorted. It looked a little like half-melted wax. There was a vision enhancer strapped over his right eye, glowing blue.

"I took a chance, letting you come in here. Make it worth my while or I just might flood this cabin with cyanogen chloride gas." His voice was filtered through a vocal simulator, giving it an odd rhythm when it emphasized the wrong parts of words. "We'll stuff your corpses in the torpedo tubes for safekeeping. How does that sound?"

That didn't sound too good to me. I would have thought

about how much I hated Javier for getting us into such a bad situation, but I guessed it was a better use of my time to figure out how we could get out of it. And other than not making Mutagion mad, I wasn't coming up with any ideas.

"Well, the point is," Javier started, "we believe the so-called heroes are nothing but a bunch of tools and henchmen, working for fascist governments to suffocate the—"

"If you came here thinking you were going to impress me by reciting some political lecture you got from a book, you made a big, big mistake. When you first made contact, you said you wanted to do business with me. What do you think you have that I need?"

"We did pull off that incident with the building. You know that was a Justice Force surveillance lab?"

"Of course, I knew that. Big deal. They got more. That showed me you can get stuff done, but it doesn't mean I want to get in business with you." Mutagion leaned forward. Now I could see how big he was. His head was almost twice the size of a normal man's, with a large lower jaw and heavy, almost apelike brow.[60] He put his enormous hands on his knees. His fingers were huge and flattened at the ends. "Let me make this perfectly clear," Mutagion said, a gurgling undertone in his electronically modulated voice. "You have twenty seconds

---

[60] I'd suspected it was acromegaly, and I was right. His gigantism was more like the human hormonal imbalance that causes crippling pain and death, rather than a mutation that results in a tall and muscular physique. This was a prime example of what happened when you tried a do-it-yourself mutation: you ended up as a Phaeton.

to convince me that you're more use to me alive than dead."

"We thought we could work with you. Since we have a common enemy—"

"I don't need more partners and I don't need friends. You got ten seconds left."

There was one thing I could think of that I had that he might want, but there was no way I could make that offer. Not and still be able to live with myself.

"Here's what we have," Layla said. "We go to school in the same building as the Academy. The Monroe Academy?"

"Yes, well, I'm not looking to finish my high school education, so—"

"We have access to all the information on the hero families of every student."

It was all I could do not to snap my head around to look at her. *Are you crazy?*

Hush.

You can't—

I know what I'm doing. Just follow my lead.

Mutagion cocked his huge head, and that big jaw moved as he ground his teeth, thinking. Not all Phaetons had limited intellectual ability, like Gravel-Voice. No, Mutagion didn't become one of the most dangerous and doggedly hunted criminals in the world by being stupid.

"What do you mean by 'access'?" he asked.

Good question. I was wondering that myself.

"We can get access to all their information," Javier said.

"How?"

Layla jerked a thumb at Boots. "She's a genius with computers. Me, I'm a genius with biomech merge. And him," she said, tilting her head toward me, "he's just a straight-up genius."

Mutagion began to cough, a horrible sound like a piece of wood getting snarled up in a table saw, from deep in his chest. He turned away from us and put his face over some kind of bowl while he coughed some more. The steel walls of the cabin didn't exactly soften the sound.

When he turned back toward us, the exposed part of his face seemed to have darkened. "Yes, so. That's terribly interesting. If I wanted to invite them to a party or send them e-mail, that information might be quite useful. But other than that, I'm not so sure what you have that I need."

"Well, if you think about it," I said, again surprising myself, "there's a whole lot. There are more than a hundred kids in the Academy. Taking siblings into account, conservatively, we can say that there are around seventy-five families directly connected to the school. Then you have all the alumni. My colleague here just proposed sharing intel about some of the most famous and most important heroes in the whole country. Are you telling us that getting access to their private information—secret identities included—isn't something that has a lot of value to you?" I still don't quite know where this all came from. As much as I couldn't stand so many of the Academy kids, I wasn't actually planning to sell them and their families out to Mutagion. But this salesmanship seemed to flow out of me without the slightest bit of effort. "If you don't want that information, we can definitely find other people who do."

He moved in his chair, and I winced when I heard sounds like thick sticks snapping from inside his body.

"Relax," he said. "I never said I wasn't interested. I said I needed to know more about what you had. So let's say I do want this information. What do you want from me?"

I didn't know exactly what the answer was, but it didn't matter.

"Endorsement," Javier said.

"Public recognition," Boots said.

"An alliance," Layla said.

Me, I just wanted to get out of there alive. I didn't say anything at all.

CHAPTER 37

Big League

Javier was so delirious with excitement while he was driving us back that I worried he might crash his car. We had already changed out of our costumes and stashed them in hidden compartments he had built into the car doors. Javier hadn't stopped talking about our meeting. Finally he wound down and smiled while he shook his head to himself a bunch of times, lost in thought.

Boots was also excited. "Boy, was that, like, right out of a movie or what? It was just like *U-Boat Patrol*, only cooler."

"So is he, like, handicapped or something?" Peanut asked.

"No, no. He's just too big to stand up in that low-ceiling cabin," Javier said. "Believe me, he is not crippled."

"He *might* be," Layla said. "And that coughing? What was that about?"

Javier nodded. "*Ja*, that was from when the Victory Squad trapped him in that São Paulo apartment building and burned it down. He got permanent lung damage before he escaped."

Suddenly Javier was an expert on Mutagion.

"I think he was going for some amphibian type of mutation," I said. "That could explain the breathing problems."

"He looked kind of decrepit," Layla said. "I wonder if maybe that's why he's talking to us at all. Like, maybe he's breaking down and needs some dumb kids to do his dirty work for him?"

"No," Javier insisted. "He is talking to us because he is awesome, and because he realizes *we* are going to be awesome, so he wants to encourage young talent."

"What's so awesome about us?" I asked.

"What a nice attitude," Javier said. "That kind of confidence is exactly what we need on this team."

Boots spoke up. "I think Brad is right. What makes us so special? Why are we so much better than all the established villains already out there? Lots of people want to work with Mutagion. Why would he pick us?"

"What the hell is wrong with all of you? We just got into business with one of the top villains in the entire world, and all you can do is criticize? Why can't you be happy that we're going to make it in the big leagues of villainy? What a bunch of whiners. Let *me*, at least, savor this sweet moment."

He's a little over the top, don't you think? I thought to Layla.

Yeah, he gets like that.

For the record, I have no intention whatsoever of sharing all that info with Mutagion. Too many people who did nothing wrong will end up being collateral damage.

Yeah, there are tons of great kids in the Academy. They're cogs in the giant hero wheel.

I thought to her, *They're kids of heroes. The little ones in the lower school, they didn't do anything wrong. I'm not giving Mutagion the records. No way.*

Then why'd you go along with the offer?

Because if I didn't, it seemed like there was a good chance we would have ended up at the bottom of the river. There's something about this arrangement that seems off. Are you getting that, too?

What, you mean aside from you making a deal that you're not going to follow through on? she thought to me.

Yeah, aside from that.

Not sure.

I don't know why we even got involved with Mutagion, I thought to her.

Javier wanted to.

So whatever Javier wants, Javier gets?

Easy now. Down, boy.

This whole night was pretty scary. I'm wondering if we got in over our heads.

A little late to be thinking about that.

No kidding. But we're dealing with a really dangerous guy. I think we're playing with fire.

Then we'd better play carefully so we don't get burned.

Mutagion and his ilk are sick in their souls. That's why these Phaetons tried to change themselves physically: they weren't satisfied with what they were. They wanted to be more, to be like us. They tried to take on nature itself, but they failed. They failed because their basic evil cannot be changed, by themselves or anyone else. The only choice is to extinguish them."

FLATLINER,
Co-leader of the Justice Force

We are not interested in perpetrating crimes, per se. We are devoted to bringing down the fascist institutions that support individuals who call themselves heroes. We will do whatever is necessary to achieve this aim. If that requires tearing the whole system down and starting anew, so be it."

THE HELLIONS
Public message

Fight on, Phaetons!"

GRAFFITI SEEN IN MANY U.S. AND BRITISH CITIES;
Slogan of "Operation: Reset"
computer virus

CHAPTER 38

Forget It

I had a hard time paying much attention in English class. Wittman was talking about *Finnegans Wake*, which was pretty boring and incomprehensible even if you were inclined to study it. (And I was not.) I was more focused on replaying our visit with Mutagion. It seemed almost like a dream: I couldn't quite believe that we had met him, infamous as he was. And we'd survived it.

One big problem, though. I had made a promise to get information about the Academy students and their families. Without question, Boots could easily hack into the school's database, but no way was I in favor of that. Even though Layla had brought it up, I was the one who had made that bad promise. I felt it was up to me to find something else we could offer Mutagion that he would want more than names and addresses of the hero families with kids enrolled at school.

"Okay, guys," Wittman said. "The period's about over. I can tell from the conversation that you haven't been keeping up with the reading. So I think it's time we pick up the pace a little. And since we're about to go on break, instead of reading up to page 240, I want you to finish up the book before we come back. That means all 665 fun-filled, action-packed pages, friends. And read it carefully. We'll have an in-class essay as soon—"

He stopped talking suddenly, and his face went a bit blank. That was due, no doubt, to my stealth mind incursion and clandestine command projection.[61]

He blinked, then smiled. "You know what? I changed my mind. Any objections if we just call it quits on this book?"

A chorus of shouts of "No!" and "Dump it!" and "*Thank you!*"

"Yeah, to tell you the truth," Wittman said, "I never liked it much anyway. No homework. Have yourselves a good break."

That was almost too easy. Then it occurred to me: maybe that's what I could offer Mutagion. I was becoming a pretty good telepath. Maybe he would want to use my skills. There were just a few more that I wanted to hone.

That night at the lair, I wanted to try something. Layla, Boots, and I were politely listening to Javier go on about how *magnifique* it was that he'd gotten us into business with Mutagion and how lucky we were to have him leading the

---

[61] The difference between regular telepathy and CCP is that in telepathy, writing is easy: the person basically hears the inserted thought in the voice of the sender. In CCP, the aim is to have the receiver think the thought is his *own*. To do that, you have to find the person's individual psi form and project the thought using that pattern. So in this case, I didn't want Wittman to think *I* was telling him what to think; I wanted him to think the idea was entirely his own.

team. I wasn't paying too much attention; I wanted to get my little experiment started.

Peanut was on the floor, his back up against the couch and his massive legs straight out in front of him, crossed at the ankles. He was studying the video game he was playing with the same concentration you'd expect to see in someone performing microsurgery. I walked over and sat on the couch, looking at the back of his big head.

"Hey, Brad," he said, his attention still riveted on the monitor. "What's going on?"

"Nothing much. How are things with you? How's your little brother doing?"

"Pretty good. He's going to another school now."

"Yeah, you mentioned that he might. How's that?"

"A whole lot better for him. I'm glad he got in."

"That's great." I wrote a feeling of physical warmth to him. After a minute, he took one hand off the game controller and used his shirt to wipe his forehead. "Damn! Is it hot in here or what?" he asked loudly.

Nobody responded. Layla and Boots were still listening (or pretending to listen) to Javier's self-aggrandizing bombast about his great feat of making the initial contact with Mutagion. "Feels fine to me," I said to Peanut. "Maybe even a little chilly."

"Really? I feel kind of hot." He shrugged.

I'm thirsty, I thought to him. I had been working hard on this skill, clandestine command projection. It had worked easily on Wittman earlier, so I figured it would take practically no effort to make it work on Peanut.

"I'm thirsty," he said, and he got up to go to the little kitchen. Peanut was so easy.[62] I followed him.

"Want some?" he said. He held up a bottle of soda when I leaned against the doorframe.

"No, thanks. I'm good. Hey, I've always meant to ask you: what's the story with them calling you 'Peanut'?"

"Oh, yeah. It's pretty funny. Javier thought it up. It's because when I started on Myomeg, I had this crazy appetite and I wanted to keep my protein intake, like, real high, so I put peanut butter on everything I ate. Even steak! So Javier and the girls called me 'Peanut' because of that."

I nodded and smiled. "Well, actually, that's not the real reason. They call you that because of a condition called testicular atrophy. One of the negative side effects of taking Myomegamorpherone."

"Testi-whozit?"

"Testicular atrophy. It's when your nads shrink up from taking steroids. In other words, small nut leads to the name Peanut."

"Who told them my nuts shrank?"

"I don't know. Either they just guessed or maybe Javier knows somehow."

---

[62] As one would guess, people with more sophisticated thought processes have mind patterns that are harder to duplicate accurately. Not to be mean, but there's really no way that anyone could honestly use the word *sophisticated* in reference to any aspect of Peanut.

Peanut looked confused. "He told me it was because of the peanut butter I ate. Wait, so Boots and Layla don't know about this, do they?"

"Of course they do."

Peanut's cheeks turned red from embarrassment. Then they turned dark, along with the rest of his face. "Javier said it was because . . . and he told the girls this crap about me having . . . peanuts?" His jaw set and he started to move past me.

Stop. He did.

Now I'm hungry. "I'm hungry," Peanut said.

"So why don't you grab something to eat."

He nodded and opened the refrigerator. While he was looking inside, I went into his mind and found his memory of our conversation, right out on the surface. If thoughts had colors, that memory would have been dark red.

I wiped it clean, easy as blotting a drop of water with a bath towel.[63]

He stood up from looking in the refrigerator, blinked a few times, and said, "I forgot what I was looking for."

I shrugged. "Hey, I meant to ask you: why do they call you 'Peanut,' anyway?"

"What?"

"Why 'Peanut' of all things?"

He looked at me, then smiled. "Are you kidding me?"

---

[63] This is called thought-erasing or, more colloquially, mind-sweeping. Very, very useful. . . .

"What?"

"I thought you knew. It's a good story. See, when I started taking Myomeg, I was hungry all the time, and whenever I had something to eat, I always had peanut butter with it."

I listened to him repeat the story, as if our earlier conversation had never happened.

CHAPTER 39

Tell the Truth

ike I said: Peanut was easy. If I wanted my skills to be really useful, I had to be sure I could make them work on more challenging subjects.

"I'd like to try something," I said to Layla. It was just the two of us, parked in Javier's car with the engine running a few blocks from my house. "Something we haven't done before."

"Excuse me?" she said with an arched eyebrow.

"A telepathy skill."

"What is it?"

"Let me try it, and then I'll tell you."

She squinted at me sideways. "Hm. Sounds a little suspicious."

"Nothing to worry about. I promise." I reached over and turned off the ignition.

"Okay," she said really slowly. "I'll trust you." *Go ahead.*

It's about us.

Pause. *What about us?*

I was nervous. If this didn't work out the way I planned, the way I hoped, it could cause a lot of tension between us.

What's wrong? she thought to me.

Well, it's like this, Layla. I think I'm kind of falling in love with you.

The conscious part of her mind went blank for a few seconds, locking up, while various thoughts competed for dominance. Total mental confusion.

I sent a CCP—clandestine command projection—to her. *Let your guard down*, I made her think. *Tell him the truth.*

I thought you were. Falling for me, she thought.

How do you feel about it? About me?

I don't know.

Ugh. Not the answer I hoped to get. *You don't know? You don't know if you're in love with me? At all?*

Maybe. I think so. Oh, I don't know. I'm confused.

How? What are you confused about?

I mean, I think I have feelings for you. I just don't know if I'm totally in love with you.

Okay, forget totally. How about a little?

I don't know if it's a matter of degree. You're either in love or you're not.

So which is it, then?

Brad?

I needed to use all my will and concentration not to dwell on what she was thinking, that she didn't love me back. I had to renew the CCP to keep her telling me the truth.

How can you not know how you feel?

Because I'm not used to the feeling. You may not believe it, but I haven't really had too many relationships. Nothing serious, anyway. Is it love I feel? Maybe. I just don't know. Maybe it's not. I'm confused.

It should be simple. What do you feel?

I feel . . . like this is going to make things really awkward and weird between us now.

That won't happen.

How do you know?

Because. I just do.

The conversation was there in her mind, right in front of me. I wiped it clean and left no trace.

Layla's eyes looked a little fogged, dazed. I withdrew from her mind. She blinked fast three times. Her eyes were bright and alert. "So? Go ahead?"

"Go ahead what?" I asked.

"Do that telepathy thing you wanted to try."

"No, it's okay. Never mind."

"What was it?"

I shook my head. "I forget." I reached to the keys and turned the engine back on. I didn't want her to see my face.

CHAPTER 40

Like Minds

I may be evil, but I'm not a total bastard. I did feel guilty about getting Layla to tell me her feelings, erasing the conversation, and keeping the whole thing secret from her. That said, though, mind-sweeping it away would prevent any conscious awkwardness that would result from remembering everything that had passed between us.

Awake in bed, I admitted it to myself: I loved her. Being in each other's minds as much as we had been—well, that was an intimacy I'd never, ever had with anyone else. I was pretty sure it was the same for her. So why wasn't she in love with me?

She definitely liked my personality. A lot. I was sure of it. She thought I was funny. And we believed in the same stuff, as far as right and wrong, heroes and power, and all that. We liked spending time together.

What didn't I have? What was I lacking?

It was obvious. Of course. I didn't have cool powers. Sure, she liked my telepathy and thought I was a great guy. But apparently that wasn't enough. I knew what she wanted. I mean, what girl didn't want a guy who had shoulders three feet wide, who could crush a brick in his hand, who could fly?

I figured that if I had Blake's powers and my personality, she'd fall for me totally and without question.

Sure, I basically couldn't stand his personality, but why did Blake get all the great genes for looks and powers?

How the hell did that happen?

I believed there was an explanation, and I was confident that I could find it by comparing my DNA with Blake's. I had tried to get Mom to answer my questions, but the conversations always got derailed. They ended up with her feeling bad for me and me feeling frustrated.

I had Layla ask Boots if she could help. And now it was looking a lot like she couldn't.

"I'm sorry. I tried everything," Boots said. "I can't get in there." She sat back on her heels and stretched her neck. I was between her and Layla, the three of us gathered around Mom's computer.

We had been there for over two hours, since three o'clock. It wasn't often—or ever, actually—that I had seen Boots so frustrated by a computer.

"You said, 'There's not a computer system made by man or machine that I can't bust into,' and now you're telling me you can't get into this?" I said.

"I said that there wasn't a system I'd ever *heard* of that I couldn't crack. I've never come up against the kind of security that GenLab has." She waved her hands in a helpless gesture in front of the machine. "I've never seen anything like it."

"Is this the kind of thing you could research or something?" I asked.

"My guess is that whoever set this megafirewall up has a whole bunch of alarms that'll be triggered by any kind of search into its security."

"And you don't know how to avoid that," I said.

"I'm not gonna take a chance. If GenLab security catches us, it's a big, big deal. Sorry, but it's too dangerous."

"No, I understand. You tried. Thanks."

"Now it's gonna bother me. I'll keep thinking, but no promises." Boots pulled out the hijack cable that connected her computer to Mom's. She started packing up her equipment.

I looked over at Layla. *If anyone could do it, it would have been her,* Layla thought.

I know. I think we'll have to approach this another way.

I'm not approaching anything anymore until you tell me what you're trying to find.

I didn't respond.

Don't ignore. I know you read me.

"We should get out of here before we leave serious heat signatures for the thermo-cameras to record," I said.

"I'm blocking the therm-cams, but anyways, I'm done," Boots said. She snapped her computer case shut.

"What's going on here?"

I swear my heart skipped a beat when I heard Mom's voice. "Um . . ." I said.

"What are you doing?" she asked, her voice getting louder.

"Um . . ." I repeated. I had nothing. Nothing that would sound remotely believable. "You're home early," I said. Brilliant.

"Yes, I am, and this is not what I expected to find. You know that you and your friends are not allowed in my study when I'm not here." She looked over at the computer. It was still on. "What are you doing with my computer? Have you been trying to use my work—"

"Mom, you look really tired."

"What? Don't you worry about how tired I am. I want to know right now—"

You're really tired. You can't stay awake for another second.

I caught her under the arms before her knees touched the carpet. I can't say how I did it, but I had slowed her thoughts down and made her fall asleep. I set her down in a chair. Her head lolled to the side.

"I have an idea. . . ." I said.

CHAPTER 41

Tapping In

Y ou think you can do it?" I asked.

Boots shrugged. "Well, yeah. She'll do all the tough stuff. I just have to record everything she does. That's easy."

"And then you could duplicate it on your computer?"

"Any computer. If she does the heavy lifting, I can do the rest, no problem."

"Are you going to tell me exactly what this is about or what?" Layla said.

"Let's just get it done and then I'll explain."

Mom began to stir. I sat on the table next to the chair and started to examine her mind patterns while Boots connected her equipment to her computer.

"Are you set?" I asked Boots.

"Give me, like, one more minute," she said. She was hooking up all kinds of cables between the three little mano-computers she had brought with her and Mom's computer on the desk.

I'm pissed at you, Layla thought to me.

I know. I'm sorry. I promise I'll explain, but we have to work fast now. "How are we doing over there?" I asked Boots.

"I'm basically going to record every single keystroke, password, link—anything, really, that goes into and out of her computer. Now let me just finish . . . this . . . part . . . and . . . oh . . . kay. Yup. Whenever you're ready."

I managed to pull Mom halfway out of her sleep. She sounded groggy when she asked, "What's going on?" Still looking barely awake, she scanned the room with her half-closed eyes. "Who are these young ladies?" she slurred.

"They're friends, but never mind about them. I need you to do something for me. It's important."

"All right, what?"

"Log in to your GenLab account and pull up Blake's gene map and then my gene map."

"Honey," she said, looking lazily at the girls, "I can't just pull that information up. It's a security issue."

You have to pull up that information right away, I sent her way. *Do it now.*

She got up from the couch and went to her chair.

I stood a few feet behind her as she started logging in. I looked over to Boots, but she was concentrating on her screens. Layla looked up from the displays and nodded to me. *She's getting it,* she thought to me.

Mom leaned in close to the computer and opened her right eye wide for the retinal scan. Boots would now have a digital recording of Mom's retina, which she could use or manipulate, if necessary.

While Mom typed into her computer, Boots kept getting *Aha!* looks on her face, obviously when she saw how to get past the firewalls that had stopped her before.

I looked over Mom's shoulder as she navigated through screens. There was a word that kept appearing, many more times than I would have expected: Phaeton. It showed up in various phrases: *Phaeton Research*; *Phaeton DNA Examination*; *Phaeton Reversion*, and *Phaeton Disposition*, among others. Why would GenLab have so much interest in Phaetons? It was well known that GenLab was a contractor for the U.S. government. Maybe the DOD and BOMA[64] had the GenLab geneticists analyze information about how Phaeton mutations went wrong.

The thing that got to me, though, was that with all the information GenLab must have gathered, they couldn't even try to *help* the Phaetons instead of hunt them down? Maybe reverse the faulty mutations? Hell, no. The government and corporations weren't about to do anything to help anyone if it didn't yield any profit for the big boys.

But I knew it wasn't the best time to be thinking about social injustice. We were breaking into the GenLab database, and this might be our last chance to get the info that would allow us access on our own.

"So, now, what did you want to see?" Mom asked, her voice just a bit dreamy.

"DNA profiles with gene ID. Blake's and mine. How do you do a search?"

---

[64] Department of Defense and Bureau of Metahuman Affairs. They worked jointly and with various hero teams—Justice Force being one of them—in the effort to hunt down Phaetons.

"Just like this."

I watched carefully as she typed some more and navigated through a few screens before reaching Blake's DNA profile.

"You got all that?" I asked Boots. She nodded.

On the screen was a 3-D model of DNA that could be rotated, magnified, exploded.

"I need to know how to display the gene color codes," I said. She showed me the commands. Blake's DNA lit up with all his powered genes.

"Okay, now let's bring up mine."

And as if on cue, we all looked up when we heard the front door open and Blake bellow, "Hello? Anybody home?" followed by the sound of the door closing.

"We have to stop right now," I said. I turned to Boots and Layla. "You got it all? You know how to get in again?"

"I got it," Boots said.

"You sure?"

"I got it."

"Okay. Then gather up your gear, fast." I turned to Mom. *Log out and make sure not to leave a trail or set off any alarms in the system. When GenLab asks you tomorrow what you were looking up, you can tell them you're doing research for a journal article you're writing.*

Blake kept calling out to see if anyone was home. I swiveled Mom's chair away from the computer. I crouched so my eyes were level with hers. This was going to be the key part, and I had to make sure I didn't screw it up.

I looked in her mind and found the center of her thoughts about our little group research project. I tried to make that central memory disappear, but I could feel that there were still traces of it, maybe because Mom had a very complicated thought pattern. It was taking a while to scrub every last bit of the memory from her mind.

"Mom? Anyone? I know *some*body's home," Blake called.

"Go on out," I said to Layla and Boots. "I'll be right behind you."

"You sure?"

"Yeah. I just have to finish up here. Go on."

While they left the room, I did one more scrub of Mom's memory of the last hour or so. As far as I could tell, it was gone except for the faintest trace, which probably would feel to her less real or detailed than a dream.

I put her back to sleep again and then carried her over to the couch across the room. I laid her back, put one of the journals on her stomach, and slipped her thumb in it, so when she woke up, it would seem like she'd stopped reading just for a minute to close her eyes and ended up drifting off.

That was the best I could do.

CHAPTER 42

Critical

On my way out of the study, I stopped at the bathroom in the back hall. I flushed the toilet, ran water in the sink for a few seconds, then opened the door a little louder than necessary.

". . . know him from school? You're in the A-program, right?" Blake was saying when I got to the living room.

"Yeah, we have some of the same classes," Layla said.

"Oh, hey. Didn't know you were home," I said.

"Ah, here he is," Blake said. "I was just meeting your little friends. Now, you, Layla? You're not related to Kitty Keating, a.k.a. Felinity?"

"She's my sister."

"Ah. I've worked with Felinity a bunch of times. She's great. A super member of the Power Division. So, how does she feel about you being in the A-program instead of the Academy?"

Layla looked at me. *Wow*, she thought. *He doesn't even pretend to be subtle.* Turning back to Blake, she said, "I don't know how she feels. We don't talk much."

"Well, that's a shame. I'm guessing you're pretty much

in the same ship,"[65] he said to Boots. "I don't know. It doesn't really matter. See, you may be wondering why I think it's my business what your relationship with your families is. And you'd be right to wonder. It's really not my business. What *is* my business, though, is what goes on in my own family. And like it or not, Brad is in my family.[66] So I'll tell you, I'm not happy about him being in that program. And like I told him, I'm also not happy about him hanging around the likes of you. So if you don't mind, it would be super if you would leave now and, no offense or anything, but not come back again."

"Hold on," I said. "You can't just—"

Blake turned on me. There was none of that amiable friendliness the public was used to seeing in his sparkling eyes. "No, little brother, the best thing for you to do is to just let them go out. See, if they stay while I talk to you, you're gonna be real embarrassed, because—"

"No, it's okay. We're gonna go," Layla said.

"See you in school," Boots said.

He's just like you said he was. What a dick, Layla thought. *Go on to the car. I'll be right out.*

I waited for the door to close before I turned back to him. "What is your problem?"

---

[65] In the same *boat*, he meant. I had to wonder whether he realized what a moron he sounded like half the time.

[66] I still don't know if he meant whether *I* liked it or not or if *he* liked it or not. Works either way, I guess.

"*You're* my problem. One of them, anyway. And I got a whole bunch of them, so I sure don't need to worry about you, too."

"Good. Don't, then."

"I'm not going to let you bring dishonorability on this family—"

"That's *dishonor.*"

"Okay, fine. Dishonor. You think you're so smart, but let me tell you: intelligence isn't everything. If it were, people all over the world would worship *you* instead of *me.*"

"Hey, I don't need—or want—people all over the world to worship me."

"Yeah, sure. That's just you rationing[67] because you know you won't ever get it to happen. And anyways, that's not my point. I told you before and I'm telling you now and I'm not going to tell you again: I don't want you being with losers like them."

"As far as what you want goes, I really don't give a flying f—"

"Watch it there, chief. We don't use language like that in this house. You can talk that way with your trashy friends, but not here."

"Fine, then. I'll go and talk that way with my trashy friends." I walked toward the front door.

---

[67] He meant . . . oh, forget it. You know what he meant. I'm not going to bother explaining him anymore.

"Hey. Don't walk away from me," he said, keeping his voice just under the volume that would have made the glass in the windows tremble.

"You want me to stay so we can continue bonding?" I asked.

"I want you to stop running away from your responsibility."

I stopped at the door. "Stop running from my . . . ? Listen. You don't determine what is and isn't my responsibility."

"Well, *you* sure don't. And that's your problem. You always think about what you want, instead of what is *needed*."

"Well, please tell me, Blake, oh wise one. What is *needed*?"

"What's needed is people like me, little brother. I wouldn't expect you to understand, since you only think about yourself. But it's true. The world needs heroes."

"Yeah, well, who says I have to be one?"

He was about to speak, and then he stopped. He looked totally stunned, like someone had just suggested that the sky is really green, not blue. It didn't make one bit of sense to him. "What?"

"Not everyone wants to be you."

"Wait—*what*?" he said again. And he still had that dumbfounded look on his face when I left him there. I slammed the front door shut behind me.

CHAPTER 43

A Theory of Relativity

After we dropped off Boots, Layla drove up the street, pulled over, and touched the steering column to kill the ignition on Javier's car.[68] She turned to me.

"Okay, I've been real patient. Why were you so desperate to see your brother's DNA and your own?"

"I think it has some information that I want."

"Duh. Which is?"

"It's complicated."

Layla shook her head slightly and turned away to face the driver's side window. *I'm getting sick of playing Twenty Questions with you.*

"Okay, listen," I said. "Mainly, I want to get raw data on my genome and my brother's."

Layla turned to me, then faced forward and pursed her lips in a way that made me want to kiss her. But I figured this was a key moment in our relationship—The Time He Proves

---

[68] Of course we didn't have the keys, because we'd borrowed the car without asking. One of the major benefits to having biomech-merge ability: you never need to ask for a ride. Wherever you are, there are always more than enough available cars.

He'll Be Totally Honest With Her—so I let the feeling go without acting on it.

"Why?" she asked.

"Because I want to compare."

"You want to compare yourself to your brother at a base genetic level? Does that sound like maybe the most extreme sign of sibling rivalry ever?"

"Well, when you put it like *that* . . ." She didn't smile. "No, see, it just doesn't make sense that, coming from the same genetic sources, he would get all those powers and I would get absolutely none."

"Except amazingly strong telepathic powers and enhanced intelligence. Let's not forget those little things."

"Well, yeah. There is that. Still, none of it makes sense to me," I said.

"It doesn't make sense? Or do you mean it doesn't feel fair?"

"Well, okay. Both."

"I don't know. I thought you were . . . I believed you were better than that."

"Better than what?"

Her face was half in light, half in shadow, which somehow made her look like someone else, someone I didn't know. And I probably looked the same way to her.

"I thought you were past this thing of admiring your brother or being jealous or whatever. I thought you had come around to seeing him for what he is. You know what all this sounds like."

"Hero worship," I said, my voice catching a little.

"Pretty much. And I thought you were with us."

"I am. This isn't about me wanting to be like him. Not his personality, anyway. But if I could know exactly where his powered genes are and then check my DNA . . ."

"Please don't tell me you're thinking that you could get DNA from him and somehow graft the powered genes onto your own DNA. There's a word for how that turns out: *Phaeton*. You can't possibly be thinking of doing anything that completely stupid."

"Okay, but I have this theory. It may sound more ridiculous than trying to gene-graft. The thing is, I have a totally different idea about hero genes."

"I can hardly wait. Do tell."

This was it. I could totally change the subject or I could tell her my theory.

No secrets.

"The Kraden Project scientists in the 1950s thought they'd *created* 'powered genes' and, by using an early version of genetic engineering, had used them to graft powered genes onto regular human DNA. But I have this idea."

She looked at me with a steady gaze. "Care to read my thoughts?"

"Um, I don't have to. I'm going to guess that they include 'I'm losing patience' and 'Just get to the important part.' Close?"

"Very. Get on with it."

"My theory is that the powered genes were *always* there.

The first heroes were not actually *created* during the 1950s; that was just when the scientists inadvertently activated *dormant* genes, genes that had been there all along. The geneticists and government agencies thought they were building new genetic material, but it would never have worked if the base genes hadn't already been present. And here's the cool part of my theory: the powered genes have been present since the beginning of man. They just became inactive. All the powered genes had been present, but unexpressed, buried in what's typically viewed as junk DNA."

I let her take it in. "Doesn't seem *completely* crazy," she said.

"Reserve your judgment. Here's the coolest part. All the legends and myths about heroes and demigods are so prevalent and found in just about every culture because, at one point, they were just about real. Samson. Hercules. The Titans. Trickster. All of them actually existed, but the most powerful ones killed one another off during prehistory. Their offspring and descendants had remnants of the genes, but the genes became latent, recessive to the growing dominance of regular genes, and they eventually turned into ghost traces of genetic material. Comatose. Like a light that's unplugged: the ability to light the bulb only happens if it's plugged in and switched to *on*." I waited for her to comment. She didn't. "What do you think?"

"Well, I think that's all very interesting. I also think it's all academic and makes no real difference to our lives."

"Unless, of course, I'm right about the idea that everyone

holds powered genes, genes that went dormant in ancient times. If this theory is correct, then it's a matter of identifying those latent powered genes and finding some way to activate them."

"Oh, is that all? Just activate them?"

"I know. I haven't figured out how that's possible. Not without hurricanes and nuclear bomb tests. But I believe there's a way. Why the genes activated for Blake and not for me is also a big question. A huge question—for me, at least. But if I can possibly figure out where his powered genes are and where they're dormant on my DNA, I have a shot at trying to figure out how to activate mine retroactively."

"Wow. That is . . . some theory."

"Insane?"

"Well . . . unusual."

I gave her a few minutes to think.

"Layla, the thing is, what if I could have all those powers?"

"You're the strongest telepath and the smartest person I've ever met. Isn't that enough?"

Not, apparently, enough for her. Not enough to get her to love me.

"Having telepathic powers is great, but what if I have a bunch of latent powers hidden deep in my DNA, just waiting to be unlocked. If I'm right, if I could activate the same strength or flight or speed that Blake has? Or maybe even something new, something undiscovered? Add that to my telepathic powers and just think. Talk about power."

She nodded a few times, taking it in. There was a sound

of laughter from outside the car, maybe fifty yards away. I glanced through the windshield, looked up, and saw a pack of six or seven middle school kids passing overhead in a game of fly-tag.

I turned my attention back to Layla. I could have read her, but I wanted to give her these few minutes of privacy. Her chest rose and fell slowly as she breathed.

"If you're right," she finally said, "it would put us in a whole different league."

"Not just a bunch of teenage villains."

"No. This would shoot us right to supervillain status. We could really make a difference."

"That's my point," I said. "Just think about all we could do."

The possibilities were limitless.

CHAPTER 44

Rogues' Gallery

She didn't have much time to mull over my theory. Her cell phone rang.

"Javier, what's up?" she said into the phone. She listened, then said, "Okay, got it." She hung up and turned to me. "It seems we're wanted."

This time we were meeting Mutagion on the loading dock of a shipyard. I figured that he liked to stick close to water so he could make a fast escape in his little submarine if he needed to.

We had gone straight from where we were talking in the car over to the lair so we could change into our costumes. We met up with the others and got to the shipyard a few hours after dark and walked through the maze of shipping containers the size of RVs, following the directions we were given. Finally, we found the location.

Not far from the water were five Phaetons sitting near what looked like a card table. The light above this section of the yard just happened to be out, leaving the Phaetons at the table in partial shadow. What a coincidence.

The huge bulk of Mutagion was sitting in a cast-off easy

chair. I still couldn't see too much of him. He had on the single blue monocular vision enhancer, and his face was half covered like last time. Without the red light that lit the inside of the sub when we first met, I could see that his skin was white and waxy, like there was a translucent layer on the surface.

There was a regular-sized man with long, shaggy hair, wearing what looked like a World War I–era gas mask. Sitting close behind Mutagion was a guy I figured suffered from some kind of dwarfism, except his arms looked to be regular length, leaving just his legs really short. He wore one of those commedia dell'arte masks with the long birdlike nose.

A woman was sitting in the fourth chair, across from Mutagion. I guessed she was in her early thirties. Her face, though, had absolutely no expression. Then I noticed her hands, which looked like they belonged on someone's great-grandmother. Same with her neck.

Leaning back in another chair was one more guy, who looked completely run-of-the-mill—except for the knobby bone projections that poked through his shirt on both sides of his torso, like an extra set of ribs, except on the outside of his body. Oh, and the other thing that was a little out of the ordinary was the enormous shotgun/grenade launcher that he held diagonally in front of him in a military port arms position.

"Greetings," Javier said to them, making me wince with embarrassment.

Mutagion spoke before Javier could go on. "We don't

have seats for you kids, but that's okay because this is going to be a quick meeting. Just so you don't think I have no manners, I'll introduce you to my crew. You've probably heard or read about most of them, but this fellow here in the gas mask is Groetesk. He doesn't talk; the speech center of his brain was destroyed during his mutation. Our lady friend is Pariah." She didn't change her gaze or expression when Mutagion mentioned her. "The gentleman back there with the peashooter is Scattershot. And of course, you already met Caliban," he said, pointing at the little guy.

"We never met him," Peanut said.

"Whatta ya mean? We was together for, like, a long time the other night, on the dock," he said in a deep, gravelly voice.

Him? "Oh. You seemed . . ." I started to say, not wanting to finish.

"Taller," he said. "Yeah, them's my legs over there." He pointed to a pair of shiny steel alloy prosthetics, wired up with myo-response computer systems.

"All right," Mutagion said. "Let's just get to the point. You said you were going to get me information about the kids in the Academy, and then I would give you my seal of approval in public."

"We haven't had a chance to take care of that yet," I said. "We didn't forget about it."

"Well, you can forget about it now. I decided there's something I want more than that information."

"Okay . . ." Layla said, her voice a little shaky.

I figured, maybe he wanted us to join his crew straight

out. I would have had to think about that one. Getting aligned with Phaetons might not be our best bet after all, not at the beginning, anyway. And not too directly. But they did have a fear factor about them; the public was more afraid of Phaetons than of human powered villains.

Mutagion had another coughing fit, made a horrible gulping sound, and then cracked his neck. "Yes, so what I want is for you to do something for me." He was pointing a huge, gnarled forefinger at me.

"What, me?"

"You." He was overtaken with that wet, hacking cough again. Whenever he tried to take a breath, he only coughed harder. The small guy, Caliban, hopped down off his chair and opened a case on the ground next to Mutagion. First he took out what looked like a gallon jug of water. He unzipped a pocket near the collar of Mutagion's coat and poured the entire contents of the jug in. I didn't see any water spill out from the bottom of the coat, under the chair, or anywhere else. Then Caliban reached into the case and uncoiled a clear, ribbed hose with a metal nozzle. Mutagion took the end and put it inside his woolen shirt, apparently attaching it to something. Caliban turned a switch in the case, and something inside made a chugging, pumping sound. Mutagion's coughing lessened, but he still struggled to get air. He nodded to Caliban, then waved his hand to the woman, Pariah.

She pointed to me. "Mutagion wants information from you."

"I'll try to help, if I can."

"Yes, he wants to know why Blake Baron is not working with the Justice Force."

"Why . . . wait, what? How would I know about that?"

"Do not lie to us, or Mutagion will have you and your friends killed instantly." This woman's face did not change expression in the least as she threatened us with death. It was like a cheap cartoon where the only part of the face that moves when the character talks is the mouth.

"Listen," I began.

"We know he's your brother," Caliban said in that gravelly voice.

Mutagion waved at Caliban and pointed at the case next to him. Once the machine was switched off, Mutagion removed the hose and shook it out. He said, "Did you really think I haven't been watching all of you? Do you think I'm stupid? Yes, many of us did lose some cognitive abilities when we—*kaff, kaff*—embarked on our course of self-initiated mutations, but I was not one of them. I couldn't have risen to the leadership position I'm in now if I had lost my intelligence or cunning. Of course I know who all of you really are. You are not dealing with some two-bit thief—*Kaff, kaff, kaff.*" It sounded like the guy was going to cough up a lung. "And you're going to get us information about the Justice Force. That's a great deal more useful to us than report cards and SAT scores from the kiddies at your school."

There was a gurgling sound from the gas mask that the Phaeton called Groetesk wore. The canister at the end of the hose swung back and forth like an elephant's trunk.

Mutagion moved in his chair. "So answer my initial question."

I saw where this was going. "You want to know why Artillery hasn't been seen with the Justice Force for a while."

Mutagion said, "Artillery. Blake Baron. Your brother, yes."

"You're asking him to betray his own brother?" Layla said.

"I don't believe I was talking to you, Miss Keating." There was a disturbing rumble in his voice. He turned his gaze back to me.

"Let me explain something to you. To all of you. Those spandex-clad morons on the Justice Force, and all of their kind, are my enemies. The public may think what they will, but to me, these so-called heroes are nothing better than savages, unscrupulous executioners, and I will not be their prey. My forces are weakening. Just in the past month, two Phaetons turned themselves in for euthanization. They were tired of fighting. They had given up. I knew both of them. Now, I don't expect you, or anyone like you, to shed a tear for us. But I do think you should understand my resolve."

Mutagion leaned forward. His head began to twitch rhythmically. He waved to me to come closer.

I took a step, but Layla grabbed the back of my jacket and held on. I waved my hand, letting her know it was okay. I took two more steps. I was maybe one yard away from Mutagion.

It smelled like a swamp when he spoke. "We believe the Justice Force has planned a major attack against us. And if that's true, your brother knows about it. You're going to find out and you're going to report to me. Cross me, and I'll have each one of you killed. If you think I can't reach you, or I don't have the stomach to kill teenagers, just try me. You wanted to be villains? This is how we play. For keeps."

He took in a deep breath and his shoulders shook with the effort to keep from hacking that awful cough.

I glanced at Javier. He was looking down at the ground. I turned back to Mutagion. "Just so I'm clear," I began, "what you're asking—"

"No, my boy, I'm not asking. I'm telling. I have no time or use for sentimentality, and I care not a whit for your allegiance to your brother and his friends."

"With all due respect, sir, you have no idea about my allegiances."

He cocked his head. "Is that so?"

"My allegiances are my own business. But I can assure you of one thing." I thought of the argument I'd had with Blake before I left home. He found the idea that I would not want to be like him incomprehensible. That arrogance and egotism, his deeply held belief that his way was the right and only way—all that only strengthened my intentions.

"Despite what you think," I said, "I have no allegiance to my brother. No allegiance to him at all."

Perhaps the most ruthless and cunning of Phaetons currently at large is the one known as Mutagion. He is the alleged mastermind behind various acts of destruction, treason, attempted government coups, and, not least, murderer of countless innocent children and women, in addition to men. An avowed enemy of all heroes, Mutagion remains one of the most wanted villains both in the United States and abroad.

From the introduction of
M Is for Monster, M Is for Mutagion
by K. J. Baker
Hyperion Press, 2014

CHAPTER 45

Linked

Peanut drove and Javier stared (or, more likely, glared) out the passenger window. I didn't have to read him to know what he was thinking. He was pissed that Mutagion's attention had shifted from him over to me. Back by the loading dock at the shipyard, Mutagion had pointed at me and said, "So I'm gonna tell you how to reach me."

Javier had cleared his throat and taken a step forward. "Actually, I handle all communications. I am sort of the . . . point person, yes?"

Mutagion didn't even turn his head toward Javier. "No. I'll decide who I will talk to, and right now, it's him," he said, pointing that long, crooked finger at my chest. "You are going to contact Caliban. He'll give you the number, and when you need to make contact, you text him the number where he should reach you."

So it seemed that, like it or not, *I* was going to be the point person. Javier was welcome to the attention; I wasn't looking for it. Once again, Blake had attracted the spotlight, even when he hadn't been actively seeking it.

I had called home to say that I was sleeping over at a friend's house, maybe for the weekend. I was going to stay at the lair. I didn't want to be around Blake after our argument. Not for a while, anyway.

Layla walked upstairs with me.

We had outfitted the place with serious stealth equipment, courtesy of our ATM withdrawals and the know-how of our technically gifted Hellion members.[69] We sat on the couch.

"Are you sure you're okay going up against your brother?" Layla asked.

"You met him."

"Yeah."

"So, if you were me . . ."

She nodded. "I get it. Okay."

"Javier's pissed."

"He'll have to get over it. He'll have to come to terms with the idea that *wanting* to be in charge doesn't mean you *are* in charge."

"It looks like Mutagion elected *me* to be in charge."

"Well, if you think about it honestly, who do you think will make the better decisions for the group: Javier or you?"

---

[69] There was thick, clean carpet on the floor. The walls and ceiling had some white spongy material that looked quilted like a down jacket and provided extra soundproofing. Behind that material we had lead-plated steel sheets on all the walls. The low lighting that had a calming blue tint was kind of a by-product of some electronic stuff we had running. Image and sound transmissions set up by Boots made it so that anybody who might try to see what was there would see an empty place. Even heroes with intersight would get the false transmitted picture. And the only sound they would hear was rats scurrying around. Basically, we made it pretty much impossible to listen or see into the lair from the outside.

Javier was reckless and vain. Given the stakes involved, cooler heads and smarter minds could be the difference between our being successful and our being incarcerated . . . or killed.

Exactly, Layla thought to me. *I knew you'd come around.* Then, out loud, "Anyway, it's time Javier understood that this isn't just some exciting adventure. Believe me: if push came to shove, I'm sure he wouldn't want to change positions with you. He's already probably thinking he got in way over his head."

"If I had any brains, I'd probably be wondering the same thing myself."

She nodded a few times. "If you had any brains, yeah."

Layla took my hand and we stared at the blank TV screen across from the couch.

"You want company tonight?" she asked.

Really? What'll you tell your parents?

Are you kidding me? They don't even notice whether I'm there or not.

I knew her well enough to understand that there was absolutely not an ounce of self-pity or sympathy-seeking there. She was just stating a fact.

"Aren't the others waiting for you downstairs in the car?"

"They left right after they dropped us off."

"Hm. Sounds like you planned to stay."

She shrugged. "Hey, if you'd rather be alone . . ."

No, no. Not at all.

Good.

CHAPTER 46

Code

I guess it's hard to get more intimate than being in someone's mind. But what happened that night—well, let's just say it was a close second.

Tired as I was, I didn't sleep well. Layla was out like a light, but I had too much going on in my mind. Mutagion wanted to do business primarily with me, and I didn't think it was just because of my connection to Blake. Clearly, Mutagion just took me more seriously than he did the rest of the Hellions.

That was part of what kept me up. Mutagion was known the world over as being a freak, a morally corrupt, ruthless villain. Heartless and vile.

But he didn't come off that way to me. I just had this gut feeling that there was more going on with him than the heroes or newspapers had led us to believe.

In fact, though I had little doubt that the Phaetons in Mutagion's crew would have blasted us to bits with no more than a nod from him, they, too, left me with the sense that they were . . . well, maybe not victims, exactly, but not quite the aggressive offenders everyone believed them to be.

If for no other reason than they just seemed too sad.

I watched the sun come up at dawn and I watched Layla sleep. I waited until eight o'clock before waking her.

She was not too pleased. "Are you kidding me? It's Saturday. Let me sleep."

"Call Boots for me."

She rolled my way, squinting against the light. "Why?" she asked.

"Because I want to see if she can get us into the GenLab databanks."

"Oh, come on. You woke me up for *that*? Seriously. You're not going to figure out the secrets of genetics this morning. That can wait till the afternoon. I'm going back to sleep," she said, and she rolled away from me.

I'll go in there and mess with your dreams. Come on. Get up and give her a call.

You are such a jerk, she thought to me, just before she sat up in bed.

"What's the big rush?" Boots asked me when she got to the lair. She was dressed more sloppily than usual—way more— and she had on glasses. "It *is* Saturday, you know."

"I need your help."

"And it has to be this minute?"

"Pretty much."

Even with her keyloggers and some kind of digital decoding system, it took her twenty-three minutes to hack into the GenLab system. Layla watched from the couch, a blanket wrapped around her.

Boots shook her head. "I'm trying to get to those DNA profiles, but I keep bumping into these top secret walls about some 'Phaeton Reversion Project' and 'Phaeton Disposition' something-or-other."

"Why would that come up when you're looking for DNA analysis of Blake and me?"

"Not sure. Maybe because they're both in high-security areas of the database, and the lockout is somehow connected? Could just be a glitch, but when it tries to bump me from my DNA search, this Phaeton stuff also comes up as blocked, even though I wasn't actually looking to get into it."

I couldn't imagine that they were linked in any significant way, but it did get me thinking. "So what's the story? Do you think you can still get into these places?"

"I *thought* I could. I mean, your mom got us through and I recorded everything, but I just can't slip into the DNA profile area. I'm thinking it might have something to do with the retinal scan that I have being taped instead of real time. Some systems can detect that."

"Great," I said. "All right, see what you can do with that Phaeton section."

"Why?"

"Because there's something I want to check."

"I thought you wanted that DNA stuff," Layla said.

"Yeah, I do. But if she can't get in, she can't get in. I'll have to get my mom to open it up again."

It took a little while, but Boots was able to work her way into the Phaeton section of the database.

"Got it," Boots said. Layla stood up, still wrapped in the blanket, to see what we had found.

The only problem was that the text looked something like this:

Lbthfæp, Fæbyft	Tyrmnokj	%^	as	YFbllbs, TX	Bt lbfgy, ASY USB
ASbf5scæ, Chbflys	P5llbgyf	æ5	as	P5tts, BL	YFycybsyyf/yfystfæyf

"What the hell is that?" Layla asked.

"It's encrypted," I said. I turned to Boots. "You have decryption software, I assume?"

She nodded and ran a program. She ran another. And another. "That's pretty weird. I've never seen that."

Layla said, "Seen what?"

"This site is basically bouncing my decryption software right off. I can't decode it. You want me to back out of this section?"

"No, wait a minute," I said. I stared at the characters on the screen, looking for patterns. I found a few, but not ones that would help to decrypt the code. "Does staying on this screen for a while open us up to a greater chance of getting caught?"

"By about five hundred percent, yeah," Boots said.

"I figured. If you can get me screenshots of every page in this section, that would be great."

She did, then settled down on the couch to watch some movie on TV.

"You can read code," I said to Layla.

"Yeah, sure, but that's not computer code."

"It's close enough. I have an idea."

I asked Layla to look at the printouts, to scan them over and over again, and not to worry about trying to make sense of them. While she did that, I started to read her, trying to combine her code-reading abilities with my limited knowledge of cryptography.[70]

Six hours later, I was typing a text to Caliban through the scrambler Boots had set up. I just sent my phone number. Mutagion had explained to me, quietly, that Caliban couldn't read.

After we sent my number, I had to wait for Caliban's call. And after four hours, there was still no response. Boots wanted to leave, so after she showed me how to work the scrambler, I thanked her and let her go.

My lack of sleep started to take its toll on me.

"Are you going to sit there and stare at the phone, waiting?" Layla asked me.

"That's the plan."

"You look exhausted. Why don't you go to sleep for a while?"

"I can't miss his call."

---

[70] Okay, yes, I'm being humble. I had gone through a cryptography and cryptology reading jag a couple of years earlier and developed a reasonable foundation in the subject. That foundation being, I figured, about as good as Regular cryptologists who had spent their careers doing it for the FBI and CIA.

because I couldn't be sure that it wasn't going to turn into a kidnapping . . . or worse. But I should have expected that she wasn't going to sit home watching TV, either. Our compromise: she would drive us there, but she would stay by the car, ready to take off if necessary, while I met with Caliban.

We were waiting by Javier's (ahem, *borrowed*) car in the parking lot of a shopping mall that had been closed years ago after the water supply for the area had been poisoned.[71] The only light came from the moon and from a factory complex on the other side of the highway.

I didn't mind it being mostly dark. We had decided to wear our costumes, even though Mutagion seemed to have figured out who we were.

There was a *thock-THOCK-thock-THOCK-thock-THOCK* sound getting closer and closer from the east end of the parking lot. Layla and I turned to look.

It was a person with absurdly long legs—at least five feet—loping toward us, fast, in an unbalanced gait. The person came to a swaying stop about forty yards away. The left leg was wobbling at the knee.

---

[71] This was when Pneumatica from the Vindication Squad had an aerial battle with Bubonica in the skies above Crow's Falls. Pneumatica wasn't thinking, apparently, when she slashed at Bubonica, which, of course, resulted in Bubonica's poison blood becoming atomized and raining down into all the reservoirs, rivers, creeks, soil. Good job, Pneumatica: you captured a minor villain, and the only cost was that you made a suburban township completely uninhabitable for decades. Go, heroes!

"You gotta come here," Caliban said in his gravelly voice. "I ain't going over there. And just you, boy. Girlie, you stay right over there."

Layla looked at me. I shrugged. "If anything goes wrong . . ." I said.

"Just give him the info and let's get out of here."

"That's the plan. But just in case—"

"I know, I know. Drive away. Just hurry up."

I walked over to where Caliban stood on his prosthetic legs, altogether well over eight feet tall. He had some kind of homemade pants on, shiny parachute-type material. When the breeze moved it, I could make out the flat, bladed form of the prosthetics. There was a metal creaking sound from what I figured was the left knee joint.

It was weird, craning my neck to look up at a person who I knew was actually only about four feet tall. It was made even weirder by that crazy white mask with the long, pointed birdlike nose.

"Okay, I'm here," he said. "You got something for Mutagion?"

"Yeah. And it's important that he get it as soon as possible."

"Kid, you don't give me orders. I'll deliver it when I deliver it."

"Okay, sure. But I'm just telling you, it's something he's going to want to see right away."

"Yeah, yeah. I heard ya the first time. Give it here."

I handed him the manila envelope. "Caliban. Listen. It's really important that nobody else sees this."

"I'll look at it if I want."

"I don't know if Mutagion would be happy about that, but I guess that's between you and him. I'm saying, nobody else."

"Yeah, yeah. I get it. It's important and top secret. I ain't a moron, ya know. I can understand a simple conception like that. I'm out."

He started to turn back toward the direction from where he'd come.

"Caliban? Can I ask you a personal question?"

He turned back and looked down to me. "You can ask, but it don't mean I'm gonna answer."

"Okay, well, I'm wondering, do you remember anything about . . . before?"

"Before what?"

There was no nice way to phrase it. "Before you became, um, a Phaeton."

Caliban's little barrel chest swelled as he took a deep breath. "What, you don't read the papers? Watch TV? Read books or nothin'? None of us got our memories from before. That's what we get for messing with things we don't know about. Ya ain't heard the preachers saying how it's our punishment for messin' with nature? Or the governments say we should leave the big-time science to them, and this is what happens when you try do-it-yourself mutations or go to half-assed hacks promising to do it in a unregulatorialized way? You ain't heard none of that?"

"Yeah, I did. I was just wondering. Maybe you had some little bits of memory that all those people don't know about."

"I got nothing, kid."

"You don't remember why you did it?"

"Like I just said, I got nothin'."

He tucked the envelope inside his long overcoat and turned. There was a grinding sound and an electronic whine from his left knee. The leg started to bow out.

"You need a hand?" I asked.

"I need a *leg*! Ha. That was good. Get it? 'You need a hand?' 'Nah, I need a leg.'"

"Do you need some help?"

"What, from you?"

I pointed back toward the car. "My friend over there? She has biomechanical-merge abilities. She could probably—"

"I know she's got biomech merge. Why you think I said I don't want her too close? She'll mess my legs up, then what do I got?"

"She won't. If you need some help, she'll give it to you."

He shook his head and tried to take a step. The knee made a buzzing sound.

"How do I know she ain't gonna shut me down?" Caliban asked.

"I'm telling you, she won't."

He took a minute to think it over, switching his gaze

between his faulty knee and Layla, who was leaning against the car.

"All right, I guess. But you tell her if she messes with me, she's gonna have to answer to Mutagion. That's more trouble than she'll want to deal with."

Layla's mech repair didn't take long. She gripped the carbon-fiber/steel alloy where Caliban's shin would be. When she was done, Caliban seemed happy to have his legs functioning again.

He didn't say a word but left at a fast clip, this time the *thock-thock-thock-thock-thock-thock* sound balanced.

"There's some pretty amazing high-tech machinery going on in those legs," Layla said.

"Yeah, well, I wouldn't trade places with him for all the high-tech stuff in the world."

He was out of sight in less than thirty seconds.

UNITED STATES, EURASIAN ALLIANCE,
UNIFIED AFRICAN NATIONS, ET AL.
V. DEFENDANT #5958375-ER/OO-M

People's exhibit 211-15b

ÆF5G5ASµL ASBASY	5DYAST5TY	BGY
Lbthfæp, Fæbyft	Tyrmnokj	%^
ASbf5scæ, Chbflys	P5llbgyf	æ5
Gfyyaswby, Lysl5y	AS5scfybt5æas	r-8
Æ'Flbhyfty, L5bas	Gfæytysk	r-æ
Ygbas, ASbfshb	Pbf5bh	r-1
ASylsæas, Fbhyyas	ASæasstfæs	ææ
ASæastbasb, Yyfwbfyf	Cbl5bbas	%^
C5ylæ, V5fg5l	Sl5pkasæt	æ1
Tfbsk, S5asæas	Væas5tus	r-0
Bfæwas, Jyss5cb	Gbffætb	æ8
ASælbas, Styphyas	Ffbctufy	r-æ
Wbll5asgfæfyf, Ffyyfyf5ck	AS5ghtasbfy	r-3
Hbasl5as, Gyæfgy	Hbasgasbas	æ9
Jæasys, Gyæfg5b	Tyffæf	a4
Stæfch, L5sb	Bbby	1n
P5ccæl5asæ, Lyæasbfyf	Blææyfbbth	æn
AScHugh, Blyxbasyfyf	Bubæas5cb	æ6
Stf5cklbasyf, YFbv5s	AS/B	a5

Original text; nonredacted, reconstructed for court

SYX	PLBCY ÆF ÆF5G5AS	STBTUS
as	YFbllbs, TX	Bt lbfgy, ASY USB
as	P5tts, BL	YFycybsyyf/yfystfæyf
f	Blbbasy, EY	Bt lbfgy (Cbasbyfb?)
as	Tulsb, ÆK	Bt lbfgy, ASY USB
f	Quyyas, EY	Bt lbfgy (Wyæas5asg?)
as	Slæbt, PB	Suffyasyfyyf, yfystfæyf
as	Cbff, ASV	Bt lbfgy, ASY USB
as	Cbft5as, ÆH	Bt lbfgy, SY USB
as	H5llsly, EY	Suffyasyfyyf, yfystfæyf
f	EY, EY	YFycybsyyf/yfystfæyf
as	Bæstæas, SB	Bt lbfgy, ASYC
as	B5llyt, CÆ	YFycybsyyf/yfystfæyf
as	Ffysasæ, CB	Bt lbfgy, ASyx5cæ
f	Wbll5s, UT	Bt lbfgy, ASY USB
f	Suffyy, GB	Bt lbfgy, SY USB
as	5sv5lly, BL	YFycybsyyf/yfystfæyf
as	ASæasvl, AT	YFycybsyyf/yfystfæyf
as	Bbyæasy, ASJ	Bt lbfgy, ASW USB

CHAPTER 48

Disclosures

We changed out of our costumes and stashed them in the car before driving over to my house.

"Have we met?" Mom asked Layla near the front door when we came in. I didn't think I had erased Mom's memory of our entire visit when I tapped her mind, but she might have pushed it into her subconscious, which can happen with unattached memories.

"Uh, I'm not sure," Layla said.

"This is Layla. You probably think you met because you've heard me talking about her."

"Ah, yes." After closing the front door, Mom asked me, "So, what was it you needed?"

"There's a book in your study I need to see."

"That's all? Well, go ahead in and take whatever you want."

"I'm not sure where it is. I need you to help me find it."

"Fine. Come on."

"I'll meet you in there. I just want to get Layla settled in."

"Of course. Make yourself at home."

"Thank you."

Mom went down the hall.

When she was out of earshot, Layla asked, "You sure you don't want me to come with you?"

"No, I have to talk to her on my own. Wait for me in there?" I said, pointing to the living room. "You'll be okay out here?"

"Uh, yeah. I don't imagine it'll be too dangerous, sitting on the couch and watching TV."

"Okay. I'll be back soon."

I stopped at the living room doorway before going through and looked back at Layla. She settled onto the couch and held her hand up. The TV set buzzed, then turned on.

Halfway down the hallway I slowed down. I had some questions for Mom about the Phaetons, among other things. And I believed Mom could answer my questions, though the answers might not be anything I wanted to hear. But I still needed to know.

I went in.

"What book was it you wanted?" Mom asked.

I closed the door. "This isn't about a book. It's something much more important."

"Sounds serious," she said, not sounding a hundred percent sincere to me.

"Oh, it is. Serious as death." I took a pause, a dramatic pause, to be honest. I had a sense that this could be an important moment in my life. And I had dreams that all this would someday become public, maybe even legendary, part of a bigger story. "You work for GenLab."

She squinted at me with a wry smile. "I don't think that's big news."

"What's the Demophon Program?"

"The what?"

"The Demophon Program. Do you work on it?"

"I'm not sure what—"

I didn't have patience or time. I needed answers, and as much as I didn't want some of my suspicions to be true, I just wanted to get this done. "Okay, let's get to it. I assume you don't know this, and though I never got rated, I think I'm somewhere around a level K telepath."

A look of genuine surprise came over her face. "A what? Are you . . . are you sure?"

Yes, I'm totally sure.

She looked like she had just gotten the wind knocked out of her.

"You had to know," I said out loud. "You studied my DNA."

"We haven't been able to map telepathy, or any kind of psi genes. They just don't show up."

"So you had no idea."

Her eyes filled. "None. I thought . . . I knew everything about your genetic makeup. But I didn't know this. Of all the powers for you to have, *this*? Telepathy?" She swallowed and wiped her eyes.

"Okay, we'll come back to that," I said. "First, I need to know some other things. It would be better if you just tell me. I'd rather not have to get the information against your will."

She recoiled a bit, obviously hurt. "I . . . I don't even know what to say."

For a moment, I thought maybe I had gone too far. I didn't mean to hurt her. But then, there was a lot at stake. I had to stay the course, no matter what. "Well, start by answering my question. Do you work on the Demophon Program?"

"I'm telling you honestly: I don't even know what *Demophon* means."

"Well, we can start with the word itself," I said. "You might as well sit down. *Demophon.* From Greek mythology. The goddess Demeter was grateful for a king's hospitality, so she wanted to repay him by making his son, Demophon, into a god."

"That's a pretty good repayment, I'd say," Mom said with forced humor.

"Yeah, well, it didn't work out. She had tried to burn away his mortal soul, but she got interrupted by his mother, and eventually Demophon died."

"Well, that's a sad tale, but what does it have to do with my work?"

I reached into my back pocket and took out a folded piece of paper. This document was a copy of the actual decoded translation of the message I'd given Caliban a couple of hours earlier. I handed it to her.

Looking at it, she said, "I'm not sure what this is."

"You're lying to me. It's very clear what it is."

I heard her swallow. "Well, be that as it may, I'm not clear on why you're asking *me* about this."

"Do you work in the Demophon Program?"

"No."

"But you know what it is."

"Not specifics, but yes. I do know vaguely what it's about."

I shook my head. "Mom, please don't do this. Trust me when I say I'm going to find out what I need to know. I'd rather you be honest, but I'll use my telepathic power if I have to. It's really up to you. Now, you're not on any of these teams working in the Demophon Program?"

"What teams?"

I was getting jumpy. This would only lead into bad directions. "Okay, based on my understanding of this document, there are several teams involved with this Demophon Program. The team that kidnaps or recruits or whatever it actually is, the people, the Regulars. Then it's obviously another team that does the dirty work, messing with these people's DNA. Once they've been changed, it looks like they either die in the process or they get released and then considered enemies. Am I right so far?"

"You're pretty close." Mom took a breath and shook her head. "Okay. I'll tell you what I know. The Kraden Project was successful exactly once. In 1952, the first set of metahumans was created. The Soviet Union and China also succeeded with counterpart programs. That was it. There are theories about why it worked, theories involving everything from weather conditions and nuclear tests—"

"I know about the theories. Let's move on. The Kraden Project was shut down in 1983. Then what?"

"The experiments continued unofficially. And unsuccessfully." By this point, she couldn't meet my eyes. "The Demophon Program started up in 1992 as a way to deal with failed attempts to bind powered genes onto regular DNA. So far, the experiments that go bad either die in the lab, or, if they live, they're bad mutations with serious problems."

"Phaetons," I said.

"Phaetons, yes."

"It all makes sense now. The first U.S. heroes fought against the Russian heroes, the Chinese, metahumans from all our Communist enemies. Nineteen ninety-one was when the Soviet Union and Communism collapsed. No more common enemies. So let's just create some. Nineteen ninety-two is the start of the Demophon Program. The failed mutations are called Phaetons. They're released and used as common enemies for the public to hate or fear, and for the heroes to attack. Is that about it?"

She nodded. "How did you find out about Demophon?" she asked.

"Doesn't matter. What does matter is how you can work with an organization that would do this. How can you be a part of GenLab?"

"Hold on. GenLab is just a contractor. We're consultants. We work for the government. They're the ones who set the agenda and run the Demophon . . . activities."

"Brad?" Layla called from the living room. "You should see this."

"I'm in the middle of something."

"Yeah, well, I'm telling you: this is something you'll want to see. . . ."

I told Mom that I would be right back. When I got to the living room, I found out that Layla was wrong: it was something I *needed* to see, but most definitely not something I *wanted* to see.

CHAPTER 49

Human-Interest Story

Layla held her hand up toward the TV. "Here, let me rewind it for you," she said. She had engaged the DVR and now ran it back a bit.

The video was of a reporter standing in the woods. "Local police were alerted by EagleEye that Caliban, a Phaeton affiliated with Mutagion, had been apprehended. During his attempt to escape from EagleEye, Caliban experienced equipment failure with his bionic legs and stumbled into the toxic creek that connects with the Crow's Point River. Police and medical personnel pronounced Caliban dead on arrival."

The video showed crime-scene tape stretched between trees and police milling around. In the far background, Eagle-Eye, in his yellow-and-green costume, was giving a statement to local police.

"I fixed the malfunction in his metal leg," Layla said. "I'm telling you, it was minor, and what I did should have made it run perfectly."

"Can you roll back the video on this again?"

She put her hand up near the TV, and the recorded news segment played backward.

"Stop! Move forward again. Stop! Right there. Is there some way you can zoom in on the upper left corner?"

"Easy," she said. She zoomed in and I was right.

"Look right there, on the hill. Those are his prosthetic legs. See anything weird?"

She examined the picture. "You mean other than that each one of them is snapped in two?"

"No, exactly that. You think those carbon-fiber alloys can be broken by a guy who weighs *maybe* a hundred pounds running on them?"

"Impossible," she said.

"Right. So somebody else broke them, which is how Caliban ended up facedown in a poisoned river."

"EagleEye," she said.

"Maybe." There was still stuff I needed to talk about with Mom, and I had a feeling that if I didn't do it on this visit, it could be a good, long time before I would have another chance.

"I need to finish talking to my mom, but we have another problem to deal with right away. Mutagion is going to think that we'd set Caliban up, that this was part of a plan. We have to make sure he knows that's not what happened."

"Okay, how are we supposed to reach him without any contact information at all? It's not exactly as if we can look his number up on the Underweb."

I had to think for a couple of seconds. I didn't like that Mom was in the study with all that information I had already given her. I was going to have to finish up with her and probably erase the whole conversation from her mind. "Okay, how's this? Take my phone. I called Caliban, and he called back. He must've had phone conversations with Mutagion. Is there any way you can get a connection to Mutagion by tracing that trail?"

"Hm. Maybe. I can give it a try."

It took her about a minute to get through. She handed the phone to me. Mutagion has a very distinctive voice.

"You made a big mistake," he said.

"Before you say anything else," I said into the phone, "let me tell you—"

"No, it don't work like that. You took advantage of the fact that Caliban was feebleminded, and you tricked him into meeting you, just to have him murdered."

"I swear to you, I didn't trick him. I gave him some information for you. And I'm guessing he got . . . they got to him before he was able to give it to you."

"Listen up, you little brat," Mutagion said. "I don't believe one damned word you're saying. This was a setup, plain and simple. And for that, you're going to pay. Dearly. I would like nothing better than to exact my vengeance immediately, but it seems that the Justice Force and some of their friends are gathering to eliminate the last of the Phaetons. Well, you can rest assured that we are not going down without a fight. I put the word out that this is going to be a last stand. I have plenty of volunteers who'll fight to take down the so-called heroes. And then, if I'm still alive, I'm coming after you. If I'm not alive, then I'll make arrangements to have you killed.

And failing that, I'll come back from the depths of hell, and I will find you."

"I found out some information about Phaetons. About you."

"This conversation is over," Mutagion said.

"It's important."

"The next time we meet, I'll watch you take your last breath. Until then . . ."

"Robert Lathrop."

"What?"

"That was your name. Robert Lathrop. You were from Dallas, Texas, when the government took you at the age of thirty-four. They turned you into a Phaeton."

"You have lost your mind, boy."

"That's the information I gave to Caliban. The government has been taking citizens and trying to genetically enhance them. Most of the failed experiments die in the lab. The ones who live get their memories erased, and they're set loose. Common enemies for the public, opponents for the heroes, who can beat them and get better press."

There was only the sound of raspy breathing from the other end of the phone.

I said, "They did this to you. I'm telling you, you didn't do this to yourself. Mutagion? Mutagion? Robert?"

There wasn't even a click when he disconnected us.

CHAPTER 50

DOC

Back in the study, Mom was on her computer. "Perfect," I said. "I need you to bring something up for me."

"What else is there to look up? I told you about my—*very* minimal—involvement with Demophon—"

"Pull up my gene analysis and Blake's."

She sat back in her chair and shook her head. "Are you still obsessed with that? I told you—"

"Just please bring them up."

She gave me a look, then typed into the computer for a while. I wondered how Layla was doing with trying to reach Javier and the others. I told her to tell them to go to places I didn't know so there would be no chance of torturing me to find out where they were.

"Okay, here they are," Mom said. The screen was split, with one double helix model on each side, color-coded and annotated for powers. Aside from the one on the left being brightly colored and the one on the right being mostly white, they were identical.

"Look at all those bright powered genes on Blake's DNA, and, except for that gene for my enhanced intelligence, mine is plain. Why do you think I got telepathy and Blake didn't?"

"It was probably a spontaneous mutation that occurred a while after conception. Though it's also possible that he got it, too. Being that telepathy is illegal, most people who have the ability don't make the effort to develop it."

"Or they do and they don't get caught."

"That, too. Some of them, though, don't even realize they have the capability. Some of these people just think they're very insightful about other people's thoughts and emotions. How did you find out about your telepathy?"

"I had some help." I looked at the twisted ladders on the screen: Blake's full of color and powers, mine pale and dull. I shook my head. "What are the odds that Blake's DNA and mine would be so completely different?"

"Not very high. They were originally . . . much more alike."

"I don't follow."

"You were part of an experiment in knockout genes, which are—"

"I know what knockout genes are. They're used to suppress traits, basically to inactivate the genes in the organism. So, what? They used knockout genes on my DNA to repress my powered genes? Is that it?"

"Yes."

"Which is why they're all white Regular genes, instead of blue and red and the rest, like on Blake's."

"That's pretty accurate," Mom said.

"So I could have had all those powered genes if they hadn't been knocked out."

"Yes."

"I would have had strength, flight, all the powers Blake has."

"In theory, yes."

"All I had was the intelligence gene. And the hidden telepathy gene."

"Right."

"I was an embryonic felon."

"You could say that."

I pointed toward the right side of the screen. "What's that mean?"

"What, your birthday?"

"No, below it." I tapped my fingertip on the screen. "What does DOC mean?"

"'Date of conception.' What does that have to do with—"

"Well, then, that's a mistake. This DNA with my name has the same DOC as Blake's."

She took a deep breath. "It's not wrong."

"How can that be? We're almost five years apart." I laughed. "So, what, you walked around with me in your belly until I was ready for kindergarten?"

Mom looked at the DNA models once more and then turned away from the screen. And from me. "You and Blake were both conceived at the same time."

"I don't follow you. How could we have been conceived

at the same time but born more than four years apart?"

Mom got up and walked to the window. "Like I said, you and Blake were part of an experiment. Blake was the control: they didn't knock out any of his genes, and the prediction was that he would develop with fully powered DNA. But they identified your powered genes and knocked them out, one by one. When you were embryos and your father found out the details of the experiment, that you wouldn't grow up to have powers like Blake, well, your father . . ." She trailed off and kept her gaze from mine.

"What?"

No answer.

"My father *what*?"

She swallowed a couple of times. "There's no way to say this without it sounding terrible. So I'll just say it. Your father didn't want to have a child who didn't have powers. He didn't want me to be implanted with the other embryo."

"Me."

"You. We disagreed about it, argued a lot. And then, well, he was killed in the line of duty. And I wanted to be implanted with you. They offered to reverse the knockout genes and give you all your powers."

"So why didn't they?"

"I didn't let them. I didn't want another hero. I didn't want another person I loved to be in the path of danger. I wanted a normal life for you."

"Didn't exactly work as planned, it would seem."

"Few things do."

"Why . . ." I trailed off, trying to put my thoughts in order.

"Why what?"

"Why would you agree to be part of an experiment like this?"

"We had trouble conceiving. We wanted children. This was offered to us, and we took it. I don't regret doing it. If we hadn't, we wouldn't have had Blake and you."

I looked at the computer screen and used the trackpad to rotate each double helix several times. "I just can't get over how, except for the colors, they're almost exactly alike."

"Actually, aside from those things, which as I said were manipulated in the lab, they *are* exactly alike."

Okay, I was no geneticist, but as far as I knew, same date of conception and same original genes could really mean only one thing. "Are you telling me that Blake and I are identical twins?"

"Something like that."

"Something *like* that, or that *exactly?*"

"Well, yes, you started out as identical twins, but with the genetic differences between you now, technically you're not identical. Anymore."

I sat down on the couch. I just couldn't take in everything I was finding out. "Five years apart and nothing alike, and we were once identical."

"Who cares what we call it," came a familiar voice from

behind me. "Whichever way you cut it, we're still brothers, right?"

Mom and I both turned to see Blake's bulky form filling the study doorway.

CHAPTER 51

Brothers-in-Arms

He walked into the room and sat heavily on the couch, staring at me. "Right? Brothers-in-arms. Like it or not," he said.

"Not."

"Ha! I feel the same way," he said. "I guess *brothers-in-arms* isn't the right phrase, anyway, right? I think it means people who fight on the same side and rely on each other. So it doesn't apply at all to us, does it, now? We've actually been on opposite sides. Is there a word for that?"

"There are a few. Opponents. Antagonists. Adversaries. Foes. Enemies. Should I go on?"

"What are you two talking about?" Mom asked.

Blake flashed her the smile. "Oh, nothing important, Ma. Just that your younger son has gotten a political side to him recently. Odd views, he's got. Very disappointing. Disturbing, in fact."

"Funny how you just happened to drop by at this particular moment," I said.

"I called him," Mom said.

I knew it. I just knew it. "Why, Mom? Why would you do that?"

"Because you were acting so . . . not like yourself. I got concerned."

"And so you called *him*? To come to the rescue?"

"Brad, he's your brother. Of course he wants to help—"

"I don't need help. Not from him."

"Ah, it's no problem at all," Blake said. "I was on my way out to a job. It was no problem at all to pop on over."

"I thought you weren't working," I said.

"I wasn't. But duty calls, as they say. Thanks to your efforts to betray the heroes and all that time spent with the lowlifes at your school, not to mention your new . . . *friends* outside of school."

"Brad?" Mom said. "What is he talking about?"

"He may look puzzled, Ma," Blake said, "but believe me, he knows exactly what I'm talking about. Right, Brad? Your new buddy? Starts with an M and rhymes with . . . um, let's see . . . *new-tage-un*."

"I'm done here," I said. I got up, but there was a blur of movement, and then Blake was standing in front of the door before I had taken two steps.

"Sit down, little brother."

There was absolutely no point whatsoever in trying to get past him. I turned and took a couple of steps to stand in front of the bookshelves. "Oh, yeah. As you heard, we're twins, so I'm technically not your *little* brother anymore."

"Well, yeah, you are. You're still way smaller and considerably weaker than me, so you'll be 'little brother' unless I decide on something worse."

"Did you just say *considerably*? That's quite a big word for you. Where'd you learn it?"

"Brad, for all your intelligence, you're not too bright. Did you look carefully at my gene map? I'm assuming you didn't, or you would have noticed that they didn't knock out my intelligence. It's all theater, genius. I act dim so people—especially enemies—will underestimate me. It gives me a considerable edge."

I said, "Well, all that's just great to hear, Blake, but I have a friend waiting for me and we have somewhere to be. . . ."

"Don't worry about your friend. Janet is sitting with Layla in the living room. They're discussing a few things, getting some info on your new colleague and his location."

"Janet is . . . I'm telling you now, Blake. If she does anything—anything at all—to hurt Layla—"

"Don't try to threaten me, Brad. You'll just embarrass yourself. And anyway, Janet isn't planning to hurt her. She just wants some information, and as long as your little girl-friend gives it up—"

I'll admit I wasn't thinking clearly when I charged at Blake and took a wild swing, a great big roundhouse punch, at his face. He didn't even bother to dodge. He let my hand connect, which only sent a bee-sting buzz up my arm, as if I had punched a tree. Of course, it didn't harm him in the least.

"That was smart," he said. "Look, no matter what you believe, we're the good guys. We don't torture people for information. We ask for it and we usually get what we ask for quickly, so we don't *have* to resort to other methods. Make no mistake, though: if it's for the greater good, we do what we have to do."

The best thing for me to do, obviously, was to get into his mind and get him out of my way. But when I tried to do a clandestine command projection, I couldn't.

Blake shook his head. "No, no. Nice try. You really didn't notice the orange plugs in my ears?"

"Actually, no, I didn't."

Blake turned his head sideways and then I could see a little orange nub sticking out of his ear canal. "Yeah, these were invented by Pneumatica of the Vindicators. They send out signals that block any kind of mind incursion. So whatever it is you had in mind, to put in *my* mind, don't bother trying. Now sit down and stop making a fool of yourself."

Again, I wasn't going to take orders from him. I stood behind the couch, leaning on it.

"Somebody needs to tell me what's going on," Mom said.

"You want to tell her, or should I?" Blake asked.

"Be my guest."

"Brad here has been having himself a little adventure. He's been playing at being a villain, but he didn't realize he was in way over his head. This may be hard to believe, but he and his little playmates have been trying to work with Mutagion—yes, *the* Mutagion—in an effort to sabotage heroes. But they've been swimming in much deeper waters than they realized, and all they've done is helped the Justice

Force and a few other teams get ready to take down Mutagion and his pals once and for all."

"You're just going to kill every one of them, aren't you?"

"Yup, just like they killed our father."

"These Phaetons aren't the ones accused of killing him. Those Phaetons are long dead."

"What's the difference? They're still part of the same evil, and they killed him."

"Allegedly. There are different theories about that."

"Oh, I've heard those 'theories' plenty, believe me. Crackpot ideas about it being a government setup, that it was a trap for Phaetons and the whole thing went wrong, ending up with Dad getting killed."

"How about that it was a Justice Force ambush of Phaetons that went wrong, and the government was really responsible because of a screwup in timing? Then the Phaetons were blamed, just like they always—"

Tendons stood out like steel cables in Blake's neck. "I don't buy it. I don't buy any of it. He was killed by Phaetons in a sneak attack at the Hoover Dam incident, end of story."

"You were three and you weren't there."

"You were nothing, and you weren't there, either! You didn't even know him. And anyway, how can you side with the Phaetons against our father?"

"It's not so much that I'm siding with Phaetons, but much more that I'm siding against you and your hero pals."

"You disgust me. I'm ashamed to have you as a brother."

"Then we're even. I couldn't have said it better myself."

"It's my fault," Mom said, true grief in her voice. "I should have told you the truth long ago. Please, though, this anger, or hatred toward Blake—you have to let it go."

Blake ignored her. "I don't have time for this. The Justice Force has some scores to settle and Phaetons to exterminate. And whether you like it or not, little brother, that's where I'm going after I leave here."

"What about your injuries?" I asked.

Mom said, "What injuries? You never told me you had injuries."

Blake glared at me for bringing them up in front of her. But as far as I was concerned, all bets were off. Especially after he pulled Layla into it.

"Don't you worry about my injuries. They were minor and they're healed," he said.

I shook my head. "Not that I especially care, Blake, but if you go into battle with the injuries you told me about, you're going to get your—"

"I said not to worry about them. There's one thing *I* have to worry about, though."

I wasn't going to ask, but Mom did. "What's that?"

"Well, our little dissident rebel here is likely to make trouble for the Justice Force and our allies. I wouldn't put it past him to warn the enemy that we're coming, which would basically be an act of treason."

"Treason?" I asked. "Are you kidding me?"

"Treachery? Betrayal? Take your pick. Anyway, I need to stop you from doing that."

"Blake, you are *not* going to hurt him," Mom said.

"Well, maybe a tiny bit, just to make sure that he doesn't do anything to jeopardize the safety of all the heroes about to go into battle. See, Brad, I was born to do this. You? You were born to do nothing."

I'll tell the truth here: I probably would have killed Blake at that moment if I could. But I couldn't and I knew it.

"Brad, lie down on the couch, there."

I looked at him.

"Listen, you can do it, or I can make you do it. Your choice."

"I'll do it if you swear to me that you're going to leave Layla alone and not harm her."

"You're not in a position to make any demands, but no, my aim here is not to hurt her. I just need to make sure that you're not going to do something stupid. So. Now. Lie on the couch."

"Blake, don't," Mom said.

"Mom, relax. I'm not going to do anything serious. Or at least, nothing permanent. Are you comfortable?" he asked me, as if it mattered.

"I'm super. Could fall asleep right now, just staring at the ceiling."

"Good," he said. He got down on one knee next to the couch.

"Why is there dried blood on your cheek?" I asked.

"What are you talking about? There isn't."

"I'm looking right at it. Just a drop, but it's there," I said, staring at the tiny rust-colored dot.

He wiped at his cheek. "It probably was from when you just hit me."

"You wouldn't bleed from that."

"Well, anyway, it's off."

"Whose blood was that?" I asked, but I already knew.

"Just relax and don't move," he said. He slid his hand under my neck.

It all made sense. "You killed Caliban."

"I don't know what you're talking about, but just don't move."

His left hand clamped down on my forehead, pinning me to the couch. He felt around the back of my neck with the fingers of his right hand, probing.

"What are you—"

"Don't talk and don't move. This may hurt a little bit, but it'll be fast."

Just as I realized what he was going to do, as I was about to speak, my world went white.

CHAPTER 52

A Pain in the Neck

You okay?" Blake asked.

It took a couple of seconds for me to remember where I was and why I had white-hot pain in the back of my neck and down into my shoulders, even if the intensity of the pain was starting to diminish.

"No, no, no! Don't move your head, not at all," he said. "Okay, now. Sorry to do this, but you didn't leave me much choice. I disconnected the titanium appliance they put in your neck to replace all the crushed vertebrae from that event on the flashbang field. So, basically, I have your spine unplugged from your brain. You want to hit me again? Go ahead."

And, of course, I couldn't. I couldn't move any part of my body below my neck. My legs and arms—I was completely paralyzed.

"Don't worry, brother," he said. "This is strictly temporary. Now, you can try to get some neurosurgeons to do it. Major surgery, probably six hours or so. But if you wait, when this is all over, I'll set you right back up. I'll even bring along the Justice Force medical team. The very best doctors in this or any other country. And we can talk then. We'll get you all squared away."

"Go square yourself away. And you can also go—"

Blake leaned a bit on my chest as he stood up, forcing all the air out of me. I followed him with my eyes as he walked to the door while I worked to get my breath back.

"Okay," he said. "Ma, I would recommend that you stay here and make absolutely sure he doesn't move until I get back."

"Blake," Mom said, "what's the matter with you? Have you lost your mind? That's Brad! You fix him right now."

"Can't do that, Mom. Believe me, he's gotten real fiery lately, and we can't take a chance of him sabotaging this battle. This is going to make history, and I can't let him wreck it. I promise, I'll make him good as new when I get back."

"You probably won't come back," I said.

"Why wouldn't I?"

"Because, you idiot, you're likely to get smashed up or killed."

This time, he just laughed out loud. "That's not going to happen."

"You're being stupid. You told me your ear is messed up and you can't fly right. You have all those joint injuries. You could get killed."

"Well, I won't. Sorry to disappoint you. Oh, I almost forgot." He walked back so he was standing above me. He held a manila envelope over my face so I could see it. "I figure you might be concerned about this falling into the wrong hands. Don't worry. I got it."

He tucked the envelope with the information I had printed for Mutagion into his back pocket. That was the envelope I'd handed Caliban, probably only minutes before Blake killed him. Blake wouldn't have found him if he hadn't been following me.

Everything was going wrong. It was all backward and upside down. And me, I couldn't even move a single muscle to set things right.

UNITED STATES, EURASIAN ALLIANCE,
UNIFIED AFRICAN NATIONS, ET AL.
V. DEFENDANT #5958375-ER/00-M

People's exhibit 211-15e

ORIGINAL NAME	IDENTITY	AGE
Lathrop, Robert	Mutagion	34
Marisco, Charles	Pillager	25
Greenway, Leslie	Miscreation	38
O'Flaherty, Liam	Groetesk	32
Egan, Marsha	Pariah	31
Nelson, Raheem	Monstros	22
Montana, Edward	Caliban	34
Cielo, Virgil	Slipknot	21
Trask, Simon	Vomitus	30
Brown, Jessica	Garrota	28
Nolan, Stephen	Fracture	32
Wallingford, Frederick	Nightmare	33
Hamlin, George	Hangman	29
Jones, Georgia	Terror	19
Storch, Lisa	Baby	14
Piccolino, Leonard	Bloodbath	24
McHugh, Alexander	Bubonica	26
Strickland, Davis	N/A	16

Decoded text; excerpt; nonredacted as per Court Ruling 349284;
reconstructed for court

SEX	PLACE OF ORIGIN	STATUS
m	Dallas, TX	At large, NE USA
m	Pitts, AL	Deceased/destroyed
f	Albany, NY	At large (Canada?)
m	Tulsa, OK	At large, NE USA
f	Queens, NY	At large (Wyoming?)
m	Sloat, PA	Surrendered, destroyed
m	Carr, NV	At large, NE USA
m	Cartin, OH	At large, SE USA
m	Hillsdale, ME	Surrendered, destroyed
f	NY, NY	Deceased/destroyed
m	Boston, MA	At large, NYC
m	Billet, CO	Deceased/destroyed
m	Fresno, CA	At large, Mexico
f	Wallis, UT	At large, NE USA
f	Surrey, GA	At large, SE USA
m	Isville, AL	Deceased/destroyed
m	Monvale, MT	Deceased/destroyed
m	Bayonne, NJ	At large, NW USA

CHAPTER 53

Heroine

Are they gone?" I asked.

"I don't know what to do," Mom said.

"Go get Layla from the other room."

"Brad, don't talk. Just let me think."

Just go get her.

She left the study. I stared at the ceiling. I knew what I *needed* to do, but I couldn't do anything at all. It was looking as if Blake had beaten me. Maybe he'd been right when he said I had gotten in way over my head. Now I couldn't even *move* my head. But I wasn't out for the count—not yet.

"That Justice Force bitch was trying to scare me into giving her info about us," Layla said. "And your mother said something happened with your brother. Why are you lying there—"

"Layla, please, just listen to me. Blake disconnected pieces of the metal appliance in my neck."

"Let's get an ambulance."

"I can't travel anywhere like this. Not in an ambulance, not in a medevac helicopter. No. One bump and it would be over. So just listen to me."

"I'm listening."

"You're going to put me back together."

"*I* am? Are you out of your mind? I'm not a neurosurgeon!"

"No, you're better. You have biomech-merge abilities. You can put this together without even making an incision."

"You're crazy. I don't even know what that hardware in your neck should look like when it's connected."

"That doesn't matter. You know it doesn't. The hardware is loaded with smart nanotechnology. Do a biotech merge. You can fix it."

"I've never done that."

"You've done enough things like this for me to have total confidence that you'll be able to do it now."

She looked at Mom, who shook her head.

Layla said, "Look. If I screw this up, it could paralyze you."

"Not going to happen. I trust you."

She bit her lip. "No. I'm not doing it unless we have a Vitakinetic here to heal any damage to your spinal cord if I—"

"We don't know any Vitakinetics, and we don't have time for that even if we did. And like I said, I totally trust you. Just please do it."

Layla got down on her knees next to the couch. She reached toward me, then pulled her hands back and rubbed them together.

"What's wrong?" I asked.

"My hands are cold. If I touch you with them and you jump, game over."

"See? That's why I trust you."

"Well, it's good one of us does."

"And anyway, I can't jump, so you don't have to worry about that."

"Wow. Big relief. Okay. Hang on. Here we go."

She put her hands on both sides of my neck, her fingers moving slowly. I could feel her fingertips, centimeters apart, at the back of my neck.

"So?" I said.

"Shh. Let me see what's going on in there." She closed her eyes. Her eyelids fluttered slightly as she concentrated. "I think I see it," she said.

Do it, then.

Are you sure?

I'm sure. Do it.

Okay, I could be wrong, but it's my best guess that nobody in the history of the world has ever written about what it feels like when pieces of metal are moving around under the skin, just barely brushing the spinal cord. I doubt anyone has ever described what it's like to keep from moving or shouting or passing out while this is happening. I'm pretty sure of this because it's unlikely anyone has ever gone through it before.

And I really had no great desire to be a pioneer in experiencing it. But I didn't have much choice.

Layla's hands got noticeably warmer as I felt the whole mess in the back of my neck tighten and settle.

A tingling pins-and-needles sensation started at my neck and extended out toward my arms and legs. There's no other way to describe the rest of it except to say that it felt right.

"I think I got it," Layla said.

"You did." I didn't warn her or Mom, because I didn't want a big argument. But I slowly, slowly moved my head to the side, just a tiny bit.

It felt fine.

I moved it a little more. No problem.

No point in waiting. I sat up and I was totally okay.

Layla let out a long, ragged breath, followed by a nervous release of laughter. I pulled her down and kissed her.

She sat up and looked at Mom, who was white as a sheet.

"I'm okay, Mom. Relax." I looked at Layla. "Do you know where they went?"

"Well, yeah, of course. I did the phone trace. I'm the one who told them where Mutagion was calling from."

I tilted my head. My neck felt okay. Sore, yes, but stable.

"We can call Mutagion, warn him."

"He still thinks we set Caliban up. He wouldn't believe anything we say, even if he would take the call. No. I'm going," I said.

"Then so am I," Layla said.

I was about to protest, but I realized there was no point. She wasn't going to take no for an answer.

"Come on," I said.

CHAPTER 54

Fireflies

Even if we hadn't known the destination beforehand, it would have been hard for us to miss the site of the battle. From a mile away, we could see streaks above the river, looking like fireflies flitting and dancing—or dogfighting—in the air around a rowboat.

It was no rowboat, of course; it just looked like that from so far away. It was the half-sunk destroyer USS *Montana*, the former museum that had been attacked by Phaetons and the Gorgon Corps ten years earlier. And of course, it all made sense. Mutagion had cut a hole in the part of the ship's hull that was underwater. A hole big enough, I figured, to fit his little submarine through. While every hero team and government law enforcement agency was searching for Mutagion's hideout from Antarctica to the smallest islands in the Pacific, there he was, hiding in plain sight. His hideout was less than a hundred yards from a major U.S. city.

After we left the car, Layla and I went down the winding scaffold that led to the dock where we had first met

Mutagion.[72] We were back in costume, figuring we might get seen.

Once we got to the end of the pier and wharves, we found a narrow wooden walkway, clinging precariously to the stone embankment of the river. The walkway shook and rattled with every step we took.

As we got closer, the tilted hull of the ship loomed bigger and bigger, blotting out a large swath of the night sky.

We took cover behind a thick piling by the dock.

I couldn't tell which Phaetons were which. They were mainly ragged silhouettes of various sizes, battling against the heroes of the Justice Force, the Vindication Squad, and plenty of others.

"What are we doing here?" Layla asked.

"I'm not sure. I was hoping we could help Mutagion. It was my fault that Caliban got killed."

"How is it your fault?"

"Indirectly, it is. Blake had followed us. Me talking to Caliban put Blake on his tail. I feel responsible. So at the very least, I can try to save Mutagion."

"He might not even be here. Right? Maybe he left before the battle even started."

"I don't think so. I get the feeling that he's not the kind of guy who would turn tail and run. He thought this was a last

---

[72]And, of course, Caliban. I was sick with guilt, but I knew it was not the time to dwell on it. I couldn't let myself think about him. Not yet.

stand, a battle of honor. He's around here somewhere."

"Now what about the fact that he kind of wants to kill us? Tell me again why we're here to save him."

"I don't really know. All I can tell you is I see probably thirty or forty heroes and maybe fifteen Phaetons and villains combined. This is why we chose the side we did."

Miss Mistral swooped down in a corkscrew roll, her silver-and-blue costume glowing from air friction. She slashed with her silver cudgel when she went into a straight dive toward a bearlike Phaeton who was standing on the edge of the ship's deck. At the bottom of her arc, she swung the cudgel at the Phaeton, but he ducked and batted at her legs. A long hook in his hand caught Miss Mistral's leg, just enough to make her ascent wobbly. She flew out, away from the ship, and over the river. Hovering, she checked her injury.

Flatliner ran up the slanted deck and lunged with a flying leap to drive his head into the bear Phaeton's chest. A spray of blood arced from the Bear Man's mouth as he was launched off the side of the boat, falling through open air to hit the surface of the water fifty feet below. Because he'd been hit hard, both by the attack and by the fall, it wasn't too likely that he would survive.

"Do you see Mutagion?" I asked Layla.

"I can't tell who's who. I don't recognize most of them."

"There goes Hangman," I said.

"Where?"

"There, fighting Meganova."

We watched them fight a prolonged battle, Meganova

taking short flights to gain distance, then diving back in. Hangman grabbed on to Meganova, weighing him down. They landed back on the tilted control tower of the ship, where they slugged it out.

There was a metallic clang and I shifted my gaze to see a body plummet into the water with a loud splash.

"That guy just flew right into the side of the boat," Layla said.

"What?"

"I saw it. He flew headfirst into the metal and then dropped like a stone."

"What color uniform?"

"Couldn't tell. It was in the shadow."

"I bet that's Blake."

"Why?"

"Flying problems." I watched the area where the splash happened. Nothing. After almost two minutes a figure shot up out of the water.

The red, blue, and gold costume was clear in an illumination flare thrown by Fireball of the Justice Force. I was right: it was Blake. He was flying in big loops, then going into a dive, then pulling back up. I figured he was doing it because he couldn't fly straight, so this was a way to hide his weakness. He had almost paralyzed me and then left to find glory, and now he was doing aerobatics instead of fighting.

Slipknot apparently noticed the same thing. I saw him setting the trap. After watching Blake fly around for several minutes, Slipknot fell to his knees near the edge of the ship's deck. His head was hanging. He made a perfect, easy target.

And Blake took the bait.

He flew at Slipknot, slowly, but almost straight. Blake put his fists together in front of him, no doubt imagining how great his winning blow would look when they made a blockbuster-movie dramatization of the battle.

What he probably didn't picture was how it would look when Slipknot dodged to the side and caught Blake's ankle.

Blake smashed into the deck of the ship so hard I would've sworn I felt it in the dock beneath my feet.

He slid down the tilted deck on his back, headfirst. Slipknot ran, downhill you might say, racing to catch up with Blake and do him in.

I couldn't tell if it was partly by accident (I suspect it was), but Blake reached to his side and somehow caught hold of a chain. He jerked to a stop and Slipknot overran him, and then lost his footing and hit the deck. He continued downward, tumbling head over heels.

Slipknot slammed spikes into the deck, stopping himself.

Blake flew at him.

And I saw Slipknot pull a fire pike from under his cloak. I was sure that Blake couldn't see it from his angle. That fire pike, I knew, could kill Blake if Slipknot got a solid stab in the vitals.

Fly hard left, I thought to Blake in a clandestine command projection. It wouldn't work if he still had the inhibitors in his ears.

But he didn't, and he did what I told him to: he took off away from the deck, well out of Slipknot's reach.

Come to me, I commanded Blake.

He was flying almost in a zigzag path. He dropped his feet below and ahead of himself to make a landing. But it was sloppy and he had to run when he reached the pier, a clumsy staggering stride. He lost his footing and fell sprawling, face-first.

I'm not going to pretend that I had a deep concern for Blake's well-being. I like to think it had more to do with wanting to keep Mom from becoming heartbroken at the loss of her older son, but whatever the motivation, I said to him, "You're done."

He looked up at me from the deck of the pier. "How . . . how are you walking around?"

"You need to hang it up. No more fighting."

"I can't just sit it out," he said. "I have a reputation to uphold."

"Yeah, that'll do you a lot of good at your funeral. Any single one of the Phaetons could kill you without thinking twice, the shape you're in."

"I don't take orders from you," he said.

"Actually, yeah. You do," I said. *Sleep.*

And he did.

CHAPTER 55

My Brother's Keeper

It took both of us—Layla and me—to drag Blake's sleeping body off the dock and stash him behind some bushes near a culvert.

"Your brother needs to lose some weight," Layla said, out of breath.

"Muscle is heavier than fat. He's a solid two twenty."

"Whatever. So why save him, after what he did to you?"

"I honestly don't know."

That's when I heard it. About halfway up the dock, a struggle.

Five heroes in their bright colors, standing in a ring. That was Flatliner, Miss Mistral, G-Force, Mr. Mystic, and Radarette. In the middle was a large, staggering, bloody mess. It took a second or two before I realized it was Mutagion.

His demimask was gone. The blue monocle was nowhere to be seen, and I could see a pale, milky eye blinking against the light from the pier. His coat was half torn off. Along the side of his neck, there were deep slits. They looked like gills to me.

"Okay, tough guy, you got any more fight in ya?" G-Force

yelled at him. He kicked Mutagion in the back. Mutagion staggered but didn't go down.

"Yeah, let's see it," Flatliner said. "Show us some of that Phaeton fighting spirit, huh?"

Mutagion tried to break through their ring, but Miss Mistral and Mr. Mystic caught him. G-Force stepped in and hit Mutagion in the face with a downward pile-driver punch.

Mutagion slammed onto the pier hard. I wasn't totally sure he would get up.

I had one shot at this and I had no idea if it would work. But I couldn't think of any other option.

I projected a suggestion that I was actually Blake. I put out a mental image that I looked and sounded exactly like him. I had never tried to project to more than one person at a time, and I wasn't exactly sure how to do it. So I just tried.

"Let him go," I said.

They all looked up.

"Let him go? Are you nuts?" G-Force said.

"Actually, I'm not," I said, duplicating the pitch of Blake's voice in my projection.

"Bl . . . Artillery, man. We've been looking to get our hands on him for years," Mr. Mystic said.

"Like I don't know that? No, the thing is, he tried to corrupt my brother, so I think I'm entitled to be the one who finishes him off."

"He's right," Miss Mistral said. "Let him do it."

I stepped in, got him to his feet (not easy: he was huge

and I had to do a command for him to get up, barely penetrating his consciousness), and I did my best to make it look like I was actually fighting with him, but mainly, I was trying to hold him up.

If he hadn't been bent nearly double, I wouldn't have been able to reach high enough to have had one arm over his neck and the other one driving powder-puff uppercuts into his gut. I thought to him, *If I get you into the water, can you get to your sub?* I took another baby shot—even by my standards—to his gut. *Where is it?*

"What are you saying?" he gasped. "Who the hell are you?"

I'm Brad. I mean, Mindfogger. Just think, but don't answer out loud: is your sub nearby?

It's right there, just off the dock.

Mutagion was leaning with most of his weight on my shoulders. I struggled to keep both of us upright.

Could you get to it? I thought to him.

"If I can get to water, I'll be okay. I could be in the sub in seconds."

"Wait," Radarette said to the JF. "That doesn't look like Artillery, does it?"

I reinforced the image projection of Blake. It seemed to be going in and out. *Is anyone else from your team alive?*

"I don't know."

I threw a few more weak punches, trying to make it look real. I wasn't sure if I was selling it. I put my hand on the back of Mutagion's neck (it felt almost scaly) and pulled his head closer to mine. *Okay. I'll get you off the pier and into the water if you do one thing for me.*

"What?"

Take my girlfriend with you. Get her far away from here so she doesn't get hurt or get caught.

"Where is she now?"

Don't try to talk out loud. I can read you. That's her over there. Bionica. Right behind me.

I see her. I think.

"What the hell . . . ?" I heard Mr. Mystic say behind me. "Do you see that?"

"Yeah," Flatliner said. "Is that Artillery or . . . who *is* that?"

I had to concentrate again and project the image of Blake into their minds. But I realized I couldn't do that and concentrate on what I was saying to Mutagion. If I could get him out of there and get Layla safe . . .

First, I took a couple of seconds to reintroduce the image of Blake. After that, I gripped Mutagion's coat at the shoulders and swung him around. It took every bit of strength I had not to let him fall.

"Artillery, finish him off!" Miss Mistral shouted.

Can you do this? I thought to Mutagion.

"I can try," he said with a gasp. "Need water."

You'll have it. But you have to take my girlfriend.

If I go in the water, they're going to jump in after me. They're not going to let me go.

Just leave that to me.

"Wait a second," G-Force said. "That is *not* Artillery! What's going on?"

What about you? he thought to me. *I have room for you.*

I can't go. I have to finish up out here. You'll take her?

Mutagion nodded. It didn't sound like he could get enough air to speak.

"That isn't Blake," one of the JF called. "I think it . . . wait, *what?*"

I whispered one last thing to Mutagion, knowing that my image projection wasn't working anymore. "Remember what I told you before: your name is Robert Lathrop and you're from Dallas. Layla can tell you more. Find out who you are and what they did to you. Don't quit until you do."

And with that, I threw a punch while at the same time heaving him into the water. I only had time to take a quick look. I saw his body rotate, then swim underwater like he was born there.

Get in the water, I thought to Layla. *Right now. Mutagion is going to pick you up in his sub.*

What about you? she thought back to me.

He's going to come back to get me after you're in. Hurry up.

Okay. You did great out there.

See you soon, I thought. And hoped.

CHAPTER 56

Closing the Circle

The battle above us on the ship seemed to be dying down. There were heroes up there, flying around and shouting to one another, but I didn't hear too much fighting. Not that I listened long, because things were pretty intense down on the pier.

G-Force and Radarette edged behind me, closing the circle. The heroes from the Justice Force closed ranks, cutting off any chance of me getting off the pier.

"Who is this kid?" Miss Mistral said. "Anybody seen him before?"

Nobody had, of course, and they said as much.

Next thing I knew, it felt as if two telephone poles had pinned my arms to my sides, then crossed over my chest and squeezed me against a brick wall. This was G-Force, putting me in a bear hug. If the fate of civilization depended on it, I couldn't have used physical strength to break his hold.

Fortunately for me, though, I didn't have to rely on physical strength.

And fortunately, G-Force was stupid enough to think, *I gotcha, you little brat* when his head was practically next to mine. This made picking up his thought patterns especially easy.

I couldn't breathe and I was getting scared. I had to concentrate and use my only strength.

Like mentally trying to lift a car, I projected every bit of my psi energy straight into his mind at once and overloaded his brain with psi energy. My guess is that it feels a lot like having ten flashbangs go off at once, but inside your head. That was a psionic blast.

His mind was overloaded, as was his nervous system, which meant he collapsed to the deck of the pier. I suspected it would be at least an hour or so before the aftereffects would start to dissipate.

One down . . .

Fight each other, I thought to Mr. Mystic and Radarette. They turned, and to my great pleasure, they started beating the daylights out of each other.

Miss Mistral took to the air and then went into a nosedive toward me. About twenty yards up, she dropped her feet beneath her to land.

Easy. I projected that the pier I was standing on was a lot farther away from her than it was, and rather than slowing down to land, she just went straight through it and into the water. I heard a muffled clang, which was probably her getting tangled up in all the scrap iron underneath.

Looking past where she'd crashed through the dock, I saw a weird and reassuring sight. Layla was walking on water.

Then she took another step and started to descend. It was as if she was climbing down a ladder, which was exactly what she was doing. She hadn't been walking on water; she had been walking on the mostly submerged hull of Mutagion's sub.

The faint glow of light disappeared when the hatch closed, and I felt the thrum of engines build up and vibrate through the pilings and into the deck under my feet. When the vibration lessened and disappeared in a few seconds, I knew Layla and Mutagion were away, out of danger.

I, however, was not.

Flatliner was running at me.

I tried another psionic blast, but nothing happened. I didn't have nearly enough psi energy left to make one.

He was close. If he caught me, he would either capture or kill me.

But he was easy. I projected into his mind, *Stop!* And he did.

I knew he wouldn't stay like that for long. I needed to do something, and fast. Then I realized that, in effect, he himself had told me what to do. It was all in his name.

I was already in his head. First I took away his sense of the present: where and who he was, what he was trying to do. Then, because I was in there and because he was a scumbag hero, I erased what was there. I cleaned out his entire mind.

It's not that I wiped his brain clean of synapses or did any permanent damage. All I did was wipe out every memory he had, putting his mind back into the state of a newborn. He would learn how to walk and talk, learn about the American Revolution and Hemingway and algebra and everything else. It would just take him a good, long time.

"Ugga, ugga, ugga," he burbled, drool running down his chin.

That was that. It was time to make my getaway. He had been the last one.

Or so I thought.

I realized how wrong I was when a hand grabbed the collar of my jacket, yanked me backward and off balance, and then forced me down in a prone position on the dock. Strong hands took hold of my wrists and pulled my arms behind my back.

The tight grip of armored flex cuffs pulled my wrists together.

"You are under arrest. You have the right to remain silent," Blake said.

CHAPTER 57

Villain

To be totally honest, jail isn't so bad. That is, there are much worse things. For example, a federal trial is a lot more unpleasant. Hearing witnesses testify, one after the other, hundreds of them, is not a lot of fun. Listening to the lawyers go on and on, trying their simplistic tactics, is pretty frustrating, especially when they're telling flat-out lies about you. And those are just the lawyers who *defended* me.

Getting used to your mother refusing to look you in the eye, even from across the courtroom, is worse than jail.

The other thing that's bad is when major information won't be revealed, with the explanation that to do so would be a serious threat to international security. Kraden, the Demophon Program, Phaetons being made and sacrificed by the government and GenLab—all of it suppressed. Oh, well. I tried. Fight on, Phaetons.

Preparation for the trial took almost a year, what with the federal laws, hero laws, my being a juvenile, and all that. The trial itself took only about five weeks. During that entire time, I was in jail, but like I said, jail isn't so bad.

Because of my powers, they kept me in strict isolation.

Every VIO[73] who had to deal with me wore anti–mind incursion earplugs so I wouldn't be able to control them. Given that I had no physical powers to speak of, it was kind of overkill for them to keep me in an underground cell that was completely encased by some kind of titanium-tungsten cured-steel cage. But it didn't make any difference to me. I was locked up, steel cage or not.

So I spent day after day, alone in my cell.

Not that I'm trying to get you to feel sorry for me. I *liked* being alone, left to think about whatever I wanted. And I did have lots to think about.

Eventually, they allowed me to write, no doubt hoping I would inadvertently give up some information that would be useful to them. But they must have forgotten who they were dealing with, that I never do *any*thing inadvertently. Not anymore, at least.

But thinking is only entertaining for so long. I began to dwell on mistakes I had made, how I would have done things differently if I had known how they would turn out. My desire to make things right became almost painful.

Layla got word to me through Mom, who had started visiting me, heartbroken as she was over my chosen path as a villain. Javier, Boots, and Peanut had dropped out of the villain track once they saw how things had gone for me. They continued quietly in the A-program, keeping low profiles.

---

[73] Villain incarceration officer, a.k.a. prison guards, jailers, hacks. They don't call them *correctional officers* for us, because it's assumed that we can't be "corrected" at all.

And when I found myself thinking more and more about Layla, time seemed to slow down to a crawl. Thinking wasn't such a pleasure anymore. Time was wasting.

One thing my jailers hadn't counted on when giving me so much time alone was that I might use the time to develop myself. Now, I don't mean the kind of self-development done in most prisons—getting a high school degree or college degree or law degree, or doing a twelve-step program to battle addictions, or even finding religion. And no bodybuilding in the yard for me. No, no. What I'm talking about is developing in a way that would truly help me.

Some inmates do pushups and sit-ups all day; some find a way to exercise using their cell bars. Some get to work out with weights in a weight room.

I didn't have to move a muscle to exercise and get stronger. All I had to do was sit there and concentrate.

No, it wasn't easy. But I didn't give up. The prison authorities had been right to equip all the VIOs with anti–mind incursion devices every time they came to deal with me, deliver anything, bring food or whatever.

The prison authorities were wrong, though, to think that I wouldn't be able to make my powers evolve.

They didn't expect that I would be able to develop mind projection to the point where I didn't need to be in the room with the target; that I could build up the ability to project to people who weren't in my immediate presence. That was a *big* mistake on their part.

Because a cook can turn a key just as easily as a prison

guard can. And once getting released into a prison's general population, it's ridiculously easy for an inmate with highly developed telepathy powers to do mind incursions and practically be escorted off prison grounds by suddenly friendly and cooperative prison staff.

So there you have it. I have a lot to do on the outside.

Layla has been traveling with Mutagion and trying to come up with ways to bust me out of prison. She's waiting for me. I want to find her and see what kind of hell she's raising. I want to look into forming another group to fight the heroes. Or maybe we'll just do it, the two of us, on our own. The Deadly Duo. Has kind of a nice ring to it.

And, of course, I need to get my revenge on Artillery, a.k.a. Blake Baron, originally my brother, then betrayer, now sworn enemy.

Yes, if you're reading this, it means I'm gone. I left this reading material for the prison personnel, in thanks for their hospitality.

By now, I'm out there. Among you. I can't tell you exactly what I'm doing, but whatever it is, you can bet on one thing:

I'm up to no good. . . .

Glossary

A-HOLE: slang term for a student in the A-program

A-PROGRAM: alternative academic program that serves students with few, weak, or no powers. Students with powers but who are considered to have a bad (unheroic) attitude are also assigned to the A-program.

ACCELERATE: a person with the power to move extremely quickly. The more gifted accelerates can move much faster than can be perceived by the (typical) eyes and mind. (pronounced *"eck-SELL-er-et"*)

AEROTRANSVECTION: flight; more specifically, the superhuman ability to fly

AURAL: a person with enhanced hearing

AVID: Anti-Villain Investigation Division; a branch of the FBI

BIO-MECHANICAL PSYCHIC MERGE: ability to touch any mechanical object or system and immediately gain a mental image of its physical inner workings. The image can be rotated and manipulated at will by the user, allowing different viewing angles and magnifications.

FLASHBANG: a sport similar to rugby, but using a ball that can randomly be triggered to detonate with a loud and bright percussive flashbang, causing temporary blindness, deafness, disorientation, pain. The "ball"

can also be forcibly attached to a player when desired.

GRAVITYGAIN: an applied electromagnetic field that causes receivers worn by individuals to feel heavier than usual by artificially creating a stronger gravitational field. Typically used for strength training.

HITTER: (alt. sp. HiTTer) slang term for Hero in Training: Teen. May be used in a complimentary way or derisively. (More insulting use is when an S is put at the beginning, supposedly to signify Super Hero in Training: Teen.)

INTERFERENCE GENERATOR: device that can partially block intersight, enhanced aural sensitivity, and other sensory powers (often referred to simply as IG)

INTERSIGHT: the ability to see through various types of substances and objects. Those with Intersight are colloquially called: *scopers*, *peepers*, or for those who are known or suspected of using Intersight to look through clothing, *creeper-peepers*.

KEVFLEX®: extremely durable material that is resistant to small firearm bullets and knife attacks. However, its flexibility makes it ineffective against blunt force.

MATTER INGESTION: the ability to safely eat or drink various types of matter and gain certain qualities of the substance. Examples: the ability to eat fire and then become blazing hot, or to drink acid and then spit caustic lye. Those with the power of MI are colloquially called *eaters*, *grazers*, or *mangers* (from the French, *mangeurs*)

METAHUMANS: humans with powered genes

MICROVISION: the ability to see small things without the aid of magnification devices

MIND INCURSION: using telepathic powers to access another person's thoughts or memories

MIND-TAPPING: slang for *mind incursion*

MYO-AUGMENTATION: artificial enhancement of an individual's musculature. Typically performed through a combination of pharmaceuticals (see *Myomegamorpherone®*) and surgical procedures.

MYOMEGAMORPHERONE®: prescription drug widely prescribed to heroes to help them achieve a muscular build, even when being mesomorphic is not necessary. Myomega is primarily used for aesthetic purposes. Essentially, it's a pumped-up version of anabolic steroids. A person who abuses Myomegamorpherone is colloquially called a *Triple-M*, from *Myomega Muscle Monster*.

NATURAL: someone who was born with powers, or with latent powers, due to genetics. Many Naturals believe that they were destined to have powers, and therefore their powers are of a higher order than powers gained through artificial means.

OSTEOMEND: a medication that accelerates healing of bone

PHAETON (*"FIE-tahn"*; also commonly—but incorrectly—pronounced *"FAY-TONN"* or *"FATE'n"* or *"FAY-uh-thonn"*): a criminal or villain who has experienced failed mutations, allegedly as a result of black market or ineptly performed genetic restructuring in the attempt to gain powers. Many are enraged or insane, deformed, have no control over powers, or are otherwise handicapped. Viewed by general public, governments, and heroes much like huge, powered, rabid pit bulls. (From Greek mythology: Phaethon got permission from his father Zeus to drive the celestial chariot, led by fiery horses. He lost control, and the out-of-control chariot set the earth ablaze. Zeus killed him.)

POWER SUPPRESSORS: devices that suppress some metahuman powers

PSI: see *Psionics*

PSIONICS: the practice or ability of using the mind to produce paranormal phenomena, specifically telepathy, telekinesis, empathicism, and precognition. Also spelled *psyonics*, and often abbreviated as *psi* or with the symbol ψ

PT (Physical Training): a general gym class

Read and write: two distinct powers of telepathy. *Reading* is the ability to find out what is in another person's mind. *Writing* is the ability to project messages to someone else's mind. For example, "I can read, but I can't write yet." See *Mind-tapping*.

Regular: a person with no powers beyond typical human abilities

Shocker shotgun: similar to a Taser, but without wires. The projectiles (typically 37–40 precharged darts per cartridge) spread in a wide scatter. Can subdue multiple people with each shot without causing permanent damage.

Subvisibility: essentially the same as invisibility. One of the powers that can result from people who can control and expand the space between atoms in their body.

Telekine: someone who has the ability to use mental force to move objects (from *telekinesis*)

Telepath: someone with the ability to read minds, implant thoughts in the minds of others, and distort or alter memories and knowledge.

Thermal Wars: international conflict that erupted shortly after WWII, during the Cold War, and the first widespread use of enhanced humans as fighting forces. Generally credited by historians as the primary factor that prevented a third world war.

Triangle Battle: epic and historic battle between Justice Force and Troika, which resulted in two members of Troika being wounded and incarcerated. The third member was killed. Widely considered by military historians to be one of Blake Baron's finest moments.

Triple-M: see *Myomegamorpherone*®

UMI: Undetected Mind Incursion is the practice of telepathically entering another's mind without their knowledge.

Undernet: a semiprivate version of the internet, highly covert, and accessible only to very advanced hackers

ViewStopper® Quartzlon®: a synthetic fiber used in clothing to resist powers of intersight

Villain: the meaning can vary, depending on the context and who is using the word. It may have the traditional meaning of someone evil or harmful, someone with wicked intentions. It may also be used as an antonym of *hero*, particularly referring to a political position or view rather than having a qualitative connotation.

Vital (also, VITAL): Villain In Training; A-program Loser is a self-chosen group nickname, originally coined by Layla Keating.

Hall of Heroes

Power supporters: many thanks to members of the families Tiven, Kohn, Bihaly, Moore, and Shenfeld; and thanks to my pal, Abi M.

My super editor, Catherine Onder, used her powers of good judgment, strong insight, and x-ray vision to see into the heart of matters, which has been invaluable to me, and she has had a strong hand in making this book the best it can be. Thank you, thank you, thank you.

I'm lucky and thankful to have the absolute best agent on Earth, Jodi Reamer. Her powers of wisdom and tenacity have been invaluable. As always, she provides judicious guidance, honest and smart critique, and constant encouragement. She is my literary advocate and protector.

Heartfelt thanks to Jake, my personal hero; and Hedy, my enthusiastic cheerleader.

And finally, very, very deepest thanks to my wife, Ellen. When she heard my idea for this story, she said, "Superheroes and villains? Really? Okay, but make it good." I hope I did. She is a mighty source of encouragement, support, and inspiration for me not only in my writing, but in every way, every day of my life.